THE KING'S OUTLAW

R. MICHAEL CARD

Gryphon's Gate Publishing

The King's Outlaw

Gryphon's Gate Publishing

550 King St. N.

PO Box 42088 Conestoga

Waterloo, ON.

N2L 6K5

ebook ISBN 978-1-988115-50-4

Print ISBN 978-1-988115-49-8

DESPITE THE HEAVY CLOUDS AND LIGHT DRIZZLE, THE DAY SEEMED remarkably bright. Where Col crouched, far below the thick canopy of the Sandren Forest, only a few drips and drops of rain pattered against his oiled cloak. The lush mosses and flora of the forest floor came alive in vibrant verdancy, from deep, dark greens to bright emerald tones.

It was too bad he was going to have to step out onto the road in a moment, where the break in the foliage above would turn the packed earth trail to mud. Not to mention he'd be under the full force of the pattering rain.

Col shrugged. He'd survived far worse in his time hiding away from civilized life.

"Ready?" he whispered to Ayneii.

Ayneii was a sprite, a small fey, who hovered next to him, hanging in the air.

The sprite didn't respond for a moment, probably communicating with the other sprites in some manner Col couldn't hear or understand.

Col shook his head slowly marveling at his companion. All fey were genderless yet despite this Col couldn't help but think of

Ayneii as a tiny woman. The sprite's body was slender, seemingly stretched, with too-long arms, legs, and torso. Shimmering wings, moving too fast to be seen, created a faint blur above and behind her. She wore no clothes but instead glowed with an inner light, which made it hard to truly see her miniscule features. The radiance which emanated from her, was a brilliant green speckled with points of gold, like new leaves dappled in sunlight. Her hair was the dark green of mature leaves and floated behind her, free and wild. The sprite's ears were tall and lobeless, tapering to a fine point above the top of her head. She wore her usual mischievous grin and winked at him as her communication with the others ended.

"All set," she said, her voice high and light. There was a bit of an odd vibration to her voice, perhaps from the rapid beating of her wings behind her, Col wasn't sure. Now wasn't the time to think of such things anyway, his prey was drawing near.

He rose and stepped out from hiding onto the road, his gait long and confident. The hood of his cloak was pulled low to shadow his face. He also wore a soft leather mask, which covered the top of his face from nose to forehead, with holes for his eyes. Under the leather hung black silk to further obscure the bottom of his face while not hindering his voice.

He held out a hand before him and yelled, "Halt!" affecting his best Malacaster accent, guttural and slightly slurred. It was easy enough as his grandfather had been from Malacaster.

On the road before him were six knights, mounted and in full-plate, escorting a carriage through the forest. With them were a dozen footmen each wearing boiled-leather armor and carrying a spear, with a sheathed sword at their side.

Surprisingly, they did stop. The horses sidled and frisked as the soldiers scanned the forest around them, expecting an attack. It was a good instinct, but Col's companions were well hidden and wouldn't be seen. There were mutterings among the men on the road. Col smiled as he heard the words "Black Bandit" whispered. His reputation was well known in these parts. Hopefully that would help him get what he wanted without anyone dying.

He threw back his hood, not liking how it limited his peripheral vision in a fight. Also, it would help to reinforce his image as the Black Bandit—his mask was rather unique. Rain, light but steady, peppered the top of his head.

He slipped three arrows from the quiver at his hip and nocked one, aiming it at the lead knight.

"Surrender your cargo peacefully, and none of you shall be harmed," he called out.

"You think they actually will?" Ayneii asked, hovering beside him. He knew the other men wouldn't be able to see or hear her. He gave a quick laugh as a response.

No, he didn't.

One of the knights called out to him. "Are you Arron of Malacaster, the one they call the Black Bandit?"

"I am!" he shouted across the score of yards that separated them.

There were more murmurings throughout the group.

The knight who'd called out looked around. His helm had a full faceplate with slits for eyes, which made seeing anything difficult.

Col added, "My men are well hidden. You won't see them until it's too late."

The knight turned back to him. "My master has a message for you," he shouted.

Before he could pass that message on, however, there was a commotion from inside the carriage. It rocked violently before one of the doors swung open and a man came flying out backwards. He landed in the mud with a heavy thud of expelled air.

The door broke from its hinges and clattered to the ground as well.

Even from this distance, Col heard the curse muttered by the lead knight as a woman, bound hand and foot, jumped down out of the carriage.

This was not what Col had been expecting at all.

He whispered to Ayneii, "Tell the others to wait."

She nodded.

Col stalked in a little closer hoping to get a better look at this woman.

Wild was the best word to describe her. She looked around, frantic. Brilliant blue eyes, filled with some inner fire, caught his for a moment as she took in the situation. An oval face with a slightly too long but straight nose and small lips was framed by a tangle of light brown hair. She wore what looked like it had once been a lady's gown of silk and lace but now was torn and dirty. She had the marks of a fight: cuts and bruises, on her face and exposed arms. Those slender arms were tied tightly behind her, and another cord bound her ankles. Whoever this woman was she seemed to have gone through some great ordeal.

For a moment, as the guards stared at her, she flexed those thin arms trying to escape the bonds, but could not. She shrugged and began hopping toward the forest. She wanted to get away from these men; that was clear enough to Col now.

But... who was she?

Col had gotten word that this carriage was carrying a cargo of great value. Could this woman be the cargo or just some hapless passenger with it? And if she was the 'valuables,' why was she so important?

And why was she trying to escape?

Col couldn't make sense of any of this.

The knights managed to recover from their shock before he

did. The one in the lead yelled out, "Capture her!" to his men, adding, "I'll take this one." The knight spurred his horse.

Apparently, there would be a fight.

Col loosed an arrow, which the knight deflected off his shield.

As he nocked his next, he said to Ayneii, "The others can join in anytime. New plan; steal the carriage and help that girl."

"What about you?" Ayneii asked, eyeing the charging horse.

"I'm well enough. I've got you." His next arrow hit the knight on his pauldron and bounced away harmlessly. "I'm assuming you can do something about the horse. I'd rather not shoot it." His third arrow was nocked and ready.

"Of course." Ayneii zoomed away and waved her arms about in front of the horse's face as it drew perilously close to Col. He stepped to one side as the mount reared.

The knight was an accomplished rider and stayed in the saddle, but had to pay attention to doing only that for a moment, which gave Col an opening. His next arrow took the man in his shield arm, near the shoulder, finding the gap in the metal plating.

The knight gave a cry. He lost control and fell backward off the horse. The mount frisked and pranced off to one side as Col drew his sword and stepped up to the prone knight.

"Surrender."

The man groaned in reply.

"I'll take that as a yes."

He glanced at the carriage to see how the rest of his men were doing... and his jaw dropped in awe. The wild woman from the carriage was successfully fighting off a dozen soldiers and five knights.

2

Tom Willow stood atop the carriage blinking in disbelief.

He'd dispatched the driver easily enough with an arrow while still safe in his hiding spot in a tree overlooking the road. He'd hit the man in the leg then swung down on a rope to knock the man from the driver's bench onto the road. Between the wound and the fall, the man was not a concern. He'd then meant to take control of the carriage and drive it away, but he'd turned at a commotion to one side and found that strange woman doing impossible things.

The soldiers had been closing in, spears pointed at her. She'd jumped, and somehow tucked her legs up high enough to bring her arms underneath and in front of her. When she'd landed, a man had tried to poke her with a spear, but she'd deftly stepped to one side and, without cutting herself, used the spear's bladed tip to slice through the ropes binding her hands. The guards had hesitated a moment, while the woman had shaken out her arms.

Tom should have done something, but he was too caught up and just watched for a moment.

A knight called for the soldiers to part and rode in toward

her. Tom thought she'd be trampled, but as the horse drew near the woman grabbed some of the tack around the mount's neck, ducked under its head and swung herself up such that she kicked the knight right out of the saddle. Then, even more stupefying, she landed crouching in the saddle before leaping away to the top of the carriage with him. All that with her feet still bound.

Tom stood there staring at her while she stole his knife and quickly sawed through the ropes at her feet. Once free, she was the one who took the reins of the carriage and started it moving.

That was what snapped Tom from his reverie. He steadied himself as the carriage began moving. Hopefully the others in Col's little band were fleeing now since their primary objective was being driven away by their newly acquired secondary objective. He wasn't sure if he wanted to sit on the bench next to her, so he dropped to his knees then slipped over the side of the carriage top to the footman's rail along the side.

Ahead, Tom saw Col standing in the path of the carriage. Col had captured the lead knight, but as the carriage barreled down on them, the knight dove to one side. Col couldn't follow without being trampled by the horses. Tom saw his captain shrug and hold out his arm to Tom, who caught it and swung the man up beside him onto the coach rail as they picked up speed down the road.

"That was... interesting," Col said slowly.

"That's one word." Tom nodded.

"Any idea where she's taking us?"

"No clue."

"I'll go ask." Col gave his signature roguish grin and headed toward the bench at the front. Tom would let Col handle the woman while he checked inside for any loot.

~

DALIA BLINKED AS HER MIND RETURNED TO ITSELF.

Where was she?

She gasped and nearly screamed as she realized she was holding the reins to a speeding carriage! She'd never driven anything like this before.

She nearly screamed again when a man appeared next to her. He was dressed all in black with a mask covering his face. She felt the terrifying sensation of The Fury coming over her again. It didn't fully take hold, but kept her ready in case this man was a threat.

He sat beside her. "Hello."

She could faintly see a friendly grin through the dark silk covering the lower half of his face.

"Hello," she replied, voice shaky. "Do you know how to drive a carriage?" she asked, feeling The Fury fade.

"Don't you?" he asked, looking at the reins in her hands.

She shook her head.

"Ah, then allow me." He took the reins and held them steady. He seemed confused for a moment, but that didn't surprise her. She was even more confused. It didn't help that her memories were always a little foggy right after The Fury had taken her. She'd remember everything in detail soon enough.

She just hoped she hadn't killed anyone this time. Even if they were evil men taking her to her death... well *they* may not be evil. They were just doing what they'd been told. She didn't really know who was evil these days. She'd seen and done too much in the past week to know anything for sure.

"Thank you," she said to the man next to her.

He grinned. "A pleasure to make your acquaintance. I'm Arron of Malacaster, the Black Bandit."

The Black Bandit!

The Fury threatened to take her again, but something stopped it. As much as this man was a known rogue who'd been pillaging this part of the Sandren Forest for over two years, he didn't seem to be threatening her in any way.

"What are you going to do with me?" she asked hesitantly.

He laughed. "I have no clue. I raided this carriage because there was supposed to be a cargo of great value on board. I don't steal people though. So you're free to go whenever you like, m'lady."

Lady? It was her turn to laugh, though after one guffaw it turned to tears.

She had been a lady only a few days ago, but now... she didn't know what she was.

She quickly sniffed her tears away. "I'm sorry, it's been a long week." After a moment, remembering he was about to let her go, she added, "Thank you."

She couldn't quite describe the look in his brown eyes. It seemed like some odd mix of pity, confusion, awe, and fear.

A wild idea jumped into her mind and, before she could think better, had burst from her lips as well. "Take me with you." It had come out partly as a question and partly as a command.

He nodded slowly. "Perhaps."

With a glance behind them, he flicked the reins and called a "whoa" to the horses. The carriage slowed then stopped.

"One moment, m'lady," he said and then called out, "Tom, did you find anything?"

A voice issued forth from the carriage. "No, Captain."

The Black Bandit turned back to her with a new, appraising look. "Well miss, it would seem *you* are the valuable cargo. I won't ask why. But if you want to come with me, now is your chance." He hopped to the ground from the driver's bench and offered her a hand to follow.

She hesitated, but only for a moment. As much as her younger self might have thought following a bandit off into the woods to be romantic and mysterious... she'd recently been disillusioned of all of her fantasies. However, going with him was better than being alone or being recaptured by those knights and sent to her death. So, she took his hand and was quickly down off the carriage.

There was a second man there, tall and lean. The mask he wore was a little rougher around the edges and didn't have the silk along the bottom, so his mouth and jaw were exposed.

"She's coming with us?" the man asked.

The Black Bandit smacked one of the horses in the team pulling the carriage, and they started off again at a trot, slowly gaining speed.

"Yes, now let's get into the forest before those knights catch up to us."

They were quickly amongst the trees. Only a faint heartbeat later the six knights galloped around a corner in the road. For a moment, Dalia thought they would be spotted, but the knights rode past without a glance.

She was breathing hard and realized she had been for a while. The memories of what she'd done during this most frequent bout of The Fury started to come to her in flashes. With it came exhaustion. She fell to her knees, crumpling to the ground and shuddered. It was a reflex. None of these memories seemed too horrible, but there had been so many in the past that had been.

"Are you alright, m'lady?" the Black Bandit asked.

She had no energy to look up at him but could hear the hesitation in his voice. He wanted to say something more. Perhaps he'd witnessed her in The Fury and couldn't reconcile the trembling woman before him with that devil.

A tender, tentative hand brushed her back and she heard the rustle of his clothes as he knelt next to her.

"M'lady?"

He kept saying that...

She couldn't take it anymore and she wept, heaving sobs.

"Hush now," he said softly. "They can't get you now."

She wanted to laugh through her tears, a hard, bitter laugh. It wasn't those knights she was worried about. It was what she might do to them if they did return. But she couldn't laugh. Her world was on its head and all she could do right now was weep for a life forever lost to her.

3

Col carried the limp woman back to his camp. She'd cried herself into a heavy slumber, and nothing he'd done could wake her. With the weight and awkwardness, progress was slow, but Tom helped clear the way for him. The entire walk he couldn't help but wonder: who was this woman who was of such great value to the crown?

Perhaps it had something to do with Ayneii's reaction to the girl. Col had asked Ayneii to help wake the woman, but as soon as the sprite had touched her, she'd flinched back. "Something is wrong with her," was all Ayneii would say. After that, she'd kept her distance.

"Are you certain we should bring her back to the camp?" Tom asked, not for the first time.

No.

"I don't think we should," Ayneii said.

Col gave her a flat stare, glad that Tom wouldn't be able to hear what Ayneii was saying. "Someone needs to help her."

"Seems like she helped herself fairly well back there. Maybe she doesn't need our help?" Tom glanced back. Col gave him the same flat stare.

"You should listen to him," Ayneii added.

"We help who we can, remember."

Ayneii frowned, pouting, and hovered a little further away from him.

Tom sighed. "I know." He muttered something after that which seemed to contain the phrase 'crazy noblewoman.'

"Is everyone else safe?" Col asked Ayneii.

"They are all back at the camp. Only Jaff was injured, but not seriously, and Kiiva has healed it."

Col nodded. She didn't seem inclined to share more.

With their slow pace, it was dusk by the time they returned to the camp. Col paused for a moment, catching his breath at the edge of the clearing, and marveled at his hideout. They had cleared an area between the larger trees such that now it almost looked like there was a small village within some great hall of nature, wooden pillars supporting a high vaulted ceiling of leaves above them. Fires without any wood floated throughout the area, a gift of the sprites. They called it fey-fire, a flickering light like a torch but with no source and no heat. Even as he stood there, Ayneii lit one nearby to help him get to his cabin.

There were three cabins as well as a storehouse. All but the storehouse had been built by the fey for the growing band of men and women who'd come to follow Col. The storehouse had been Col's original dwelling, made painstakingly by piling logs into a square. If his uncle hadn't been a woodcutter and carpenter, Col would've had a much harder time.

As it was, on his own, the small building had still taken him months to build. But by that point, he'd made friends with a curious sprite called Ayneii. So, when Tom and two other men had come to join him—pushed into the wilds by fate as he had been—Ayneii had gathered up some of her kind and grown him a new house.

Tree trunks had sprouted up in a square so close they had

grown together to make walls. Their branches had arched in and out, intertwining firmly to make a roof as well as a pleasant covered area outside the dwelling. Inside, the branches had formed shelves along the walls and stones had rumbled up from the earth to form a fire pit in the center of the cabin. The leaves and branches above the fire pit formed careful layers to let out smoke while still keeping the rain from getting in.

He'd had no furniture, but the house had been gift enough. Two more such structures—each larger than the last—had been 'grown' as more and more had joined the bandit camp. The last even had rooms within the structure to create separate spaces for women or couples. There were nearly twenty men and women here now, all exiled from society for one reason or another.

"Where will she be staying?" Tom asked.

"With me," Col said. "But if you could send Lily over with some spare garments I'm sure she'd appreciate that when she wakes."

Tom nodded with a grunt and headed for the largest cabin where Lily would most likely be.

Col made his way to his small dwelling, pushing past the skins hung over the entranceway, one on the outside one inside. The fey couldn't make doors, so he'd made large coverings from the hides of animals he'd caught for food. That skill had come from his father, a hunter. He'd been skinning pelts and making various leather and hide items since he was a boy.

He set the woman on his bed of layered blankets and asked Ayneii to start a fire. Fey couldn't actually make real fire, oddly enough. They could create their fey-fire, which was a flame without heat, and they could create heat without a flame, but not both. But the heat itself would be enough to ignite the kindling and logs placed in his fire pit, and soon a fire was going strong and the cabin grew quite warm.

He removed his mask and cloak. The mask was placed on a shelf, the cloak on a small peg beneath that.

It was late spring, and the nights could still be quite cool here in the depths of the Sandren Forest. After Lily had made her delivery of clothes, Col stepped outside with her and found out just how cool it was compared to the cheery warmth within. He wished he'd kept his cloak on now.

Before he could say anything, Lily arched a brow and whispered, "You've never had a woman in your hut before?"

Col grimaced. "She's a guest and resting. She doesn't really know anyone else. She barely knows me, but I'm hoping I can keep her calm when she wakes."

"Tom said there was something wild about her, that she easily escaped from a dozen armed men? The other men were saying the same thing; say she might be cursed or possessed?"

Col didn't know how to keep his guest's incredible actions earlier in the day from becoming some wild legend. Chances are, it was already too late for that.

Before he could form a response, Ayneii appeared next to them. "Yes, that's what it feels like. There is something not human within her."

Col glanced at Lily, who'd had no reaction and wasn't looking at Ayneii. He breathed a sigh. Ayneii could appear only to him or to everyone around. It seemed this rather inflammatory comment had been just for him. He nodded to Ayneii but spoke to Lily.

"I'm not going to judge her just yet. She certainly seemed scared and in need of help after... that incident. I don't know what's going on, which is another reason she's staying with me. I'm only endangering myself. Though I'm sure Ayneii can protect me well enough." He paused, but Lily just shrugged, so he continued. "I'd wanted to ask you to keep an eye on her for a moment while I get some more blankets and a basin of water for bathing. I'm sure she'll want to clean up when she wakes as well."

Lily grinned mischievously. "And will you watch her when she bathes? Because if you do, you're a lecherous man and if you don't, she might go wild again." Lily's arched brow rose a little more waiting for his response. She wasn't unattractive with her long flaxen hair, soft brown eyes, and a curvy figure. She'd tried to be his woman when she'd first arrived with her brother, Jaff, but despite her charms, Col wasn't interested. Col had never really met any woman he was interested in... in that way. Since then she'd become more like a sister.

A sister who was always trying to set him up with someone. According to her, he needed a woman in his life.

"I'll have Ayneii keep an eye on her, unless you want to stick around?"

Lily sighed and shook her head. "You're no fun, Colric." She shrugged. "Yes, I'll watch over her for a moment. Go get what you need. As for watching her bathe, I think she'd prefer some privacy. Ayneii's probably a better option for that."

"Thanks," he said, and hurried away.

Once he was out of earshot, he asked Ayneii, "What did you mean about the girl? She's not human?"

Ayneii floated along beside Col, easily keeping pace. "That's what it felt like. I'd have to be in contact again to be certain." Ayneii contorted her tiny facial features in confusion. "She doesn't feel like you or anyone else here. She feels more like... well like me, just... huge."

"Like you? She's a giant sprite?"

"I don't know. It doesn't make any sense. That's why I said she felt wrong."

Col shook his head. This wasn't getting them anywhere. He reached the storehouse and entered the dark confines. Ayneii made light and he searched for a decent set of blankets. He dumped them in a large tin tub along with a pitcher for water. He carried everything down to the stream not far from the camp and removed the blankets. He used the pitcher to fill the tub then carried the blankets under one arm as he hefted the now quite-heavy tub back to his cottage.

Lily was waiting for him inside. She rose as he entered.

"Nothing yet," she said. An odd set of expressions played over her face in the next instant. She seemed about to say something, her face a bit hopeful or expectant. Then she apparently changed her mind and let out a long breath, waving a hand as her features fell into a sad and sympathetic look. She looked back at the sleeping woman, then to Col. She stepped in and kissed him platonically on the cheek then left without another word.

That was odd.

But then he didn't much understand women. He shrugged and set down the tub.

He laid out the blankets to one side of the fire on the hard-packed earthen floor and moved the girl from his bedroll to the new padding. Then he retreated to his own set of blankets on the other side of the fire and watched the mystery girl. She seemed at peace, for now at least. Her auburn hair was covering most of her face, still a mess of wisps and tangles, but somehow, she was managing to look... nice.

It had been a long day and he wasn't surprised to find himself nodding off, even though he hadn't had an evening meal. He contemplated getting some food, but next thing he knew he was startled awake as someone nearby screamed.

He sat up and looked over at the woman. She was awake, eyes wide, terrified, sitting on her blankets.

"Who are you?" she asked, a tremor in her voice. "Where am I?"

It took a moment for Col's mind to clear and recall why she didn't recognize him. He'd been wearing his mask before.

"I'm..."

Who was he: Colric of Haverstal or Arron of Malacaster—the Black Bandit, his alter ego?

"I'm Col," he said slowly. "We met this afternoon. I was calling myself Arron then, the Black Bandit, but my real name is Col." He didn't know why he was trusting her with that information. She could run off and tell anyone now. He didn't think she would though. "You're in my... house... as simple as it is."

The fire had died low, the glowing embers radiating a faint, pulsing orange light. It was hard to make out the walls, but she looked around. She must have had exceptional vision as she looked around then up, eyes going wide. "It's all made of trees."

"Yes, the fey made it for me."

"Fey!" She shuddered, drawing her knees up to her chest and hugging them as she looked around suddenly.

"They won't hurt you," he said to her.

"They've done enough already," she said softly, still on guard.

The fey? Had they done something to her? Was that why she felt like fey to Ayneii? That was a question for later.

"What's your name?" Col asked.

"What? Oh." She blinked. "I'm Dalia Ath—" She clamped her mouth shut. After a moment she repeated, "I'm Dalia."

Col had caught the correction. He didn't blame her if she didn't want him to know her full name.

"It's late, can I get you anything? Food? A bath?" He motioned to the tub. "I can have it warmed for you."

She sat blinking at the tub for a moment.

He rose and went over to one of the shelves, retrieving the clothes Lily had brought and setting them next to Dalia. "Here is a change of clothes for you."

She didn't seem to understand. She kept looking from him to the clothes to the bath. Finally, a tear came to her eye. "Thank you, f... for everything."

He smiled. "Why don't I leave you for a bit and go get some food. You have a nice bath and call out when you're done."

She nodded. "Thank you... again." He rose, but she called to him as he reached the door. "You said you could have the water heated?"

Before Col turned back, he whispered, "Ayneii." She appeared nearby. When he turned, he gauged Dalia's reaction. Once again, it seemed the fey had appeared only to him. "It will be warm when you're ready," he said with a nod to Ayneii. She made a face at the unspoken command and then nodded, sighing.

"How?" she asked.

"The fey can be very useful." He glanced at Ayneii adding, "And kind, and generous."

The sprite made another face. Oddly, so did Dalia; it was clear she didn't believe him.

"Oh," Dalia said. She seemed like she wanted to say more but didn't. She just nodded.

"Holler when you're done," he said and left.

He hoped she'd still be there when he got back.

4

Lord Vandar Gariast watched the nubile form of his maid as she lit the candles around his study. The sun was fully down now with only faint traces of light on the horizon visible through the two clear glass doors which led out onto a wide veranda overlooking his estates.

His gaze slipped from the girl to the doors and the view beyond. Those doors had come at great expense to Lord Gariast. Such a large area of clear glass was incredibly hard to come by. There weren't two doors to match these anywhere in the kingdom, not even at the royal palace. But then, the royals weren't as rich as he, so they could not afford such luxuries. They had to worry about armies and droughts and feeding a kingdom. He didn't. Though in a way he did care, but only in so much as it profited him. He was, after all, the kingdom's largest supplier of grain, steel, wool, and pigs, as well as a myriad of other less essential commodities. Without him, the kingdom's army would be ill-fed and ill-equipped. The kingdom needed him and paid him well for its needs.

He reclined on a long divan of soft cushions, a wide, satisfied grin spreading across his square face as he took in the final dying breaths of the day. Soon, all of the south would be his.

He had to laugh at how easily he'd gotten away with murdering an entire rival noble family. Not only had his assassins done their job well and left no one alive at the estates, but then that Athernon girl had arrived on the scene and somehow taken the blame for the killing.

Vandar still wasn't sure exactly how that had happened. The girl would be arriving soon to spend the night in his dungeons before moving on to the capital tomorrow, so perhaps he'd ask her. He'd heard rumors of her doing strange things, being possessed or cursed or something, but he cared little. As long as she somehow took the blame from him and made everyone look elsewhere, he wouldn't question his good luck.

He looked back at the maid in her simple white dress. She knelt before one of the two hearths in the room lighting another taper to finish with the remaining candles. His grin grew.

"Come here, my sweetling."

She rose and turned, nodding. She blew out the taper she had just lit and set it aside then made her way over to stand beside the divan.

"Closer," he said, reaching out a hand lazily, and she stepped in until he was touching the soft skin of her ankle.

He slid his hand up her calf, behind her knee, then farther along her thigh until he cupped the yielding round flesh of her buttock. She didn't even flinch at his touch anymore.

He consumed her with his eyes. She was a fine creature, young and fresh and pretty. Sure, she would never rival the great noblewomen with their fancy dresses, makeup, and the latest styles of hair, but that bothered him little. She was exactly what he wanted, even if she wasn't what he usually considered as beautiful. He liked the purity of blonde hair and fair skin on a woman, pale and pristine. This girl was slightly darker of complexion, having spent much of her life outdoors before he'd acquired her. Her hair was brown, long and thick, waves tumbling down to her mid-back. Her one interesting feature was her eyes, large and green. But she was attractive enough physically, a young body with curves in all the right places, and besides she wasn't his favorite toy because of how she looked. It was who she was that made all the difference.

He pulled her closer using the hand on her buttock. She stumbled, not ready for the action, and half fell. Her knees landed on the edge of the cushioned divan, her arms catching the raised back of the long chair such that she was arched over top of him. Her hair fell over him tracing across his face. With his other hand, he reached up to her head, grabbed a fistful of that thick hair and pushed her face down to his, then yanked her forward, tipping her off balance so she fell, half sitting on him.

He forced her lips to his, hair stuck between them, tasting it and the sweet youth of her lips. She relented, knowing not to fight him. He lingered over the kiss, feeling the soft press of her body on his.

When he finally drew her head back, away from his, his tongue still licking his lips from her sweetness, he met the dispassionate stare from those large green eyes.

"One day soon," he said softly. "I will put some life back into those eyes, my dear. I will find your brother and make you watch while I break him. Or perhaps I'll make him watch as I take you. Which would you prefer?"

She remained still, unmoved, unmoving. Sometimes he wished he could get a rise out of her as he had when he'd first taken her.

"I guess I could do both," he said with a grin and shoved her off him.

She had enough grace and balance not to fall but found her feet and stood before him once again.

"Finish with the candles, then wait at the door to my bedchamber."

She nodded faintly with the bob of a curtsey then resumed her duties.

He rose from the divan and went to his desk. Just as he sat, there was a knock at the door.

"Enter," he commanded, and a moment later Lord Trentin Edwir, a knight captain who'd sworn fealty to Lord Gariast, strode into the room.

"What news, Captain? Is the girl arrived safely?" Vandar asked.

The man frowned and looked away for a moment. "Sire, we... I lost her. We were ambushed by the Black Bandit, and the girl used that distraction to escape."

Vandar pursed his lips. In truth, he cared little for the wench, though he had considered having his way with her while she was in his cells. Defiling such a young thing, and a noblewoman at that, was a rare opportunity. What he didn't like was that she would not hang as planned. The longer she was alive, the more time there was for someone to be looking for her, and hence, also looking into the deaths of Lord Rossferol and his family. No, he needed her dead... soon.

He rose slowly, savoring the effect his scowl had on the other man. Trentin was a large man, towering over Vandar, but the knight was afraid. For good reason.

"Bring up your men. All of them," he commanded, and Trentin nodded, turning on his heels and leaving.

While the knight was away, Vandar sauntered over to a rack of his prized weapons. He chose a sword, one of his favorites. He glanced at the maid, wondering if she knew this had once been her brother's sword. It was the same blade the man had used to best Vandar at the tournament at Chestley three years ago. He'd had it confiscated when the man had been arrested later that year. That had been a masterstroke of cunning, a plan worthy of him. It had lacked only the final element. The man's death. Instead, the once-captain in the King's Army had escaped and fled into the wilderness.

Vandar sauntered back to his desk, standing in front of it this time. He leaned the sword against the heavy wooden frame and waited.

Trentin returned with the five other knights and a dozen footmen.

They stood in a line before him.

He picked up the sword and stalked down the line. "I have trouble believing that a little girl could escape so many of you so easily. So, tell me, which one of you helped her escape?"

The men shifted and shuffled, but no one answered. He hadn't truly expected an answer. Perhaps he should provide some incentive. "Ten gold to any man who tells me who helped the girl escape."

A man spoke up almost instantly. "It was Ulvic, sir."

Vandar spun on the man who spoke. "Tell me everything!"

The man was trembling. His voice quavered as he said, "The girl cut her bonds free on his spear."

Vandar turned to Trentin. "Is this true?"

"I couldn't see that moment of the encounter, my lord."

Vandar would come back to him. He addressed the other five knights. "Did any of you?"

One stepped forward. "Yes, Lord Gariast. I saw what happened. It is as the man says. The girl freed herself on Ulvic's spear."

Vandar nodded. "And which one is Ulvic?"

The knight pointed down the line. Vandar spotted him, the quavering footman. He looked like he wanted to run. As Vandar approached he did try to run, but the same knight who spoke up was there to stop him. The knight held him firm.

Lord Gariast slashed the blade across the man's throat, cutting deeply in one quick attack, and the knight let the man fall.

Vandar wiped his sword on the dead man's armor. "You, knight, what's your name?"

"Lord Kerrik Tandor, sire."

Vandar nodded. "You may go, but I appreciate your keen eyes and swift action. Return here in one candle-mark for a reward."

The knight nodded and left.

Lord Gariast returned to pacing in front of the men. Killing one of them had been satisfying, but there needed to be some repercussion for their leader as well. "Lord Trentin Edwir, come to me."

The large knight stepped forward and strode confidently to Vandar. If he thought he was about to die at least he was facing it like a man.

"You failed in your mission."

"Yes, sire."

"I want to hear you say it."

"I let the girl escape. I failed, sire," the man said stoically.

Vandar grabbed the other's throat. Trentin was taller and stronger, but he was also a true nobleman. Lord Gariast knew he'd never think to lay a hand on a superior, so Vandar squeezed, hard. Feeling the man's life-beat pulsing beneath his fingers.

Trentin sputtered and gasped.

Vandar smiled. He wasn't going to kill his captain—he still needed the man—but that didn't mean he couldn't teach him a lesson. Besides, he just really wanted to see the man's eyes bulge out as he drew close to death. So, he squeezed a little harder, reveling in the strained sounds of pain and desperation.

Finally, he let go, and Trentin fell to the carpeted floor of the study gasping.

For good measure, Gariast kicked him in the head, satisfied with the crunch of a breaking nose.

Trentin rolled to his side with a groan, failing to stop the blood pouring from his nose from splattering on the floor.

"Don't get blood on my carpet," Gariast said, kicking the man again so that he rolled away onto the cold stone of the floor close to one of the hearths.

"Perhaps," Gariast said, kneeling beside his captain, his tone soft and deadly, just loud enough for the others to hear, "You now see the price of failure." He drew in a steadying breath. "Tomorrow you will report to me here. I will tell you where the girl is being kept. You will fetch her back for me. Do you understand?"

Trentin nodded feebly.

"Good." Gariast pried the captain's hand away from his broken nose. He then used the thumb of his other hand to press down on the red, swollen flesh that had once been a straight nose. He pressed until the other man screamed. "Because, if you fail me again, you'll suffer far more than a broken nose. I will take your lands and I will make you watch as I have my men rape your new wife then beat her to death. Then I'll very slowly and carefully flay the flesh off you so that you'll suffer for weeks before you die. Do you understand me?"

The man nodded.

"Good, now get out of my sight and get to a healer."

Vandar rose and turned away. He heard Trentin scramble to his feet and flee the room.

"The rest of you may go." He waved his hand dismissing them. They too fled with all haste.

Gariast's gaze fell upon the trembling form of Rissa, his maid, standing by the door to his bedchambers.

Good. She was scared. Let her be. Tonight, he would make her scream as she had in the old days, though she'd probably need a little more incentive than usual. He considered using a whip or cat-o-nine-tails to rend the flesh off her, but no, he wanted to keep her mostly intact for now. Besides, it would be so much more rewarding to use his hands and feel the tender flesh give way to his rage.

He smiled and stalked over to her. She looked like she wanted to flee, but there was nowhere she could go. With each of his steps, her terror grew and so did his grim smile.

5

DALIA DRESSED QUICKLY. THE FIRE WAS BURNING LOW AND THE chill of the night was seeping into the small, odd cabin. The dress was a sturdy one, if by no means fashionable. It was a little large on her, the hem brushing the floor where it probably went to the ankle of the woman who'd provided it. It was gray and mostly formless except for a tie under the bust, which helped create the illusion of a high waist and fuller figure. There were sturdy woolen stockings as well and a knitted shawl. She looked like some old beggar woman, but right now that's what she was —well, everything but old.

The dress was comfortable enough but just didn't feel right. Nothing here felt right. Nothing had felt right for days now: not this dress, or this house, or having been blamed for murdering a whole family or... The Fury—

She could put her finger on one thing that definitely made her uneasy: fey.

Fey had built this house, had warmed her water, and could have been watching her bathe. She'd never thought ill of the fey, well not too ill anyway. Not until a week ago, when her life had changed forever because of one.

Though some small voice in the back of her mind told her she'd wanted this. That the fey had only granted her a wish. She'd just never expected it would turn out like this, all wrong and upside down.

She tried to shake those thoughts from her head as she called out, "I'm finished with the bath!" As some strange afterthought, she added, "Thank you!"

A moment later, Col—or Arron, the Black Bandit, whoever he was—entered with two wooden bowls filled with something steaming. She caught his appraising look as he laid eyes on her. It was something unintentional most men did, looking a woman over. Many noblemen had done the same thing when she'd been introduced to them. The odd thing was... Col smiled kindly after. Here she was in a bag of a dress with her hair still a mess, despite how hard she'd tried to wash it out. She'd never considered herself pretty, even in her old life. Yet now, dressed as a peasant, he seemed to be pleased with how she looked? It baffled her.

"Here," he said, handing her one of the bowls. "Venison stew. It's not the tastiest thing you'll ever have, but it's warm and filling."

She nodded her thanks.

He glanced at the fire. "I should build that up."

"That would be nice," she said, hearing how tentative and soft her voice was. She sounded like she had before she'd been cursed.

He set his bowl down and left, returning a moment later with a bundle of kindling. After several trips, he'd brought in enough wood to keep the fire going for some time. He set about building it up again as she ate. As he'd promised, the meal didn't taste that great. It was good enough, but there were no herbs or spices, which made it bland. As she ate, she watched him.

He was... precise, yes, that was the word. It seemed everything he did was intentional and purposeful. There was an efficiency of movement and action, which surprised her. She wasn't sure why. She'd not expected some forest-dwelling bandit to be so meticulous.

"How did you come to be here?" she asked after a moment. "To be the Black Bandit?"

He chuckled, but then oddly turned somber. "That's a long story." He stopped what he was doing and looked up at her. "I suspect yours is an equally long and interesting story? Perhaps when I'm done we can share our tales."

She didn't give any indication of agreement. She wasn't sure if she wanted to share her tale with anyone. It was still a fresh wound and would not be easy to recount.

Once the fire was going strong, he sat back and picked up his bowl to eat.

Perhaps he saw the hesitance in her eyes. He said simply, "I don't think you're willing to talk just yet, are you?"

She shook her head. Whatever else he was, he was also quite perceptive.

He nodded. "I don't know what you've been through," he said slowly. "But I know there are things I've been through that even after a couple of years are still hard to talk about. So, whenever you're ready." He ate a few bites then added. "Perhaps a good night's rest will help. It's late, and once we're done eating, we should probably get some sleep. How does that sound?"

She tried a tentative smile. "That would be appreciated. Thank you." Despite having slept most of the day, she was still exhausted. She'd been far too active with little rest these past days.

He finished his meal and threw a few more logs on the fire to keep it going, and then they settled on their blankets for what sleep they could.

The ground was hard, little cushioned by the layers of blankets beneath her. There was a bit of a pillow for her head made from several blankets rolled together, but it was nothing like her bed at home. It was, however, far better than the bare wooden cot she'd been on the night before in the dungeons at Fort Hiliar. She settled as best she could and did eventually find some peace.

LORD TRENTIN EDWIR DIDN'T LIKE THIS AT ALL.

A few strands of morning sunlight filtered down on him and a dozen footmen as they crept through the Sandren Forest toward a place they'd been told the girl should be. The underbrush was thick, so they'd left their horses behind. Now he was just another man in heavy armor. He led a group of footmen, no other knights. He hoped he had enough men to bring the girl back. Failure was not an option he wanted to consider. He'd known Lord Gariast for several years now and the man's threats were never idle. Trentin was very aware that failure would mean a painful death for him and his wife and daughter. He was a low enough ranking knight that there had been no marriage of convenience for him. He'd married for love, and Hana had been a ray of light in his otherwise dreary life. Working for Lord Gariast was not how he'd hoped to be spending his days. The knights of old fought to protect their people. They were honorable and valorous. Gariast wasn't any of those things.

Then there was Lord Gariast's pet wizard. That man scared Trentin even more than Lord Gariast himself, and that was no easy feat. The man was aloof and... odd. He wasn't tall, but his large, dark eyes seemed too intense, like he was staring into some unknown place within your soul. He displayed little emotion, which was fine enough, but Trentin had seen some of the things the man had done with his foul magic. Terrible things. Yet the man remained stoic, as if such acts were of no concern, or beneath him. Yes, that was the feeling of the man: that Trentin, and the whole world with him, were nothing to the wizard.

It was the wizard who'd pointed to a spot on the map of the Sandren Forest after sniffing at a scrap of the girl's dress, which had been torn and left behind in the carriage—which they'd eventually recovered. It was like the man was some sort of magical hunting dog. He knew exactly where she'd be. Only it was Trentin who was actually doing the hunting.

As if that didn't bother him enough, there was the girl herself to think about. Trentin had picked her up at Fort Hiliar to transport to Gariast's dungeons, then on to the Capital. He hadn't witnessed her feats before that... he'd only heard tales.

'Possessed' the other soldiers had said of her, 'cursed'. Her list of deeds was significant. She'd killed one of her father's soldiers and crippled two others when they'd come to take her home after she'd run away. Then the truly gruesome events had transpired. She'd apparently ripped the entire family of her betrothed husband to shreds and been found eating the corpses or drinking their blood, or some such thing. The men who'd taken her then had also suffered grave injuries, but she'd relented after a short fight apparently.

Then there had been the escape from his men the previous day. He hadn't seen any of it, having been flat on his back after his tangle with the Black Bandit. Yet his men spoke of the woman in hushed and terrified tones. She hadn't injured anyone, but to hear their tales, she'd done things no person should be able to do. Trentin wasn't particularly looking forward to trying to apprehend her. If any of the tales were true, she was to be feared as much as Lord Gariast or his wizard.

But what choice did he have? If he didn't bring the girl in, he and his family would perish.

And yet... if he died trying to bring her in... his family would still probably suffer for his failure.

A part of him wanted to take his men—they were loyal to him not Gariast—and return to his keep. He could steal his wife and child away in the night, even the families of his men, and run. If it wasn't for his oath of honor to his liege lord, he would have. Honor still meant something to him...

Even if it didn't to Lord Gariast.

COL LIKED THESE SPRING MORNINGS IN THE FOREST. A CLOAK KEPT the chill away well enough as he patrolled the camp and spoke to his men. A light mist clung to the ground and the trees, swirling around his feet. Sun filtered through the thick canopy above and where it hit the misty air there were long diagonal shafts of light. It was beautiful and still. He had time to think and plan.

He'd return to his cottage soon enough. Dalia had wanted another bath. He laughed at that. He must be a bit pungent as it had been a day or two since his last washing. She'd been here two days and had bathed on both days. He highly suspected she was a noble of some sort, though she'd still not said anything about what had brought her here. Her mannerism and posture along with that tattered dress she'd worn yesterday all pointed to a noble upbringing. Either that or perhaps some wealthy merchant's daughter?

She'd asked for a brush for her hair before the bath, which one of the other women had provided. Being 'presentable' wasn't something most of those living here worried about, but it still meant something to her apparently.

Ayneii popped into existence beside him. He flinched but

settled quickly. She'd been doing that for two years and he was *almost* used to it.

"The weird woman is done with her bath and now dressed and brushing her hair, if you wanted to return."

"Thank you, Ayneii." He turned to head back. "Last night, while she rested, did you get a chance to investigate her condition any further?"

Ayneii shook her little head. "No, I still feel awkward just being near her. I'd rather not have to touch her if I don't have to."

Col laughed a little. "You're waiting for her to tell me what happened, aren't you?"

"Maybe."

Col reached his cabin and knocked on the solid wood beside the door coverings. "How are you doing, m'lady?" He figured the title might put her at ease.

It was several moments before she answered. "You may come in."

He did.

She was finishing up with her hair and... he had to admit he was quite taken with the image before him. Her head was tilted to one side as she finished brushing the ends. It fell in waves now, not tangles. Soft brown in color, the fire adding tinges of red, or perhaps those were natural shades; he wasn't sure. It fell to just past her shoulders. Her face was clean, and she wore a small, distracted smile. Her eyes, slightly hidden by a half-curtain of hair, were clearest blue, pale like a summer's sky. She wasn't tall or particularly curvy, but she had a fineness of features, slender and delicate, which even the simple dress she wore couldn't hide.

She caught him looking at her. "Sorry, m'lady. I don't mean to stare. But you are well transformed from the woman I rescued yesterday."

Her smile grew at that. "You are kind to say so." A few more strokes and she finished with her hair. "Thank you for the use of the brush." She closed the distance between them and held it out for him. He raised his hand to hers. Her skin was soft. He let his hand fall away.

"I'm sure the other women have others and wouldn't begrudge you this one. Keep it."

Those blue eyes fixed on his. "Again, you are too kind." She turned away and placed the brush on a shelf.

Losing eye contact seemed to break the spell she'd had on him, and he drew a sudden breath. Had he been breathing? He shook that off.

"Would you like to walk?" he asked.

She turned back to him with a nod.

"Perhaps," he said as she drew near and rested her hand on his arm, as was common for noblewomen to do when being escorted. "Perhaps I can tell you my tale. Then, if you feel up to it, you can tell me yours?"

"Perhaps," she said softly.

He didn't expect much more.

They left the cabin and he started her on a wide circuit around the camp. "My story begins... well if I go all the way back it begins in a forest, not unlike this one." There were others that knew his story, but it felt good to tell her, even if he knew it would still be... difficult in places.

"As I mentioned, my name is Colric of Haverstal. If you haven't heard of it, Haverstal is a village in the Sellian Forest, north of here."

She nodded and when he glanced over, she was watching him. There was an odd look in her eyes as if she was searching for something within him. He didn't know what to make of this. He looked away and went on.

"My father was a hunter, a good one. He kept our family and

the village well fed, and our furs were even sold to nobility in the capital."

"Truly?"

"Yes. We had a contact there who took in our wares and sold them to nobles, even at the palace."

"Oh."

"It was a good life, looking back on it now, but as a boy I wanted something more. I wanted to join the King's Army and help defend our kingdom from the Orcs in the north, or the Forsean in the south, even Santhine in the east. I will admit it. I felt like I was destined for more than hunting."

They were nearing the small stream where Col had drawn the water for her baths. It burbled and babbled along, and a ray of sunshine shone down through a still patch of water showing several fish lazily swimming against the current, seemingly unmoving.

"I'd learned the bow before I was ten and could land a deer at a hundred paces by the time I was twelve. By that point, my two younger brothers were helping my father a lot, so I decided to make the three-day journey to the capital and test for the King's Army. Even I was surprised at making it in. I was naturally quick and agile, and even though I'd never trained with weapons other than the bow, I could best older boys simply by seeing what they were going to do before they did it and being quick enough to find a way to counter it. The tester, Lord Quillian, said I was a natural and took me under his wing and began my training."

"I remember old Lord Quillian," she said softly. "He was a nice man, always laughing and smiling."

Colric nodded. "That he was." Her knowledge of the man almost certainly meant she was nobility. "He—"

Col was cut off by Ayneii suddenly appearing before him. "Someone's coming!"

Dalia let out a clipped scream. Apparently, Ayneii had appeared to both of them. Whether from some fear of the fey, or just the surprise, Dalia retreated behind Col as Ayneii went on.

"There is a group of thirteen men sneaking through the woods. They're coming from the north, and they'll be here shortly. They have weapons and armor. I don't think they mean to join us. They feel... aggressive.

"Have the others been alerted?"

Ayneii nodded.

"We'll go to our defensive positions." They had long ago developed a plan for how they would defend the camp. They knew the forest and the camp well and would use that against any attackers. "I'll meet you there after I return the lady to my cabin."

Ayneii nodded and vanished.

Col turned to Dalia. "I'm sorry about that. I'd hoped you'd meet Ayneii on slightly less startling terms." He took her hands. She was trembling. There was a mixed look of terror and restraint in her eyes.

Dalia shook her head. "I'm sure she's a nice fey. My experience with others was not so pleasant."

He wanted to ask what had happened, but now was not the time. He started her back toward the cabin.

"They're here for me," she said suddenly. "Those men in the forest, I know it. They've come to take me away."

Col turned her to face him as they reached the doorway of his cottage. "I won't let them." He laid a hand on her shoulder.

Her trembling was worse now.

Her next words caught him by surprise. "If I start to fight, you need to make sure you and your men are well away from me." Even the manner in which she spoke was odd, jaw tight, body rigid. Everything about her was tense.

He put his other hand on her other shoulder. "If you stay

here the fight won't reach you." He tried to calm her, but it didn't seem to take.

"I don't think I'll be able to." Something changed within her then. Her eyes seemed to glaze over, not seeing him or perhaps anything else. "I'm sorry," she whispered, then broke free of his hold and ran.

In some ways, he didn't blame her for running... until he realized she was running toward the attackers... not away.

6

DALIA HOVERED IN THE STRANGE PLACE SHE FOUND HERSELF WHEN The Fury took her. The world was, at the same time, both a narrow tunnel in a focused direction and completely open and revealed to her. Every noise was registered and monitored: was it a danger? Was it important?

She ran with a speed she didn't know she possessed, crashing through bushes and brush, tearing her new dress. A part of her registered this, but that part wasn't in control right now.

There were men ahead of her, a knight and twelve footmen with spears. She saw their surprise and knew exactly how to use that against them. These first few moments, while they were disoriented, would be key.

She reached the first man, knocked his hastily thrust spear aside and struck at his throat. He fell choking.

Another man turned to her. He would fall next.

∼

TOM STOOD ON A PLATFORM UP IN A TREE. THREE QUIVERS WERE

nearby as well as a rope to swing to another platform or descend to the ground. His bow was in hand and an arrow ready, pulled back to his ear as he sighted one of the men approaching.

That was when some blur of gray ran into the fight and dropped the man with a single blow.

"What in the—?"

The blur stopped for just a heartbeat. It was that girl. She certainly looked a damn sight better than she had the day before, washed and hair brushed, as it settled behind her.

Another man attacked her. He adjusted his aim to take this one down, but the girl moved too quickly. Tom didn't even see what she'd done, but suddenly she had the man's spear and he was on the ground holding his stomach.

Who was this woman?

"She certainly can fight," Riiku said, hovering nearby, the golden and red colored sprite, like a bright splash of autumn leaves, spoke a little dispassionately. Riiku usually didn't care much for fighting. "I've never seen you move like that. You'd be a lot more interesting if you did."

"Thanks," Tom said flatly. He chose another target, far away from where the girl was fighting and released. The arrow took the man in the shoulder. The soldier dropped his spear and fell to his knees holding the wound. He wouldn't be much of a concern now.

Tom drew another arrow, but the targets were rapidly dwindling. Other archers had taken down a few men, though it seemed the girl was doing the bulk of the work.

She'd just finished with her fifth man and turned to the knight, the only man still standing. The knight roared and charged her. She ducked under the man's swing and spun around so she was behind him. Tom could have fired at the knight, but watched, fascinated.

Dalia kicked the knight in the back, sending him stumbling

forward into a tree. He turned. Three more rapid kicks hit the knight, the first pushing his sword away, the second causing him to drop the weapon, the third to his chin, knocking his head back and his helm off.

Then the fight was over.

The knight was somehow pinned against the tree, gasping for air with the girl's foot pinned on his throat. She was doing a standing splits to reach the neck of the much taller man, leaning in slightly, planted and firm. His head was tilted back, and his arm flailed for a moment before he went limp.

She released him, and they fell to the ground at the same time. She fell to her knees, panting hard. The knight was still.

Tom verified there were no other threats, then put the arrow he'd been holding away and went to the rope to go down and help with the cleanup.

"She certainly is something," Riiku said.

Tom couldn't deny that.

DALIA ALTERNATED BETWEEN GULPING BREATHS AND RETCHING.

This time had been different.

The first time The Fury had taken her, she hadn't been able to recall anything for half a day. The second time it had been hours before she remembered any details, and the third shorter still. Yesterday it had been only minutes. This time she'd actually been fully aware of her actions and recalled everything clearly. The sounds and sights and smells of battle lingered in her senses. The snap of broken bones, the screams of men in pain, the sight of blood, the smell of worse as men lost control of their bowels.

A hand on her back startled her. She knew it wasn't a foe, but still The Fury threatened to return for just a moment. She liked to think she forced it down, but truly, she knew she had little control over it.

"Are you well?" Col's voice was concerned. "You're hurt."

Was she?

She sat back on her heels and looked at him. His gaze was on her arm. There was a clean, straight cut on the sleeve of the dress with blood stained around it. She didn't feel hurt. She probed with a finger to find the wound. It stung, like a sliver, but only when touched.

"I don't think it's that bad."

He nodded. His gaze drifted up and away to the bodies around her. "You... have an amazing ability," he said, though a hesitancy in his voice belied his words.

Amazing or terrifying?

Others were joining them now, more of Col's band, each surveying her handiwork in silence. There were whispers too. She wasn't sure if it was an effect of her fey curse, but her senses were sharper now. She heard nearly all of the comments they made.

"Who is she?" one man asked another.

It was the other man's reply that hit to the core of her fears. "*What* is she?"

Col squeezed her shoulder in a reassuring way. Then he rose and took charge. "Everyone, let's get these men tied up and tended. We don't kill if we don't have to, so patch up who we can."

That set the others in motion and Col returned to her. "Do you think you can get back to my cabin?"

She nodded, rising a little unsteady. "I'll... I'll see you there."

She left the scene, not daring to look back.

~

COL WATCHED DALIA MOVE AWAY, HER STEPS UNSTEADY. HE should have offered to help her, but he had things here to take care of.

Tom came to Col's side. "Did you see her fight?" he asked. There was no need to ask who 'she' was.

"Yes."

"Still think it's wise to keep her here?"

Col didn't hesitate. "Yes."

Tom gave him a questioning look.

Col sighed. "Why not keep her here? Why not help her? She obviously needs a friend in this world, just like the rest of us. It's clear to me now she won't attack us unless we give her provocation, which I don't plan on doing. She only attacked these men, not us. She's been civil the rest of the time she's been here."

Tom gave a half nod to that. "You make a good point, Captain." He still added, "you sure she won't be... unpredictable?"

"No, but that's what makes life interesting. I can't control what you do half the time."

"True, but I don't try to kill you."

"And neither has she."

Tom shrugged.

"Can you take care of gathering up these men?" Col asked his friend. "Just put them anywhere for now. Keep that knight separate and strip him of his armor. I'll want to speak to him." He grimaced. "And we'll need to leave soon."

Tom nodded. "I'd been wondering if you'd give the order to leave. We'll head to the second site?"

Col nodded. "Can you get that underway as well?"

Tom grinned. "Will do, Captain." He moved off to see to his duties.

Col took a moment to survey the enemies being rounded up. Oddly, the only ones who were seriously hurt were the ones who'd been hit by his own men's arrows. The ones Dalia had fought were all just stunned, winded, or unconscious.

Analla, an older woman who had come with her son after their lands had been taken from them, served as the healer for Col's men. She was arriving to inspect the attackers and do what she could for them.

Once the enemy knight was stripped of his armor—leaving only the silks and padding beneath—Col had three men tie him up and place him on the ground leaning against a tree. He made a quick trip back to his cabin to get his mask and put it on before he returned to interrogate the man.

Col threw water on the knight's head to wake him.

The knight sputtered and looked at Col who still held the pitcher of water. The look in the man's eyes after he'd regained himself was defeated. The rest of his face didn't look much better. His nose looked to have been recently broken and reset, which left his eyes swollen and bruised and his nose a red angry lump.

"We need to have a talk," Col said.

The knight sighed. "It matters little now."

"Why?"

"I failed. I and my family are dead. It only remains to see whether it's you who kills me or Lord Gariast."

"He'd do that to one of his knights?" Col knew Lord Gariast was a brute and felt rage bubble inside him at the mere mention of the man's name. But killing his own men...?

"He has done, and will do, far worse than just kill a man for failure. As I said, my family is in danger now."

"Your family?" Though Col should not have been surprised. When he'd escaped Gariast, he'd found out his family had been taken in his place and slaughtered. It was one of the things that haunted him to this day.

The knight nodded. "My wife and daughter."

Col changed his tactics. "What's your name?"

"Lord Trentin Edwir of Thornkeep."

"Why did you come today? How did you find us?" Col kept his tone lighter, not as pressing, the man didn't seem to be resisting that much anyway.

"The girl. Gariast wants her. I don't know why. He told us where you were hiding, where to find her. He has a wizard who used magic to find the lady."

"A wizard?" This was news indeed. It would drastically change how he dealt with Lord Gariast if ever the time came. Col had always thought magic was only for the fey, but there had been legends of wizards in the past, and if Gariast had one now... that did not bode well.

His mind was working, spinning through a thousand thoughts, trying to settle on something that would help him get out of this mess.

"We'll have to find a new camp," he said, mostly to himself. But he wondered if this wizard would be able to find them wherever they went.

The knight pleaded with him. "Does the girl mean anything to you? Let me take her in, for the sake of my family... please."

"Gariast will never have her." Col was adamant. "But..." An idea was forming. "What if your family wasn't in danger?"

The knight looked at him oddly. "How do you mean?"

This was a risk, but Col went ahead with it. "If you and your men join with me, we can go and get your family, bring them... well not here, but we'll find another camp."

"Live like this? In the forest?"

"Live free, without having to worry about what Gariast or any other lord is going to do to you."

The man gave a halfhearted nod.

"I can't guarantee a long or easy life, but it will be longer than if you reported back to Gariast with another failure. Am I wrong?" Trentin shook his head. "And your family would be... safer."

Another nod.

Perhaps a bit more convincing was in order. "Do you know who I am?"

"Arron of Malacaster, the Black Bandit."

"Yes... and no. Does the name Colric of Haverstal mean anything to you?" This was a risk, a big one.

"I think I recognize the name." He seemed to be thinking, perhaps trying to recall where he'd heard the name before.

Col removed his mask. "I am Colric of Haverstal." He peered into the man's eyes for any recognition.

The knight looked at him a little more carefully. "You look familiar..." After a moment, his eyes went wide. "You!"

Col smiled. "Me it is."

"From the tournament at Chestley and... oh... If Gariast knew..."

"Exactly. I have as much reason to hate the man as you, perhaps more."

Trentin nodded. There was something else in the man's look, something he was hiding. Col let it go for now.

"So, will you join with me against Gariast, against the king?"

"What is your plan?"

"The first step is to get your family and see if any other men at your keep will join us. What say you? Will you join me?"

The man sat there for a long moment before he finally nodded.

"I will. I swear fealty to you, Colric of Haverstal."

"That's nice, but I'm no lord. I'll earn your fealty as you earn my trust. Just to be safe, we'll leave your men here as we go to get your family. How far away is your keep?"

"Not that far actually, at the edge of the Sandren to the east. Perhaps a half-day's ride from here."

"We have no horses here. It would take some time to walk."

"My men and I left horses at the edge of the forest. We could use those."

Col nodded. Turning to the guards he said, "Untie him and give him some new clothes. Keep a sharp eye on him; I need to make preparations for a trip."

"Thank you," Trentin said softly.

Col helped the man up.

We'll see if you'll be thanking me when this is all over.

7

DALIA PACED THE CABIN.

Gods! What must Col and his men think of her?

She hadn't said anything when he'd come to get his mask. She hadn't known what to say then. But now...

"I should go," Dalia said in a rush when Col arrived. More words tumbled out before he could speak. "I am only endangering you. Between my curse and those looking for me, I am nothing but trouble."

She didn't have anything here. She would have loved to ask for some clothes and personal items, but she doubted these people had much they could spare. She'd go and find her own way in the wild.

Col stood there. He looked a little stunned. His mouth hung half open as he listened to her. When she finished, he shrugged. "I won't stop you. You are free to go when you wish."

She'd expected as much.

"But I wish you would stay."

That she hadn't expected.

"Why?" The word slipped out before she could rein in her tongue.

He laughed a little. It was a soft, sympathetic sound. "I think you need someone to help you. It doesn't seem like the rest of the world cares much for you at the moment, and well, that's what this place is: it's where people come when the rest of the world doesn't want them or is hunting them." He took a step toward her. "Dalia, I don't know what's happening with you, and that's fine. You can tell me or not as you wish. But I can see that you need help, and I... would like to help you. If I can."

This time she did take a moment to think before she asked, "Why?" Her voice was quiet, her emotions bubbling up at this man's kindness: fear and thankfulness mixed with curiosity at why someone... anyone would help her. At the same time, she felt so alone and afraid and uncertain. She desperately wanted someone to hold her and tell her all would be well. She just still couldn't understand why he wanted to help her when no one else did.

He stepped closer still and laid a tentative hand on her shoulder. She resisted the urge to just collapse into him, hoping he might hold her. He was still so much a stranger to her. They'd only met yesterday. But... there was something calming and tender about him that drew her to him.

He spoke slowly, tenderly, "I get the feeling we are kindred souls, you and I." She looked up at this. His eyes were soft brown pools, understanding, inviting. "We've both lost a great deal and simply want to return to what lives we had, but we can't. I'm only guessing that's the case for you, but it seems logical."

She nodded. It was true.

"Thank you," she said softly. "I'll stay."

He smiled and rubbed her shoulder a little. "Unfortunately, I have to go, for a little while at least."

"What? Where?"

"That knight who attacked us is... well he's also like us and needs some help."

"You just help everyone, don't you? Even your enemies?"

"I don't think he's our enemy anymore. I hope so at least. Now he needs my help to save his family."

"What if it's a trap?" She couldn't let him go. A strange thought came to her then. She'd never wanted The Fury and loathed what it made her do, but... there could be situations where it might come in handy. "Let me come with you. I can help if it is a trap."

He gave a bit of a laugh. "I don't doubt that." He seemed about to say more, then pursed his lips, thinking for a moment. "I've already said you're free to do as you please. I will not trap you here if that's not what you want. You are free to come and go as you please."

"Then you'll let me come with you?"

He nodded. "Though to be honest, I think some of my men might think I've gone crazy to let you come along. Half will wonder why I'm taking a woman, the other half... well I think they're scared of you."

"I know." Her voice had gone to whispers again. She looked away, but not for long. His eyes were so comforting. Her gaze returned to them. "But you aren't." It wasn't a question. She just knew he looked at her and didn't see what she was when The Fury took her. He saw who she was now. "Thank you."

He drew a long breath. "We have a lot of preparation to do and not a lot of time. Will you be ready to go shortly?"

It was her turn to laugh if a little pathetically. "I have nothing but my clothes. I'm ready now."

He gave a nod. "I'll come get you when we're heading out."

An impulse took her and she quickly stepped in to give him a quick, chaste kiss. "Thank you again."

He seemed stunned, then he smiled. "You are most welcome."

TOM STUFFED THE LAST OF HIS BELONGINGS, MEAGER AS THEY were, into a large pack. He looked around the small 'room' that had been his for over a year now, nearly two. There wasn't much here. It wasn't much of a room to begin with. This was the second house the fey had grown for the refugees who lived here. It was larger than Col's but not by much. It hadn't been grown with separate rooms like the last one, so areas had been defined for those who stayed here by hanging 'walls' made of hide. Tom's 'room' had two outer walls and two hide walls. There were shelves for the few things he possessed and a small fire pit he could use to warm himself in the colder times. It was just large enough to hold his blankets laid out on the floor with a little extra room. It wasn't much at all, but he'd come to like it.

Col pushed aside one of the hide walls. "All set?" he asked, entering.

"I'll get people moving. How much time do you think we have?" Tom asked.

"I'd say a few days, but let's be gone from here in a day to make sure."

Tom nodded. "I overheard your conversation with the knight. You're going to help him?"

"We help those who need help. And he needs help."

"Your big heart is going to get you killed one of these days."

"Probably. You're good with handling the move?"

"Yeah. With a little fey help, we'll be gone in no time."

"Oh, thank you for reminding me. I need to talk to Ayneii before I go."

"When are you leaving?"

"As soon as we can. I'll have the knight with me, the new girl, and two others. I'm also taking two more to bring back some horses those men left at the edge of the forest. They could be useful."

Tom looked around, saw he had everything, and followed Col out of the cabin.

Riiku appeared nearby. "I've scouted the second site, and all is well. No unwanted guests... anymore."

Tom gave the sprite a questioning look.

Riiku shrugged. "There may have been a bear or four in the caves."

"Good to know."

"Riiku?" Col asked. He must have seen Tom staring off into space.

Tom nodded. "Go, I'll handle things here. How long do you think you'll be?"

"Hopefully no more than a day. If I don't come back, you're in charge. He tossed Tom the Black Bandit's mask."

Tom held the item reverently. A surge of pride and fear welled within him. He didn't want this. He felt honored, but he was no leader. "I can't."

"You'll have to. These men look up to you, and if I'm gone, then you're all they have."

"Col—"

"I don't want to hear it. You deserve this... and I know you can handle it, Tom."

Tom sighed. "I'll do you proud. But that's a long shot anyway. You'll return, and I'll happily hand this back to you."

Col nodded. "I look forward to it." Then he turned and left.

Tom felt a great weight settle on him.

"Does this mean you're important now?" Riiku asked, her tone denoting she didn't think so.

"Will I ever be important in your eyes?"

Riiku sniffed. "Perhaps, one day."

Tom laughed. "High praise!" And it was. Riiku had always made it clear she didn't think much of Tom. She was happy to help out and be his go-to sprite, but as a human, he'd never felt he'd impressed her. Well he knew he hadn't, because she'd told him so...often.

...but perhaps that was changing.

"WHAT DO YOU KNOW OF WIZARDS?" COL ASKED AYNEII AS HE finished preparing his things. In truth, like Tom, he didn't have much; it filled a pack and that was it. If they were moving the camp, he didn't want to leave anything for others to take. He'd take what he had with him.

He hefted his pack and looked around. The cabin was empty. Dalia had stepped out to clean herself up in the brook by the camp before they left.

Ayneii made one of her scrunched up 'You're using weird human words' face. "What's that?"

"A wizard? It's a human who can use magic."

"Oh." She didn't sound impressed or excited about that. "That's just wrong. That's probably why we don't have a word for it."

"It's happened in the past though, hasn't it?" Col had heard legends of such things, but he had no idea how much truth there was in them.

"Yes, but they are rare. A fey would have to willingly give up some of their power to a human. We can..." She seemed to search for a word for a while. "We can share magic, but usually the fey takes it back once the human is done with it. Also, there haven't been any humans with magic for..." She frowned. "Your concept of time is always confusing."

"Can you count the seasons?"

She shrugged and there was another pause. "That would be thirteen-thousand-four-hundred-and-thirty-three seasons."

Col had to stop to do the math. That was over three thousand years! "Oh." No wonder the fey didn't have a word for it. It was curious that human legends stretch back that far. It must have really made an impact on society.

"And that one was the first one in many thousands of seasons as well."

"Well, there is another one now."

"What! Where?" Ayneii looked around as if the man might be in the room with them. It made Col smile. Her rather innocent and childlike nature for one who was ageless always surprised him.

"Not here, but not far away either. Apparently, magic was used to find our camp."

"Oh," she said, calming a little. "That's not good."

"No, it isn't. What I'm wondering is whether there is any way to stop someone from finding us. Can the fey shield a place or a person somehow so they can't be found?"

Ayneii seemed lost in thought for a moment before answering. "A place, yes, that's not that hard. We already have places we don't like humans going and ways to keep you out. But a person would be a lot harder. You'd need to have some sort of charm."

"I'll settle for just a place for now. You know where our new camp is going to be?"

She nodded.

"Can you make that place so no one can find us, even with magic?"

Another nod.

"Please do that then."

"I will. It might take a little time though."

Just as Ayneii had trouble understanding 'human' time, Col had never really understood how the fey tracked time either.

"Can you do it in a day?" That was a generally agreed upon period they both understood, and also the time in which the task needed to be done.

"I'd need a lot of help, but yes."

"Thank you Ayneii. I'm in your debt."

"You've used that word before, and I still don't know what it means."

"I owe you a favor." But he knew as soon as he said it that word wouldn't work either. The fey were eternally helpful and didn't keep track of who might be one-up on another or 'owe' anything.

"A what?"

"You're the best."

"Oh, I knew that."

He grinned. "Apparently, it's me who sometimes needs to be reminded."

"I'll be sure to tell you more often."

He laughed. Debts and balances were lost on them... as was humility apparently.

8

THE FIVE OF THEM RODE WITH AS MUCH HASTE AS THEY COULD, given their limitations.

Dalia was trained in courtly riding, which for a woman usually meant a more relaxed seat with one leg around the pommel. The use of stirrups was new to her. It looked like Col and Trentin knew how to ride quite well, but Trentin's horse was tethered to Col's, just in case the knight had any thoughts of trying to ride off. The two others, Jaff and Nik, were commoners and had little experience on horseback. All in all, it made for an awkward progression.

During a heaven-sent break from riding, as they walked the horses, Dalia moved closer to Col and Trentin as they struck up a conversation.

"Tell me more about yourself," Col began.

Dalia didn't need to be too close to hear well. Her senses were definitely much more acute since she'd been cursed. She stayed behind them and off to one side.

Trentin took a few long breaths, but then shrugged and began his tale.

"My father was a good man, but never much of a knight. He

was more of a scholar than a warrior. We were not a powerful or wealthy family. Our holdings are small and have no key strategic or productive value. We were surrounded by more significant families: the Athernons to the south and the Rossferols to the east."

Dalia stiffened. She wondered if anyone saw it. The mention of her family had startled her. To make matters worse, the second family mentioned had been that of her betrothed, Padran, now dead—and she was accused of their murders.

"And then there was Gariast to the north," Trentin said, finishing his introduction.

"When the lords petitioned King Thoron for greater power and the creation of a Council of Lords, my father was at home buried in his books. So, he had no say over how his land was divvied up or who became his overlord. Our lands were split. We lost a lot and we ended up the vassals of Gariast. So I grew up only knowing the one overlord. Being a good knight, I made sure I was unerringly loyal to him. Yet the more I saw of the man, the less I liked. I've known many lords and ladies. Many are petty and cruel, but Gariast is another step beyond that, more than one step. He revels in causing pain and claiming things from others. He takes anything he can, and what he can't take legally, he finds another way to take. He is as close to pure evil as I have ever met. But I was his man, and there was nothing I could do about that except follow his commands as best I could."

His voice changed then, going soft, his shoulders slumping with it. "I will admit. I came to like being a bully after a while. It was just easier to take on that role than try to justify the things I was doing. I started to become like him, and there was a part of me that enjoyed it." He shook his head.

"If he hadn't threatened my life, and had I not failed in my mission, I would probably still be that man. But now—" Again his voice changed, picking up spirit. "I have a second chance, thanks to you."

Dalia wasn't sure what she thought of that speech. Here he was admitting he was an evil man, or 'had been' if she chose to believe he had so quickly reformed himself. She didn't believe it, not yet. But having met Gariast she had to admit Trentin's assessment of the man was accurate. She couldn't imagine what it must have been like to work under such a terrible man. She wasn't sure whether that excused Trentin's behavior though.

As she mused over the ex-knight's words, Col asked, "So, you say you have a second chance now. What do you intend to do with it?"

"I don't have much choice in that, do I? I am bound to you now. I will do as you command."

Dalia spoke up. "Even if it's to the detriment of your family?" She wasn't sure why she said it, but she had, and the words were out now.

Trentin glanced over at her then back at Col

"Colric doesn't strike me as the type of man to ask that. If he did, well, I'd have to reconsider my vow to him. But at that point, the only option left to me would be fleeing the kingdom."

She nodded. So, he wasn't the type of man to put his loyalties above all else. That was good. It meant he truly might not be loyal to Gariast anymore.

"Family is important," was all she said on that matter.

He nodded.

THEY ARRIVED AT TRENTIN'S KEEP LATE IN THE AFTERNOON.

The sun was most of the way toward the western horizon, or at least it was when they could see it through the thick layer of clouds that had moved in. A light rain had begun to fall, and a mist hung over the valleys between the rolling hills now that they were out of the Sandren Forest.

They had stopped riding again. Dalia and the other two, Nik and Jaff, had requested another spell of walking. This had not worked out well for her. Dalia's boots were secondhand and well-worn. They did not fare well in the moist conditions, quickly soaking through after a short while of walking through the long, wet grasses. She was starting to feel like she was wading through a shallow pool by the time they came within sight of the keep.

She could tell it was near to evening the same way she knew they were drawing near to Trentin's home. The deep clang of chapel bells resonated through the thick, foggy air.

With the next hill they crested, Dalia caught sight of the fortifications.

It was a basic structure, far more utilitarian than her family's holdings. It was a fortress built in the motte-and-bailey style. It must have been old. It looked old from this distance, dark, rough stonework, well covered in moss and ivy. Strongholds of this style hadn't been needed for generations, since Rovalia had settled these lands more than two hundred years ago. Any family with any money had long since torn down such keeps and rebuilt elegant estates with large lawns. The exceptions were keeps in the north, where the mountains held Orcs, or the far south, where the Forsean Raiders were a constant threat. But here in the southeast, there were no such issues. The nearest other kingdom was Santhine to the east. True, there had been battles in recent years with Santhine, but they had been minor skirmishes over borderlands after the death of their crown prince.

The keep must have been a cold and drafty place. Yet, when she looked over at Trentin as they stood atop the hill together, he had an odd look of poignant relief as he gazed at the structure.

They descended the hill to the keep, moving once more into fog so thick they lost sight of its walls for a while.

When they emerged from the fog into a rather vast cleared area, the keep was right there, only a short distance away. Trentin called out as they drew near the gate. There was the creak of wood and metal as the gates were opened.

The sound of horses from the other direction made Dalia turn. From another fog bank, a few hundred feet away, mounted men emerged. They were wearing Lord Gariast's crest, a black crow on a red field.

It appeared Lord Gariast had acted quickly to seize Trentin's keep.

"Quickly, to the gates," Trentin hissed, turning to run for the keep. The gates were so close, beckoning, but Dalia didn't move... more precisely, she couldn't move. As much as she wanted to be safely behind those walls, another part of her wanted to run and engage Lord Gariast's men. That part had control now, so that was the way her body turned.

A hand on her shoulder and Col's voice made her pause. "Dalia?"

"Run!" was all she could say, a breathy urgent thing as she tried to resist the pull of The Fury.

She swiveled her torso to look back at the gates and Col's eyes. His gaze was torn. She tried so hard to make herself turn and join him, but the compulsion was too strong, and she only kept moving away, breaking contact with him, his hand slipping from her shoulder. She released the reins to her mount as well. Col caught them easily.

"Please go," she whispered, her face hopefully showing her torment. She didn't want to be doing this, but she definitely didn't want him around when she did.

"Dalia," he said, but he was shaking his head.

"Go, please!" she insisted.

She didn't know much of combat, but it generally didn't seem wise to engage a dozen knights in the open. Perhaps he came to the same conclusion as he turned and made for the keep.

She looked back at the riders and with a reluctant sigh, let her body loose. She began to run toward the twelve knights.

The hood of her cloak caught wind and flew off. She could feel her dark hair streaming behind her like the rest of the cloak.

One of the riders ahead remarked, "It's a girl," and sounded surprised.

As she drew near the riders, one of them called out to her. "Girl, why do you flee from the keep?"

She didn't answer out loud; she wasn't sure if she could. *I'm not fleeing from them*, she thought grimly, *I'm coming for you.*

They seemed a bit taken off guard when she didn't slow as she came upon them. They were even more shocked when she leapt, caught hold of the lead rider's horse's neck, and lifted her feet up and around to kick the man from the saddle. She released the horse's neck and spun in the air to land standing in the saddle in his place. It was the same thing she'd done the day before, and some of these knights must have been there as shouts erupted around her.

"The devil woman!"

"Dalia Athernon!"

"Ware!"

Weapons were drawn, but only by some of the men. The rest didn't seem to know what to do with her.

She turned, took two light steps, and leapt off the back of the lead horse. The next man—too stunned to react in time—took both her feet in the chest. This one didn't fully fall from the saddle; his boots were well in his stirrups. He bent back over the horse's hindquarters with a grunt from the force of her attack. She took one light step on the man's chest, jumped, and kicked out at the man next to him. This one she caught in the side of the head, sending him falling to one side, off his horse. Landing again on the man still leaning back on his mount's hind-quarters, she stepped off him, catching his chin in both hands as she dropped behind the horse. He didn't come out of the saddle, instead his neck broke with a sickening crack.

She stepped lightly away from the now frisking mount.

The man she had kicked out of the saddle wasn't far away. She skipped over to him and kicked down hard on his neck as he tried to get up. He gurgled, eyes wide, and then lay still.

Three down, nine to go.

There were shouts of definite alarm and warning now. She even caught a few distinct words.

"—possessed—"

"—spirit of vengeance—"

"—She can't... she didn't... impossible—"

Oh, it was possible.

Tears began to roll down her cheeks as she continued. Her mind peered out through indifferent eyes, horrified at what she was doing, but unable to stop any of it.

The horse of the man she just killed was milling about and she jumped up into the saddle. She kicked the mount and was quickly away from the others. But if they expected her to run, they would be disappointed.

She swung the horse around and charged back at them. Where she'd been a tentative rider that morning, she was a skilled horseman now. It was innate. She knew how to handle the beast and did it with ease.

The first man she'd attacked was standing next to his horse, attempting to remount as he yelled commands at the others. They swarmed forward around him and came at her. They all had swords or light lances at the ready.

The first one to reach her swung a thick-bladed sword with

all his might. She laid herself flat against her horse's neck and ducked under the blow. At the same time, she kicked out to the side, catching her attacker in the midriff. He wore armor, but it was a large breastplate that protected him mostly from frontal attacks. She hit him in the side and he folded slightly, the weight of his sword fully extended was too much. He'd lost his core stability. She heard him yell as he fell from the saddle behind her. The next man lowered a lance and she had barely enough time to throw herself sideways and avoid the strike. She kicked the side of the lance as it passed through where she had been, sending the weapon wide. She regained her saddle as more came at her.

There was a man directly in front of her, but not moving toward her. He sat still with a crossbow ready. But his aim was low. As he fired, she kicked away her stirrups and leapt to the side. The crossbow bolt took her horse in the neck and the poor beast went down thrashing.

She caught the neck of another horse as its rider moved in to attack her. She, being small and light, swung around the horse's neck in a ball, then exploded upward with all the momentum of her swing, both feet taking the attacker by surprise as her attack came from the completely wrong direction. Her kick sent him back out of the saddle, and once again, she swung up into his place, sitting quickly this time. She heard a scream behind her as the man she'd just unseated was trampled by the next rider, too close behind him.

Now she was going the same direction they were.

She took the barest of instances to get her bearings.

The keep was not far away. The gates now closed. A few men on the walls readied weapons, but those men looked like stable hands and servants, not warriors.

There were seven men still mounted around her and the leader had just regained his mount.

Something swept over her then. She always felt a little possessed when she fought, like something else was controlling her actions, but this was new. It whispered ideas into her mind as she felt her limbs strengthen and tense, ready for action. There was no fear when she was in the grips of The Fury, but still the mere thought of what she was about to do shocked even her, yet she had no hesitation when it came time to do it.

Still riding hard, she once again lifted her legs up under her to stand in the saddle, but she didn't stay there for long. Men were all around her. She stepped lightly off her mount to another man's, like a deer gracefully bounding over a hedge. That man she kneed in the back of his head, just at the base, where it met his neck. His head snapped back, then forward. He slumped over, slowly sliding from the saddle.

She was already moving on, running over him and up the horse's neck with a couple light steps to fly to the man in front of him, who was not expecting an attack from behind. She landed with both hands on the back of his horse, then flipped over to wrap her legs around the man's neck and head, then spun up and around, twisting his head to the side forcefully before releasing her legs as he fell from the saddle.

She landed lightly, standing sideways, legs sturdy on the charging equine's back.

Next to her now was a man with a lance, who was trying to poke at her with the long weapon. She was pretty sure that was not how lances were supposed to be used. She hopped up and landed, both feet on the wooden pole, forcing it down onto the back of the horse she'd just been standing on. Then, before the man could realize his mistake and release the weapon, she ran with feet like feathers, up the lance and kicked the man under the chin. He reeled. She took another step off the top of his head and spun like a leaf in the wind high into the air landing on a riderless horse.

From there, she simply stopped even trying to keep track of the improbable things she was doing. She watched amazed as her body did things even she would have thought impossible until now. Men fell before her, tossed from saddles either stunned or dead. Her heart was pounding so loudly there were no other sounds around her, even the thundering of hooves seemed distant. She was a thing of deadly grace and impossible agility. Every attack at her seemed slow and clumsy, and she knew exactly how to avoid it, or use it to her advantage. Those who she'd knocked from the saddles still alive remounted and came back at her, but she could not be stopped. They were fools to try again.

Then she finally did stop.

She stood, breathing like a hurricane, blood boiling and raging, ready to move with the barest thought and provocation, but there were no more attackers.

Only the leader remained. He was on his horse but had not charged in to engage her. When she spun to face him, she could see the look of sheer terror on his face. He turned his mount and ran.

She looked around slowly.

Horses ambled around aimless or stood grazing. Men in Gariast's colors lay all around her, dead.

She slumped to the ground as reality flooded back into her and her frenzy wore off. Once again, she was violently ill, heaving up what little she'd had that day. She leaned over heavily onto weary arms, but they gave way, and she dropped down to her elbows.

Her entire body throbbed with a numbing ache, and once her stomach was empty, she threw herself over onto her back and lay on the wet and muddy ground staring up at the gray sky above. There was a single small patch of clear blue sky above her. It seemed to mock the brutality of what she'd just done with its purity and beauty.

Tears escaped her eyes, but she could not truly weep, she had no energy to do so. She was completely exhausted and fell asleep there on the sodden muck of the battlefield.

9

DALIA AWOKE IN FITS AND STARTS.

It was dark.

She came to herself slowly. Her body ached, but it was a dull throbbing, a minor inconvenience. She was in a bed with warm thick blankets covering her, though... she was undressed. She pulled the covers up a little higher, even though they'd been at her chin already.

The bed was large and soft and nearly filled the room. There was little else but a wardrobe, a small chest of drawers, and a large hearth, which flickered with a dying fire.

She lay there for some time enjoying the feeling of simply being still. Flashes of memory returned to her of her fight that day, and it was lucky her stomach was still empty. Of course, that was causing a different problem; she was incredibly hungry at the same time as feeling ill.

She would need to do something about The Fury. It was clear to her it wasn't going to go away on its own. Which left her two options: either find a way to control it or learn to live with the brutality she reaped on so many. She lay thinking about that for some time.

She'd found no solution by the time the door to the room opened. Dalia said nothing at first, wishing to see who it was.

A girl stepped inside. She looked to be half Dalia's age, perhaps eight or nine. She held the door for a woman of rounded figure, older and matronly with dark hair. The woman carried a load of wood and bustled over to the hearth to lay it there.

"Mama," the girl said, and when the woman looked, the girl pointed at Dalia.

"Oh!" the woman said in a hushed voice. "You're awake. It is a pleasure to meet you." The woman bobbed a quick curtsey. "I am Hana Edwir, Trentin's wife." She motioned to the girl. "And this is Sahras, our daughter."

"I'm Dalia... It's a pleasure to meet you too." The pleasantry came out easily, though it was still hard to suppress her family name. She wasn't an Athernon anymore. The next question came out probably slightly too accusing and defensive. "Where are my clothes?"

The woman smiled. "Worry not, my dear. You were filthy after laying in the mud. Sahras and I cleaned you up a little and removed your clothes, so they could be washed. But they also needed mending, so we brought you some new dresses. They were mine when I was young. I had hoped to pass them on to Sahras, but they should fit you well enough. They're on the foot of the bed."

Peering up over the blankets, Dalia saw several bundles.

"Thank you."

"Is there anything else you need?"

This had been meant as a quick trip. "When are we leaving?" Was she the one who was holding up their departure?

"It will take a little time for the people here to ready themselves. Your man, Colric, has given us until dawn. We probably won't be sleeping much tonight."

Dalia relaxed a little. "So, I can rest?"

"Your man wanted to see you when you woke."

Her man? "Col?"

Hana nodded.

Dalia almost laughed at that. She didn't feel like she had anything at the moment, let alone a 'man.'

"You can send him in." After a quick thought, she added, "But do you have a nightdress or something?"

Chuckling, Hana went to one of the dresses and unfolded it. "Yes." She separated out an underdress, brought it over, and set it at the side of the bed. "I'll build up the fire a little, so you can dress." She added some logs and made sure they were catching before turning to go. She looked around for a moment. "Sahras must have slipped out already," she said.

Dalia hadn't noticed the girl leave.

Hana brushed herself off absentmindedly. Something occurred to Dalia. Hana seemed hesitant to leave. There was something about the look she was giving the room, and it connected with a longing within Dalia herself.

"This is your room, isn't it?"

Smiling sadly, Hana nodded. "Our room, ever since I married Trent nine years ago." She kept rubbing her belly. Dalia looked closer. What she had thought was the other woman 'brushing herself off' earlier, was actually her caressing her stomach.

"You're pregnant, aren't you?"

Hana snapped out of her reverie and her smile grew. It was still a sad smile, but it still made her seem younger than Dalia had first thought. She guessed this woman was not even thirty yet.

"Yes. The Wise Woman who travels these parts says it will be a boy. I hope she is correct."

That accounted for the woman's rounded appearance.

Suddenly Dalia felt awful. "I'm sorry we're taking you away
from your home and your life and... everything, especially when
you're with child. I wish..." She wasn't sure what she wished. Yet
none of this was Dalia's fault, except in so much as the knight
Trentin had been coming for her and failed and now needed to
flee with them into the forest.

Hana's expression changed, eyes softening. "Oh, young one,
do not worry for me. I come from hardy stock, and I've still got
quite some time left before this one comes out." That, with a pat
on her belly. "I can make any trip we need to. Our life will
change, yes, but we'll do well enough." After another look
around the room, she sighed. "I'll leave you to dress and send
your man up. I'll tell him to wait outside the door for you."

Hana left. Dalia lay there for a moment under the comfortable sheets, which Hana would never enjoy again, and mourned
for everything these people would lose. Then she took a long
breath and forced herself up and into the nightdress. It was silk
and sheer on her skin, cool, and comfortable.

There was a silvered looking glass over the chest of drawers.
She stepped over to look at herself. The fire flashed red and
orange on the white underdress and made it sparkle. The nightdress was a little revealing, leaving her shoulders and arms bare
as well as her calves. Her hair needed brushing again, but she
was mostly presentable otherwise.

A knock sounded at the door.

She thought to answer it, then modesty got the better of her,
and she crawled back into the bed calling for Col to "Come in,"
once she was settled.

He entered and closed the door. "I wanted to see how you
were doing."

"Well enough." She shivered though, recalling the day's
fighting.

He came to sit on the bed, one bent leg up so he was turned

toward her. It was a large enough bed that there was still a fair distance between where he sat at the side near the foot and where she half-lay at the head.

"You're certain. I..." He seemed to be having trouble. She could see his concern and something else... guilt? "I'm sorry I left you out there today."

She almost laughed, but she could see how much this was affecting him. "You didn't have a choice." After a moment, she added. "Neither did I."

He sighed heavily. "I know that, but... still..."

"You did the right thing. I was the one being crazy."

He'd been looking down, not meeting her eyes, but finally lifted his gaze. The fire caught the brown of his eyes and turned them to gold. "I know, but I'm sorry. Please accept my apology."

"I do."

He smiled for a moment before his face turned somber again. He sat there for a long moment before starting to rise. He mumbled a "thank you."

"Wait!" she said, reaching out for him. He turned back, head tilted, eyes questioning. "Please stay... for a moment..." She searched for a reason. "Tell me the rest of your story."

He smiled again and nodded.

"Where did I leave off?" he asked as he retook his seat at the foot of the bed.

She tried to recall. "Lord Quillian, your training?"

"Yes, thank you." He took a moment before continuing his tale.

"Lord Quillian trained me with a group of recruits, most of which were older than I. Yet I learned quickly I could do just as well as they, and more often I was better. I passed the basic training in under a year. To my surprise, Lord Quillian sponsored my joining the King's Guard, not just the army. I'd never thought to join the king's own forces, but I was accepted as a junior guard.

"By the time I was seventeen, I was a full guardsman. I was aware enough to notice I was better with most weapons than some knights, except for a lance. I never saw any need to train with one as I was primarily trained as a footman, not on horseback.

"The next four years were the best of my life. I rose through the ranks quicker than any man before me. I trained relentlessly, mastered weapons quickly, and seemed to have a natural knack for leadership. I became the youngest captain in the King's Army after only five years of service. I even came to know the king himself as he was quite impressed with my abilities."

Youngest captain... yes, that seemed to jog a memory loose. Did she know something about him? It took a moment, but then the name came to her, and after that, several other things fell into place.

"Oh, gods! That was you!"

He seemed taken aback by her outburst. "Yes?"

She laughed. "Sorry... I just recalled... I knew you from before." She frowned, shaking her head. "I'm sorry. Yours has become a cautionary tale to any who would cross Lord Gariast."

It was barely there, but she noticed him flinch at the mention of that name. She couldn't blame him.

He blinked. "Truly?"

She nodded. She knew at least a part of his tale now. "You bested everyone you went up against in the tournament at Chestley three years ago. All the ladies were talking about you for months after that," Dalia said. "They couldn't believe some commoner had bested their fathers or brothers and made it look so easy. They all wondered where you had come from. More than a few made some rather suggestive comments about where they wanted you to end up."

Colric blushed and looked away. "Is this the truth?"

"Oh yes. You were the talk of every ball and party until Mid-Summer's Eve when Lady Alimira was caught in a rather uncomfortable position with a stable boy at the Grand Ball at Lord Gariast's estate."

"I never knew I was so famous."

"Oh yes." Then another piece fell into place for her. She raised a hand to cover her mouth as she breathed another, "Oh!" A moment later, she added. "You were the one who killed the Crown Prince of Santhine!"

He nodded. "It seems my story is quite well known." This with a rather bitter tone. "But allow me to tell it right. I suspect Lord Gariast has hidden the truth about that event."

Dalia's father had heard a rumor once that Gariast himself had been behind the murder. The details had been unclear however.

"Please, yes, go on," she said. She was at the same time relieved and worried. She felt like she knew more about the man across from her. True, he may have been a bandit for the last three years, but somehow that made him more human. After all, she was a murderer now. She should give him the benefit of the doubt. Perhaps then he'd do the same for her when she told her story.

"Yes, I fought in the tournament at Chestley. I'd thought the point was to show our skills. I'll admit I didn't heed the warnings not to best certain noblemen, Lord Gariast among them. I was naive. I didn't think anyone could be so petty. I'd thought they'd want to know their limits. That's how I saw the event." Col's eyes wandered and his voice was wistful. "I remember the tournament like it was yesterday. It was a beautiful day, and I was at the peak of my abilities. The golden stag statuette, which was my prize, was more wealth than my family would have seen in their entire lifetime! I felt invincible." Another sigh. "I remember being surprised when everyone was avoiding Gariast in the grand melee. So, I went to face him. He's really not that good."

"No, but he's powerful. You don't need to be good with weapons when you're as powerful as he," Dalia said softly.

"I know that now." After a moment, he shook his head. "I'm curious. How powerful is Lord Gariast? I'm guessing he has great wealth, but..."

"He's not just 'wealthy.' His riches far exceed any other nobles in the kingdom. Even the king must bow to the man's wishes, for without Gariast, the king loses his largest supplier of grain and steel."

"Truly?"

"Truly."

Colric sighed heavily. "That explains much then." After a long breath, he went on. "I wish I'd known then what I know now. I'd never imagined anyone could be so angry over being beaten at a tournament."

Dalia almost laughed but stifled it. This was not the time. Yet she couldn't imagine anyone who wasn't aware of the Lord's wrath. "I supposed you were a commoner. You probably didn't know Gariast as the nobility did."

"He seemed well respected." Col shrugged.

"He is feared, not respected."

"As I said, that is clear to me now." He seemed a bit deflated.

Dalia knew it wasn't polite to ask him to continue, but her curiosity tugged at her. She tentatively ventured a question: "What about the prince? What happened that day?"

"That was the day everything ended," he said evenly. His jaw twitched.

"You don't have to tell me if you don't want to." Even though she was desperate to know.

After a moment, he shook his head. "I will." It took still another few breaths for him to go on. "I'm guessing Lord Gariast never mentioned that I didn't know who the prince was when I killed him? It was a trap. I didn't know he wanted vengeance for the tournament. He told me he wanted to congratulate me for my win." The story must have agitated Col too much. He rose and began pacing. "When I arrived, his doorman said he was waiting for me in his gardens and he had a guest visiting. It was someone important who wished to see a display of my prowess. He told me to expect a contest, a duel."

"I found the gardens, and immediately a man in black challenged me. I accepted, and though I didn't see Lord Gariast around, I assumed this was all a part of his show. But as you already know, the man in black was the prince himself. I don't know what Gariast had told the man, but it became clear that this wasn't a test of skill. He was trying to kill me. I simply defended myself. I defeated him, though to his credit, he was one of the most challenging men I'd ever fought. But even after I'd disarmed him and made him yield, he did not submit. When I offered my hand, he came at me enraged. I should have engaged him hand-to-hand, but I still had my sword and instinctively used it to defend myself. He died on it. Then Gariast and a score of his men came out from the bushes and arrested me for treason, saying I'd killed the Crown Prince of Santhine.

"I was shocked and confused, and they took me easily enough. But I was sure I could explain this to the king. I knew the king and thought I had his respect. But when Gariast brought me before the king, the man looked at me with such pity in his eyes and refused to listen to my story. But if what you say is true, about the king being so dependent on Gariast, then perhaps he could do little to defend me. I had thought he had betrayed me, and in truth, he did, but at the time, I could not fathom why. Now I know.

"They took me to the royal dungeons and there I sat, a defeated man, ready for my death. It was only by the kindness of a couple of my own men in the King's Guard that I escaped. They knew me and, curse them, they would have followed me anywhere. They helped me escape, then they covered for me." He stopped his pacing. His shoulders fell. "I've since heard they were both executed." The words came out hot and embittered. He sat again, heavily, shoulders slumped. She could tell this was a wound on his soul, even after so much time.

"I'm so sorry," she said. Her heart went out to him.

Something changed inside her then, softening.

Her next words were tentative; she found herself stammering a little. "W—would... you like t—to hear... m—my story?" She was at the same time terrified and hopeful at the prospect of finally telling someone of her trials.

His head had been down, chin to chest and he looked up. "Only when you're ready."

"I think I am," she said, then realized how uncertain that sounded. "I am."

He sat back against the tall poster of the bed. He still looked haggard, but he seemed to relax a little. "I'd like that."

She drew in a long breath to steady herself.

"I should start with my name, my full name. I am Dalia Athernon. My father is Lord Athernon."

Col reacted only by raising a brow, remaining quite still. She was thankful for that. Having been the daughter of one of the more powerful lords in the south had somehow made this whole experience worse. It was hard to even say it. It brought back so many memories of the time... before.

She was silent for some time, trying to find the right words to go on. Col waited, silent. His patience was amazing.

She began, "It all started just six days ago when I was walking through the woods at the far edge of my father's estates near Hovern." An image formed in her mind of the day. It had been a brilliant sunny day with a pristine blue sky and a warm wind from the south. She'd escaped the boredom of her after-noon stitching lessons pleading a headache and the need for fresh air. She'd walked for some time across the long fields of low cut grasses to the sparse woods that bordered the Athernon estates. She'd explored the forest many times. The underbrush was cut down regularly to create a pleasantly shaded area for walking. But she wished to venture deeper into the forest, past the cleared areas. "I found a path through the underbrush which led me further into the forest than I had ever gone. The scents and sounds were wonderful, birds all around me, the wind tousling the trees above." She sighed.

"Then I met *him*." She put as much vehemence into that one word as she could. She could not get the image of the fey out of her mind.

"There he was, standing as plain as day on the path before me where there had been no one a moment before. A fey, though I know not his name or what to call him, but he was one of the wee-folk I am certain. His skin was gray as slate. His body was mostly slender but with a round potbelly. He wore no clothes, but his features were indistinct, so it wasn't that brazen. His ears and nose were both far too long and both ended in sharp points. He wore a grin and said, 'hello' in a cheerful way which dispelled my shock at seeing him."

Col made a face, looking away. Perhaps he was thinking.

"What?" she asked him.

He shrugged. "I won't know until I can talk to Ayneii. She would know more of the different types of fey than I do, but the one you saw doesn't sound like a sprite at all."

"Do you know a lot about the fey?"

"Mostly about sprites, and that was all learned from Ayneii."

"Oh," she said.

"Please, go on. I'm sorry I interrupted."

She nodded. "He bowed and called me beautiful, a 'beautiful

lady.' I will admit I was taken by his charm. Then he said something that surprised me. He said, 'I know what you want,' and he winked at me. I was a little shocked, but he continued. 'You want an end to your boredom. You want excitement and adventure!'"

She sighed heavily, gathering her legs up in front of her under the blankets. She hugged her knees, leaning forward a little. Another shiver took her. She'd been such a fool.

"He was right. That's exactly what I wanted... what I thought I wanted." A single tear traced its way down her cheek.

"I'm sorry," Col said, true compassion in his voice.

She sniffled and forced a smile. "Oh, it gets better, well worse, actually, but for a short while, I had everything I wanted. You see, my life was boring. All I did all day was meaningless drivel, stitching, manners, learning all the noble families and their history. It was horrible. My only joy came from the little time I had to myself after dinner. I would run to my father's library and read and reread all of the poems and heroic tales my family possessed. I loved the idea of some dashing man sweeping me off my feet and taking me away for adventures in far-off lands."

She let out a harsh little laugh. "Did I mention I was betrothed?"

"No." Col's expression didn't change. If he was surprised by this, he didn't show it.

"He was boring too, definitely nothing close to adventurous, and not much to look at." Her shoulders slumped a little. "But he was gentle and sweet. His name was Padran. I was to marry him on my seventeenth birthday. The date was getting closer, and I wasn't excited at all. So, when the fey asked me if I wanted him to grant me a wish, I said yes.

"A life full of adventure and excitement is what I asked for and what he granted me." She shook her head slowly. "I had no idea what that really meant.

"That night a wandering minstrel came to our house. He played for us. He was handsome and dashing and he sung of heroes and adventures. Then there was the way he looked at me whenever he mentioned the 'fair maiden' in his tale. Sometimes he'd wink at me. I was certain the little fey had conjured this man up to take me away to a life of adventure. And so, he did.

"The minstrel came to my room late that night, climbed up to my balcony and knocked softly on the outer door. I hadn't been sleeping, though it was late. I knew he'd come. He swept me up and kissed me. Oh, it was so wonderful! Padran had never kissed me like that before, with so much passion and urgency.

"He said I'd stolen his heart and he had to run away with me. I instantly agreed, and we were off on our way in the darkest hours of the night."

Col gave a breathy laugh. "Let me guess. He abandoned you for the next pretty face who came along?"

"Actually, no." Dalia smiled faintly, sadly as she shook her head. "No, he stayed with me. He was truly taken with me, I believe." She let out a long breath, feeling her shoulders slump as she did. "No, it was my father's men who drove him away. They caught up with us two days later. Jorin, the minstrel, may have been loyal... but he was also a coward. As soon as he saw armed men coming for him, he ran. I had thought... had hoped he would protect me, defend me, fight for me, but..."

"Ah, I see."

A tremor sliced through Dalia at the thought of what had happened next. "But that wasn't the worst part of my father's men finding me."

"Oh?" The light of the fire was growing steadily, revealing genuine concern and curiosity on Col's face.

The tremor grew and turned into a full, jarring shiver that she couldn't stop. She couldn't think back on that day without the shakes. Even with all that had happened since then.

"When my father's men came for me, I fought them. I didn't want to go back." She had to stop for a moment. Her teeth were starting to chatter with her intense trembling. She drew in several breaths to calm herself and went on. "I'm a small woman, I'm not strong. I've never fought anyone before, and yet..." The shakes returned, and she could hear it in her voice, a tremulous tone. "I... I..." Her breath kept catching.

Col moved to her, sitting next to her on the bed and putting a strong arm around her. His voice was soft, quiet when he said, "Don't worry, you don't need to tell me any more if you don't want."

She laughed, and it came out in fits, a little hysterical. "Something came over me. I didn't know what it was. I fought back. Six large men, and I crippled two of them and killed another!"

10

Col's heart contracted for Dalia. Still so young, yet so tormented. It seemed cruel what the fey had done, giving her some fighting ability she couldn't control. He'd seen it in action enough to know how dangerous it was. He wasn't surprised that men had suffered. Yet the effect of such a thing on a pure soul like hers must have been devastating.

"I'm sorry," he said. It seemed he'd been saying that a lot.

She was still trembling and had started sniffling, tears on her cheeks. He used the hand he had around her to rub her arm, soothingly, and made hushing sounds. "There, there."

After a long moment of tears and quiet sobs, when her shaking had lessened somewhat, she said, "I call it 'The Fury.' It's this feeling that comes over me whenever I or others are in danger. I can't control it. It takes hold and I must fight. I've been trying to take control, but..."

She sniffed back a few more tears. Once these words were spoken, she seemed to calm a little.

"This was my gift from the fey. Some strange ability to fight without weapons. I move so quickly even I don't know what I'm doing at times. I can throw men twice my size around a room or

even run up walls or along narrow surfaces. It's miraculous...
and terrifying."

"Sounds horrible," Colric said to Dalia. He could only
imagine his body acting of its own accord and doing things to
harm others.

"It is." After a moment and several long breaths, she went on
with her tale. "That first time, I think the shock of killing a man,
hearing his neck—" She swallowed hard. "It forced me out of
The Fury. I simply stopped, but it still took everything I had to
not fight back. I just stood there and let them grab me. I knew I
could slip their grasp if I wanted to, but I was so shaken at the
time I couldn't do anything."

He held her a little closer, a little tighter. It seemed to calm
her, and he had to admit it felt good. There was something
about her which connected to something deep within him.
Perhaps it was their unity in being broken, their tortured pasts.
Hers was just a lot fresher than his was.

She leaned into him, her head on his shoulder and went on.
"My father couldn't believe I'd killed anyone. He assumed it was
an accident. Even afterward, for myself it didn't seem real. It was
like it had happened to someone else. My father refused to
believe anything the others told him. He forgave me for running
off but still locked me in my room and told me I wasn't coming
out until my marriage day."

She sighed heavily. "But I'd learned more than just fighting
from that damned fey. I learned other crafts as well, including
the ability to sneak like a mouse and unlock doors without a key,
using only hairpins or other such instruments."

Col thought this quite interesting and useful, but said
nothing.

"I was terrified of what I had done, but I had not learned my
lesson about having too much adventure in life. So that night I
snuck out of my house. It was far too easy, even with the locks

and the men my father had set to guard me. I saddled a horse and rode to the estate of the family of my betrothed, Padran. I wasn't thinking straight. I thought perhaps if I told him what I wanted, he'd see things my way and run off with me. It had been so romantic and exciting the first time before my father's men found us. I thought, maybe if I did it with my betrothed, there wouldn't be an issue. But..."

She'd been shivering more and more violently as she spoke, and finally a great tremor took her. He held her tighter still, and the trembling stopped.

"Thank you," she said, her voice barely audible. She shook her head where it lay on his shoulder. "You can't... he... all of them... it was horrible!" she buried her face in his shoulder, arms reaching out and encircling him, holding him tightly now. He used the arm still around her to press her closer to him. She wept for some time at whatever horrifying memory plagued her.

Again, he felt that deep connection with her. Tears came to his eyes, as his emotions played in sympathy with hers. His own horrible memories dragged to the surface. Chief among them was the intense regret and loss at what had befallen his family. He'd escaped Lord Gariast's clutches... but they had not. They'd died in his place, and that was something he could never forget, a tear in his soul.

His own tears were gone and dried by the time she finally extracted herself from the crook in his shoulder. She was facing him now, close, those clear blue eyes rimmed with red and still moist. He could feel her breath, warm on his face, when she spoke. "He was dead. They were all dead, his entire family. Cut up... there was so much blood. I couldn't help but get some on me." Something changed in her voice then, it became hard, resigned. "And that's where they found me. Surrounded by blood and death."

She laughed, but there was no mirth in it. "This time they

were knights, not my father's men, and I didn't resist. I thought they were just going to take me away from that horrid place; I couldn't imagine that anyone would think I could have done all of that.

"But when they said they were arresting me, something broke inside me. I fought back." A grim, stiff smile spread across her face. "And they weren't expecting anything like me. I didn't kill anyone this time. They were in steel armor, it was harder to hit their soft spots, but I did break a few limbs. I escaped, but didn't know where to go. My father had not believed me possible of such violence before, so I went home. But they came for me the next day. This time, my father, whether he believed me or not, didn't have a choice. There was a warrant for my arrest."

She turned away from him then, taking her arms from around him and hugging herself. She settled back with her head on his shoulder. There was a certain calm to her now.

When Dalia started again, it was a cold accounting of the rest of the events, the emotion wrung from her. There wasn't too much to the story after that point though. "They took me to a keep. I was locked there for another day before they came to take me to the capital. Crimes against a high noble are tried in the king's own court. I didn't resist when they came for me. The Fury didn't kick in. I don't know why. I know I'd had a lot of time to think, and perhaps I just wanted to die in that moment. Then as we travelled, the carriage stopped in the middle of the Sandren with some commotion outside: you. I felt it then. Something snapped inside me and I needed to be free. I didn't want to die. You know the rest from there."

Something seemed to release inside her then. Her shoulders slumped, and she went slack in his arms as if something within her was collapsing.

"Thank you," she said quietly. "For taking me in... for listening."

She turned her head to look up at him then, her face once again close to his. He took in that face for a long moment, those pools of blue, that straight but slightly too-long nose and small mouth. He wasn't sure what possessed him, but he kissed her forehead. She didn't flinch away.

He spoke, his voice a whisper. "No one should have to endure what we have. We are kindred souls, I think."

She said nothing, but he felt her head make a nodding motion against his shoulder.

They stayed that way for some time before she said, "I should get some more sleep if we're to be off by dawn. I'm exhausted."

He sighed. She was right. He began to pull away from her, but she stopped him with a hand on his arm.

"Please... can you stay? Just until I'm asleep. You don't know how much I've just wanted someone to hold me."

"I'll stay," he said, and together they adjusted so she was laying down on her side and he was next to her, behind her but above the covers, with an arm over her.

"Thank you," she said, her voice already slurring with fatigue. It wasn't long before she had slipped into unconsciousness.

He rose carefully and left the room. Well, his body left the room. He was fairly certain he'd left his heart back there with Dalia.

≈

COL WAS ALSO EXHAUSTED BUT DIDN'T SEEK SLEEP. DARK thoughts plagued him.

Despite Dalia's forgiveness of his abandoning her outside the keep that afternoon, he still warred with himself about it. He kept playing that moment over and over in his mind. His hand on Dalia's shoulder, hoping she'd come with him. He'd been torn. Every inch of training he'd ever had told him he'd die if he'd engaged those knights. They'd had full plate-mail; he'd been unarmored. They'd been mounted with horsemen's weapons. He'd had a mount and possessed only a long sword and bow. They'd outnumbered him and Dalia six to one. Then there was Dalia's warning to 'run.' She was clearly terrified of hurting allies when she was under the influence of what she called The Fury. She might be able to forgive him, and logic said he had made the right choice, but he still hadn't forgiven himself. He should have helped her... somehow.

Once he'd been safely within the gates, he'd readied his bow and rushed to the top of the high walls in hopes of picking off a few of the foes, but by the time he'd gotten there, Dalia had been flying like some fell spirit amongst the attackers. He hadn't known where to shoot. He'd loosed a few careful shots, but only one had done any significant damage, and that man had already been thrown from his horse. All he'd done was assure the man didn't rejoin the fight.

It had ended so quickly. One small woman against a dozen mounted knights, and she'd slaughtered them. Once it was over, and those within the keep had ventured out to get her, they'd found only a few light cuts on her, like the previous time. That had been when Col had thought to check her cut from earlier in the day and found nothing there—the flesh was pale and smooth with not so much as a scar. It seemed she healed incredibly quickly. Perhaps some gift from the fey as well?

He wished Ayneii was here so he could ask her about the fey that had afflicted Dalia, but she didn't like leaving the forest. He could try to call her, but he'd be back there tomorrow, and it could wait for now.

Col found himself in the kitchens searching for something to eat. He knew that he wasn't hungry, that the void he felt within was something else, but for now, he'd try to fill it with food.

Trentin was there, sitting by the guttering cooking fires at a long table, a flagon in his hand and large tray of food before him.

"Care for a drink of Thornkeep's finest ale?" he said, raising the flagon.

"Thank you, yes."

Trentin rose, grabbed another tall metal cup, and filled it from a keg in the corner of the room. "This is one of the few things we actually produce on these lands, and one of the many things I'll miss." He turned and handed the flagon to Col. A grin slipped onto this face. "Though there was room on a wagon for a single keg."

"Thank you," Col said, and lifted the flagon to his lips. It was chilled and the beer inside was full-bodied and hearty, dark and thick as he drank.

"Not afraid I'll poison you?" Trentin asked after a swig of his own.

Glancing into his flagon, Col shrugged. "Not unless you poisoned that entire keg."

Trentin grimaced. "Not a bad idea, actually. I wouldn't want my new enemies enjoying something I worked so hard on. Well, something my brewmaster worked so hard on."

There was a certain logic to that, and Col could understand the sentiment and resentment that came with knowing your enemies were enjoying the fruits of your labors.

They sat together at the long table for a time. Trentin pushed the tray of food to Col. It was laden with roasted chicken, bread, cheese, and fruits.

Col ate a little but found his appetite waning quickly. The food seemed to sink into his stomach like stones, weighing heavily. Another drink of the ale didn't help dispel the feelings.

"What's bothering you?" Trentin asked.

There was so much.

Dalia's tale, and even his retelling of his own, had dredged up so many conflicting emotions. But they kept returning to Lord Gariast and from there spiraled into darkness. Yet perhaps there was something Trentin could help with, a worry the man could quell.

He tried to keep emotion from his voice when he spoke next. "You've been with Gariast for many years you said?"

"Yes."

"Were you there when my family was taken in? Did they die quickly?" From what he'd heard of Lord Gariast, he feared the worst.

Trentin didn't reply immediately and Col, lost in his own thoughts didn't notice right away. When he did realize the great lag, he looked over at the ex-knight. "What is it?" A growing dread filled his stomach, a cold ball of fear.

Trentin put down his mug and sat forward, leaning heavily on the table. His head was down, and he couldn't meet Col's eyes. He drew in several long breaths before replying. His words were slow, a great regret filling his voice. "They... are not dead."

Col's heart nearly stopped. He tried to form words, but for a moment, he couldn't.

His family was alive!

But in the next instant, he knew that this was probably an even worse fate than death given Trentin's hesitation.

"What has he done with them?" He couldn't say the man's name, not now.

Again, it was a long, long moment before Trentin spoke. When he did, he hummed and hawed a little, which caused Col's fear to turn to anger.

"Tell me!" he shouted, slamming down his flagon. Ale spilled. He didn't care.

Trentin spoke. "Your parents are in the royal dungeons, the king did what he could for them, but your siblings were left to Gariast's care. Your brothers lay in his personal dungeons, broken men, tortured regularly. Your sister..." Trentin swallowed hard. "She is... Gariast keeps her as his personal maid and... plaything."

The ball in Col's stomach turned from ice to stone and sat heavily as his emotions swirled from rage to fear and a torrent of others.

"No." It came out as the barest of breaths. He found energy enough to rise suddenly. "I have to help them. I need..." To do what? Go charging into Gariast's estates and free them? It wasn't going to happen. What he needed was a thousand more men and a plan. "Gods," he whispered.

"I'm sorry, Colric."

Col ignored him. For the moment, Trentin didn't exist. In that instant, he wanted to be gone, but he knew he had to wait for the rest of the keep to be ready. He was stuck.

He needed to act, but couldn't, not yet, which left only a deep rending pain at his own impotence.

11

Lord Gariast was furious at being awoken in the middle of the night. The servant who'd disturbed him now had a swollen lip to show for it. Vandar counted the man lucky that that had been the extent of his injuries.

Apparently, Lord Kerrik Tandor, the knight captain he'd sent to seize Edwir's keep and its inhabitants, had returned. That hadn't been the plan. He was to have sent a pigeon once he'd secured the place, not return in person. This could only mean bad things in Vandar's estimation and that, on top of his already surly attitude and fatigue, meant he wanted nothing more than to hurt the man in armor before him.

Kerrik stood rigid, jaw set. His helm was off and under one arm. "I am sorry for the late hour, but I thought you would want to know what I discovered with all haste."

"This had better be good news, Kerrik." Vandar seethed.

Lord Tandor stiffened. "It is both good and bad I am afraid. I'll begin with the bad. Trentin has betrayed you and taken up with the Black Bandit. He seems to be working with the rogue... as well as the Athernon girl. They had returned to his keep, probably to save his family." The man hesitated for a moment.

"When my men attacked they defended themselves from the walls of the keep. It is a fortress and with only a score of knights, we had no chance. I barely made it back with my life."

Gariast trembled with rage. No one had ever dared betray him. He was tempted to strike Lord Tandor but held himself back. He rarely showed such restraint, but it would be a shame to break the man's jaw and not get the good news. He just hoped it was very good news indeed.

"And the good news?" he prompted.

Tandor smiled. "I have found Colric of Haverstal."

Gariast's eyes widened and he leaned forward on his desk. "Tell me!"

"As we attacked the keep, before their forces rebuffed us, I caught sight of a man with Trentin. At first, I thought it was the Black Bandit. He was the same build as the man who'd attacked the carriage the day before and moved in a similar manner. But unlike all previous times, he wasn't wearing his mask. I knew that face well enough from all that had transpired years ago. It's definitely Colric of Haverstal. And I think he *is* the Black Bandit. That would explain a lot. The Bandit only showed up after Colric had gone into hiding."

That was true.

Gariast's rage was tempered for the moment. Everything Tandor said made sense. The Black Bandit hadn't started his raids until the spring after Colric had fled. Vandar had never made any connection between the two events, but now it seemed quite possible that his prey was the man who'd been plaguing his roads for two years now.

"And where is he now?"

Tandor swallowed hard. "As I said, my men were all slaughtered, and I was forced away. Last I saw him, he was at Trentin's keep. I don't expect them to stay there for long though. I fear they will flee back into the forest to hide.

Vandar glared at Lord Tandor. He would teach the man a lesson for letting such a prize escape, but for now other thoughts consumed him. He was certain he could find Colric. If Trentin had taken up with him then he'd be able to use some blood he'd collected from the previous night to find the once-knight; and if he found Trentin, he found Colric. He'd also get the Athernon girl as an added prize. All of his foes were together. He'd just need a little magic to find them.

Now for Lord Tandor's punishment.

"Remove your gauntlets." Lord Gariast stepped out from behind his desk and strode over to the man. Tandor did as commanded if a bit hesitantly.

"You hold your weapon with your right hand correct?"

"Yes."

"Then give me your left."

Kerrik held out his hand; it was shaking. Gariast took it in one hand and grasped just the last finger in his other hand. He then bent it backward... slowly. He'd spent most of his adult life practicing torture and was quite good at it. He made sure to break every bone in the finger, before pressing it to the back of Lord Tandor's hand.

Tandor was sweating, teeth clenched, but he hadn't screamed. A hardy man he was. So, Lord Gariast did the same with the next finger in. That brought a satisfying scream from the knight. And it would leave two fingers and a thumb to still grip a shield with; that would do.

"You may go now."

Tandor turned and headed for the door. Gariast thought of one last item and stopped the man, saying, "One moment."

Tandor froze and turned. "Yes, my lord?"

"I've heard your daughter is quite beautiful, Lord Tandor. What's her name?"

"Valeesa, sire."

"A pretty name. Where is she now?"

The knight eyed Vandar for a long moment. "She's in the capital. In a few days, her mother will be presenting her to society."

"So not yet betrothed?"

"No, my lord."

"Good. Well once she is... presented... bring her to me. She will become my ward to ensure you don't betray me like Trentin did. Is that clear?"

Kerrik's teeth unclenched. "Yes, sire." He turned to go, but Vandar called him back.

"I'm not done!"

The knight turned back once again.

"When you go to fetch your daughter from the capital, I have another task for you. Spread word that Colric's family is alive and with me. I don't care what you say exactly—make it as vile as you'd like." Vandar let out a short laugh. "The viler the better. Just make sure lots of people hear it. I want to make sure the news finds its way to Colric's ears. I will prepare a surprise for him in the meantime." This was a necessary back up plan. If he couldn't find Colric using arcane means, then he'd make the man come to him!

Lord Tandor nodded and stood there stiffly.

"You may go now," Vandar said, and watched the beaten man flee.

Vandar fumed. He wanted to hurt someone, kill someone, but alas, his usual plaything, Rissa, was still healing from his last session with her and according to his healers, wouldn't be available for anything for a few days.

Luckily, he always had a 'project' or two on the go in his dungeons. Perhaps he'd go check on one of them.

He rose and made his way down into the bowels of his estate.

The dungeons themselves were in a far-removed sub-basement accessible only through a secret door in the wine cellar. After that was a long hallway then another thick metal-reinforced wooden door. Through that was an antechamber with several doors off it. The one to his left led to one of his favorite places, his second study: a large room, which only he and a few others knew about. The books and scrolls on the many shelves down here were a collection on the study of pain and death. He'd searched far and wide, using his vast resources to find what he could on the topic. He always enjoyed learning new ways to make people scream. He didn't need anything from there for the moment. The door to the right led to the chambers of Zatharyn, his pet wizard, a small, ancient man, who had just as much interest in pain and death as he did. The man had an added bonus of possessing magical powers, which came in very useful in subduing victims and ensuring no one ever escaped this place. The door straight ahead was the one he went through, leading into the torture chamber itself.

This room was vast, with a great array of machines and devices meant to elicit the most exquisite pain. On the far side of the room was another door leading to the dungeons themselves.

Zatharyn was here, behind a small desk making notes in a thick, leather-bound book. Some poor soul, a commoner plucked from his home for not paying his taxes, was strung up nearby with a hatchwork of lash marks on his back.

"What are you working on?" Gariast asked, making his way around the many instruments of torture.

The small man's head bobbed, distracted. He was an odd-looking man. Other than his diminutive stature, there was his angular face and large eyes which made him seem always inquisitive. He had long, limp, dull-gray hair, and a long, tangled beard of the same color.

He smiled as Gariast drew close, though in truth, the only way Gariast knew the man was smiling was from the rise of the cheeks as he could not see the man's mouth through the beard. When Zatharyn spoke, his voice was like strung wire, tremulous and high. "I've been testing lashing, specifically how many lashes, and how long between lashes, so as to induce the most pain without a man succumbing to unconsciousness. Alas, this particular man is proving a weak and feeble subject." He motioned to the man hanging by chains facing the stone wall. "I cannot get more than a few lashes off at a time without him fainting. It is really quite frustrating." The small man peered at Gariast for a moment. "You seem frustrated. Have you come to work off some aggression?"

"I have. Anyone in particular you'd suggest I work on?"

"Depends what you're looking for. If you simply wish to rip a man limb from limb and care little if he experiences any pain, then I'd suggest using this fellow." Again, he motioned to the limp form nearby. "If it's the exquisite delicacy of a nice refined torture you seek, then there are a couple more, heartier souls, in the dungeons which might suit your purpose.

Gariast considered for a moment. As much as he did just want to tear a man's fingers off, there was something deeper and more visceral he sought as well. "The second option, I think. Why don't you go get one of those 'hearty souls' you mentioned? I'll ready the Rending Machine."

The small dungeon-keeper chuckled. "As you say, master, and might I say, an excellent choice. I've been hoping to test that out for some time now, but I wouldn't consider it without you here."

"Much appreciated, Zatharyn."

The small man nodded and shuffled off toward the dungeons.

Gariast made his way over to one of his newest acquisitions. It was a machine based off the concept of the rack. Where the rack stretched and tore at a man in two directions at once, this one could do up to five different directions. The complex system of pulleys and ropes was meant to simulate being drawn and quartered, with the addition of a fifth pulling rope, which could be set around the victim's neck. In addition, as opposed to simply securing the ropes around wrists and ankles, it had the option of using hooks instead, which could be sunk into the flesh of the victim's hands and feet. This would most likely mean the poor wretch's skin would give way long before he was stretched too far, and the hooks would simply tear their way free, damaging the limbs, but leaving the rest of the body mostly intact.

Gariast considered his options and decided he wished to see the effect the hooks had. He retrieved the four metal hooks and the short chains on which they were affixed, then took them over to a brazier, laying the hooks in amongst the burning coals. Apparently, it was recommended—and he agreed—that, for best effect, the hooks needed to be red-hot when put through the victim's hands and feet so as to cauterize the wound and minimize blood loss, which might kill a victim or make him lose consciousness before the overall experience was complete.

Zatharyn returned with a prisoner following along behind him in a daze. That was one of the more useful abilities of the wizard, making him the perfect dungeon-keeper. He never needed to prod or beat a man to get him to do as he wished. He simply used his magic to stupefy the wretches and they followed his commands to the letter. It meant they weren't already in pain or suffering before the torture began, which might taint the venture.

Zatharyn brought the man over and commanded him onto the Rending Machine. He and Vandar made sure the man was secure before the wizard released his hold and returned the man to his own wits.

This was a good specimen indeed. He looked strong and hale with good muscle tone and a large build.

"Where did you find this one?" Gariast asked.

"He's from the Rossferol estates, one of the servants. I know your command was to leave none alive, but I figured if I stole a few away... well they would be safe enough here and probably would not stay alive for too long."

Gariast chuckled. "Well done, good thinking. Shall we begin?"

The little old man was practically shivering with glee. "Yes, master."

They had to wait a little longer for the hooks to be ready. When they were, Gariast used special thick gloves to pluck them from the brazier. He brought them over to the man strapped to the Rending Machine and took his time, slowly pushing them through the flesh of the man's hands and feet, reveling in the screams as he did so. And this was only the beginning. Once all the hooks were inserted in the victim, their chains were attached to the pulling ropes and the real fun began.

The entire device was strung such that the torturer only had to turn one large wheel at the side to make all four or five ropes retract. Gariast took his time of course. He turned the wheel slowly, notch by notch, pulling at the man.

He would stop at times to let the man's screams soothe his frustrations, taking long calming breaths to the sweet music of pain. Yes, this was exactly what he'd needed.

ZATHARYN WATCHED HIS 'MASTER' WORK. IN TRUTH, HE WAS FAR less interested in the pain of torture so much as the feeling of power and control. That was his true motive. He'd chosen Lord Gariast very specifically when he'd decided it was time to rejoin the human world. The man had an insatiable lust for power that matched his own.

For some time now, he had been feeding the man thoughts, sometimes consciously as his advisor, sometimes magically into the man's subconscious mind. 'Build your army' or 'ally with these lords'. He'd been very precise with his plans. Lord Gariast was content to be what he was. He liked having all the power without the responsibility of being king.

Zatharyn wanted it all. He would rule these humans and make them pay for what they'd done to him, nobles and commoners alike. But that took time and planning and... he was nearly there.

Lord Gariast paused in his torture to ask Zatharyn, "My two special prisoners, are they well?"

Zatharyn knew of whom the man spoke. There were two in the dungeons that had become a special project for the lord over the past couple of years.

"I have healed their physical wounds. They are ready to be broken again. I fear, however, that the mind of one is too weak. He is next to madness now. I do not know if he will break well the next time."

Gariast shrugged. "With luck, I'll have caught another to join them soon enough. I don't think I'll be working on them anytime soon, but I may need them for a plan I have. First, I'll need you to locate someone for me. I'll bring you some blood when we're done here. That should be all you need to find a man, is it not?"

"Yes," Zatharyn said simply.

"Good. Find him and let me know where he goes. There is one who travels with him whom I shall hunt down and kill. Or perhaps I'll let him die slowly." Gariast chuckled at the thought.

Zatharyn listened to the lord's scheme and nodded at the

right places. He didn't much care for the lord's petty vendetta against some commoner.

Though as Lord Gariast went on, an idea started to form within Zatharyn's mind. Perhaps this plan could be turned to his favor. But he'd need to influence some men first.

Once Lord Gariast had finished with the man on the Rending Machine and left, Zatharyn retreated to his study. On his desk was an ornate wooden box, inlaid with iron and silver. To any normal human, it would seem an odd thing, with no visible lid or way to open it. They would never be able to see its full glory.

To him it shone like a dazzling rainbow of colors. There was no lid, no opening. This box was magical and had been created by him for a very specific purpose. He held the box and felt the power within it. He siphoned off that power, drinking it into himself. As he did, he heard the distant screams of the boxes inhabitants. Perhaps it was a trick, an imagining that he heard anything, but he liked to think that when he drew from their power, it hurt them.

He chuckled as he put down the box and began a spell to take him to the estate of one of Gariast's more powerful banner-men. Perhaps he was interested in pain after all.

Soon, the entire kingdom would suffer as he had.

12

DALIA FELT MUCH MORE COMFORTABLE IN THE SADDLE TODAY THAN she had yesterday. She'd mounted easily and was getting the feel for moving her horse with just her knees and heels. Trentin, a trained knight, had even commented on her ease while riding earlier.

"You seem to be mastering what it took me the better part of a year to learn," he'd said.

It helped that she had some adequate clothing. Before they'd left the keep that morning, she'd asked to see if there were any men's or boy's clothes she might have. As much as she liked and wanted to be wearing dresses and beautiful things, it was no longer practical. If she was going to run off and fight at any moment, then a sturdy pair of pants would be best. They'd found a set of clothes for her, even new boots. They were drab in color, brown, tan, and gray, but they fit well enough and made riding a lot easier.

She used her newfound skills to urge her mount forward now to catch up to Col. He'd been urging them onward at a hard pace all morning.

"Col, please slow down," she pleaded. "These people have

been up all night. Some are only children. They're tired and on foot. They won't be able to keep up this pace much longer."

He did ease up a little, but the distracted look of grim determination didn't leave his face, and he only looked more aggravated as he slowed.

She hesitated to ask it but..."Perhaps we could dismount and walk? You could offer your horse to some of the weary. It might help us all move a little faster?"

He sighed out heavily, his shoulders falling. "Yes, you're probably right." But he still didn't look happy about it. He did dismount though.

"What's wrong?" she asked. They'd shared so much last night, emotionally and physically. Even now, she didn't know how to express her thanks for how he'd simply held her. It had been the only comfort any person had shown her in days. That, combined with finally being able to get her story off her chest, had meant so much. But despite the connection she'd thought they'd had last night, he seemed so distant now.

He fidgeted, looking around. They were well ahead of the rest of the group. They'd have to stop and wait if he was going to offer his horse to anyone. The wagons and walkers had fallen behind some time ago, which was why she'd come to ask him to slow. They were alone for a moment.

It only seemed to hit him then how far ahead he was. He seemed a little stunned when looking back at the others.

"I'm sorry, Dalia, but... it's just so very hard to be so still now. I can't seem to move fast enough."

"Why?"

His face slid through a series of emotions, from pain and sorrow to anger and determination, and even what seemed like fear. In the short time she'd known him, he'd always seemed so confident and controlled. This conflict within him was new.

"Last night, I learned that my family is still alive."

She blinked, surprised. She'd heard his family had been killed in his place, which must have been horrible for him, but this news... she could understand his eagerness to get to them, but why fear and anger? What wasn't he saying?

"Gariast didn't kill them. He has them, he's..." Col's jaw tightened, tears came to his eyes.

"Oh!" She realized what Col was saying and his urgency. If a horrid man like Gariast had kept his family alive, it could only be for foul reasons. Now his haste fully made sense to her, but... this brought up a more concerning train of thought. "You can't mean to go and get them."

"I do, and I will."

"Gariast has his own army and a well-fortified estate. You won't get anywhere close."

Col's jaw tightened again. "I must." He swallowed hard. "I will, or I'll die trying." He looked away. She'd seen the tears on his cheek before he'd turned.

She lifted a hand to his shoulder. She wanted him to know she supported him, even if his actions were crazy. After all, he'd done as she wished the day before when she'd rushed off to fight a ridiculous battle.

He visibly relaxed at her touch.

"I'm so sorry, Colric."

He turned back to her, his emotions clear on his face, so torn and hurt. "So am I," he whispered. He laid a hand on hers on his shoulder and squeezed it. After a moment, he cleared his throat and wiped away his tears. "But I am set on this path now. No more raids or thievery for me. I am done hiding, done with the Black Bandit. I am Colric of Haverstal and, by the Octave, I will bring bloody vengeance down on Gariast and any others who defy me."

She nodded. He had a purpose now, that was clear enough.

There would be no turning him from this path. Though perhaps she could... help him?

"What is it?" he asked, and she realized she'd looked away.

It was her turn to squeeze his shoulder. "Col, I... my life is meaningless now. I have no idea what I can do, but..." She faltered, unsure what to say exactly. The uncertainty only lasted for a moment. If he, who had helped her so much when no one else would, was set on this path then so was she. "If you could use a fey-cursed woman with abilities even she doesn't understand, then... I'll help you find and free your family." She smiled faintly. "I'm already condemned to death. How much worse can things get for me?"

"Are you sure of this?" Concern replaced the determination on his features.

She shrugged. "No, but like you said last night, we are kindred souls you and I; both condemned by this horrid world. We condemned need to help each other, don't we?"

He gave a faint and mirthless half-laugh. "Thank you," he whispered.

He'd been the one to help her, hold her, show her a path for her life. He was the only one she knew she could trust; the only one who seemed comfortable around her.

...The only one she felt comfortable around.

She didn't know how she could ever repay that. "No," she said softly. "Thank you."

"I'M GOING TO CALL AYNEII," COL SAID BY WAY OF WARNING. HE understood Dalia's fear of fey and didn't want her to be surprised if the fey appeared to both of them.

Dalia nodded.

They had both given over their mounts to the weary women

and children from Trentin's keep and were walking over the rolling hills. It was just past midday, and they weren't far from the edge of the forest now. They were walking behind the group, still just far enough back to be considered 'alone.'

Trentin had said that it was a half-day's hard ride to Gariast's estates from his own. Col had been worried about that one knight who had escaped and how long another force might take to arrive back at Trentin's keep. He assumed they still had some time but didn't want to take any risks.

"Ayneii!" Col called out.

She appeared with a pop. He saw Dalia flinch from the corner of his eye. He usually did when Ayneii appeared without warning as well, but he'd been expecting this arrival.

"Hi!" The sprite's boundless energy and joy was hard to ignore. Even with all his dark thoughts, Col found himself smiling.

"Hello, friend. Were you able to shield our new camp?"

She nodded. "Just finished with the ritual. No magic should be able to find anyone there."

"Thank you, but I'm afraid I have another task if you're up for it."

"Always!"

He'd thought as much.

He motioned to the ground. It was churned up by so many people and the wagons. Their passage was obvious. "This group I'm escorting is rather... Well I fear we may be tracked. Can you and some of the others hide our trail? I know you said people are hard to hide, but what about just doing something about this ground? Can you make it look like we were never here?"

Ayneii bobbed her head in a nod. "Of course, that's easy."

"Are you sure? We've come a long way. There is a lot to hide."

She made a face, quirking her mouth to the side as she looked back over the hills. After a moment, she shrugged. "Still shouldn't be too hard. Working with earth and grass is a lot easier than living beings. I'll grab a few of the others to help and it will be done quick enough."

"Thank you."

She grinned and was gone, vanished.

"She really is something... isn't she?" Dalia asked. He could still hear a bit of uncertainty in Dalia's voice. It might be some time still before she trusted any fey.

Col nodded. "She was my first friend after I ran from everything I knew. She's more than a friend now. She's a companion. She's... family." He hoped Dalia would come to see that.

"You're..." She hesitated, and he could see she was trying hard to be optimistic. "You're very lucky to have her."

He nodded.

By evening, they were well within the forest, which meant things grew dark quickly. Their caravan had slowed greatly as the wagons had had trouble moving through the brush at times. They slowed more now as darkness made passage even more difficult.

Ayneii appeared to Col again. "You're really slow."

"Sorry. If we didn't have so many with us, we'd have been there a while ago. I do want to get to camp quickly though. How far away are we?"

"Not far."

"Good, thank you."

Ayneii nodded. "Anything else?"

"Yes, a few questions."

"Oh?"

"Is there another type of fey that appears as a small gray-skinned man?" Col looked over at Dalia. He had her full attention now. The young woman's eyes were fixed on Ayneii, which let him know she'd be able to hear the answers.

"Yes, those are bogeys. Very erratic and mischievous fey."

"More so than you?"

"Oh yes, much more. Sprites are the fey of life; bogeys are the fey of change itself and are often at the heart of any big upheavals in the world."

"That makes sense," Dalia said softly.

Ayneii looked at her. Col watched a realization spread on Ayneii's face. "Oh!"

"What?" Col asked.

Ayneii ignored him and flew over to Dalia. She reached out to touch Dalia's cheek, but the woman flinched away.

"Sorry," Dalia said. "I'm still a little skittish around fey."

Ayneii nodded. "Please, I need to see something... or I suppose... feel something. I won't hurt you."

Dalia looked at Col. He shrugged but said, "I don't know what she's doing, but she won't hurt you."

"Very well then, you may proceed," Dalia said to Ayneii.

Ayneii reached out and touched Dalia's cheek. Dalia probably did not see the fey's reaction to the touch, since she was so close. Ayneii flinched but kept her hand on Dalia's skin. After a moment, Ayneii seemed to settle and concentrate.

Dalia's eyes darted to Col, questioning after several long moments of this contact.

Col could only shake his head and shrug again.

Finally, Ayneii came away with a great sigh.

"I'm so sorry," Ayneii said softly to Dalia. "I think I know what was done to you now."

13

"YES?" DALIA ASKED. HER VOICE WAS TREMULOUS. SHE WAS uncertain now whether she really wanted to know what had happened. Thinking of it as a 'curse' had seemed convenient enough up until now. Did she really want to know more?

The answer came to her almost instantly.

Yes.

If she knew more, she might be able to do something about it. She felt like she was out of control. Perhaps knowing what had happened to her would mean she could manage it... that was the hope anyway.

"Please tell me, Ayneii."

Ayneii bobbed and fluttered around a little agitated but settled finally. She landed on the hindquarters of a horse Dalia and Col had been following, still bringing up the rear of the group. If the beast noticed, it gave no indication. Ayneii sat carefully, her gossamer wings slowly swaying behind her, helping her to keep her position.

This was the first time Dalia had seen the wings and was mesmerized for a moment. They were large, much taller than Ayneii and extending out in great flares behind her. They were nearly see-through, like the filmy wings of an insect, but colorful like a butterfly. They shimmered with every hue of green along with some pale yellow, bronze, even flecks of purple. There were three segments. The one at the top shot up to a fine point, then swayed back to another point before arching back down toward Ayneii's back, like some flimsy triangle. The middle segment was more diamond shaped. It followed the curve of the upper portion for a bit to a point, then swooped far out to the back, then in again to a bottom point before arching back in to join the lower portion. The lower portion had only one point, far out at the back, and curved like a leaf bulging in the center. For each of these segments, even smaller bits extended still further out or up, connected by thin tendrils and filaments. They were beautiful.

Ayneii spoke. The fey's high and light voice, with its singsong quality, belied any gravitas her words may have carried and made it sound more like some child's story. "The simplest way to say it is that... the bogey made you partly fey. So, you're kind of like me now."

"Oh?" Dalia raised a brow. She didn't feel anything like the carefree sprite.

Ayneii sighed. "But that's very much a simplification. He did more than just make you part fey..." She paused for a moment. "Have you ever heard of—" She looked over at Col. "What was that word you used for a human with magic?"

"A wizard?"

"Yes." She turned back to Dalia. "Have you heard of wizards?"

Dalia nodded. "In tales and legends."

"Well a wizard is a human who has been gifted magical abilities by one or more fey. It hasn't happened often in more recent times, but it is possible."

"And that's what the bogey did? Give me magic?"

"Yes, but even that isn't quite right. You have magic, that is clear, but you also have... something else, an... essence of fey in you. But you are not fey and are still very much human."

This was a little confusing. "Sorry?"

Ayneii pursed her tiny lips. "In all truth, I don't know how or why the bogey would do such a thing, but it is as if he gave you a part of himself. Something that is primal and uncontrolled and... very powerful. But he did it in such a way as to blend it perfectly with your human nature. Fey cannot fight or kill, but you can. I think you will find you can do far more than that as well. And everything the bogey did... it's all tied to an imperative, a... feeling within you: to protect, to liberate."

"Liberate what, or who?"

"I don't know. It's just what you were meant to do... in general."

Dalia considered this for a moment. It made sense. Every time she'd fought, it had been to free herself or protect others.

"But why?"

Ayneii shrugged. "That I do not know. I can only tell you what I felt within you. I do not know the bogey's reason for doing what he did." After a moment she said, "Did I mention how powerful it was?"

"You did, yes." Dalia had to smile a little. She didn't feel that way. She felt out of control most of the time. But it was good to know she was... powerful now, or at least whatever was within her was powerful.

Ayneii shook her head. "I don't know why any fey would give so much of their essence to a human. It seems... well actually bogeys are erratic and confusing, so maybe it is perfectly in character for them."

"Is there anything else?" This from Col.

Ayneii nodded. The small being looked up at Dalia and

there was pity in her eyes. "What you are feeling now is only the beginning. There will be... lots of changes to come."

Dalia didn't like the sound of that. Before she could ask what these changes were, Ayneii perked up. "But! I will help you. All of the sprites here will help you. We'll help you learn to control this change. You're in good hands."

Dalia had to smile at the sprite's enthusiasm, even if it was a tentative smile. "Thank you."

"My pleasure!" Ayneii rose and launched herself up from the horse, flying again. "You're almost to the camp. I'll see you there!" And she was off zipping through the forest.

"Well," Col said as Ayneii's green light faded and the darkness of the evening forest returned. "At least you know what happened now. And you have some help."

Dalia nodded. "I do." Though she still didn't feel quite right. None of this was 'right' by any means. It was just something she'd have to accept and live with.

She hoped she could do that without harming too many more people.

ONCE AT CAMP, THINGS PROGRESSED QUICKLY. THE WAGONS WERE unloaded, and people were sent to various areas to set up shelters and make space for the newcomers.

Col made sure everything was well under way, then he found Tom.

"I'm going to be heading out first thing tomorrow once again."

Tom sighed. "I can take care of things here."

"Actually, no. I want you with me. I'm leaving Trentin in charge."

"The man who was trying to kill us two days ago?"

"Yes. I have enough reason to trust him now, and I'll have the sprites make sure he doesn't do anything stupid."

Tom nodded. "I'll be ready at dawn then."

"We'll take Nik and Jaff too. They have a little practice in the saddle now. Hopefully enough to keep up."

"We'll be riding hard? Where are we going?"

"The capital."

Tom whistled with a raised brow. "Oh... haven't been there in a while."

The question of 'why' was clear enough on Tom's face that Col felt compelled to answer. Though he did appreciate Tom's willingness to go along without asking.

"I have a few things to take care of. Mainly, I need to sneak into the palace and free my parents.

Tom raised a brow.

"Let's just say I found out a few things recently which are going to change our direction."

"No more raiding?"

"No," Col said evenly. "We're going to war."

"War?" Tom's look was skeptical. "Col, you know most of the men here aren't warriors, don't you?

Col sighed heavily. "I know, and I can't ask them to fight. This is my war."

"Some of them would happily fight for you, but... I just don't know if they should. They're not trained. By the Octave, I'm not trained! I'm a decent enough thief and bandit, but..." Tom grimaced.

Well," Col said with a grin growing on his face. "That's the other reason we're going to the capital. I may need to steal an army."

Tom eyed him. "You haven't been eating the green-spotted mushrooms, have you?"

"No, my head is clear. I know exactly what I'm doing."

"I think that might be worse." Tom shrugged. "But you've never led me wrong as long as I've known you, so I'll follow along wherever you say we go. I did say I was a thief. This will be the first army I've stolen though."

"You won't be stealing it if things go right. That will be all me. I have other things in mind for you."

"Oh. Should I be worried?"

"Not at all."

"It's a good thing I trust you."

Col nodded. "I know, and... thanks, Tom." Col stepped in to embrace the man.

Once Tom had left to prepare, Col went looking for Dalia or Ayneii. He found them together.

It was late. The moon was rising. Its light filtered down through the tangle of branches and leaves above. Col had expected Dalia to be resting, but she was standing watching a cabin being grown. He stopped beside her and watched as well. There was quite enough light to see by, since the house was being created by a score of sprites. It was a dazzling show, the sprites all glowing brightly in their respective hues, each seeming no more than a ball of colored light as they swooped and zoomed around the growing structure.

"Amazing, isn't it?" he said.

"It's beautiful."

There was something in her voice. He looked from the construction to her face, lit up by the light of the fey. Her eyes sparkled. She seemed in a state as close to peace as he'd ever seen her. Something within her had changed. He said as much.

She looked at him and smiled. "Yes." Her gaze drifted back to the fey. "I was just thinking that... if I'm part fey now and... and if they can be so industrious and beautiful and magical, then... perhaps that's what I'm becoming as well. Perhaps I can be that beautiful."

"You already are," Col said softly, but his voice was drowned out as Ayneii zipped out from the build to join them and called out, "we're almost done," at the same time as his words.

He wasn't sure if Dalia had heard him, and since the moment had passed, he wasn't sure if he should repeat it. Instead, he forced himself back to what he'd wanted to talk to these two about.

"Dalia, Ayneii, I'm leaving you in charge of the camp while I'm gone." He raised a hand to forestall questions. "Let me explain first, then you can tell me how and why I'm wrong." He turned to Dalia. "I know you'd offered to come with me and help me on my quest, but I'm not going after Gariast yet. I'm going to the capital first. It's my parents. Gariast doesn't have them, the king does. I know the palace like my own home. I lived there for three years. I'll be able to get in and out alone far easier than with anyone with me. I hope you don't mind."

Dalia nodded. "No, I understand. Actually, I'd been about to say that I'd wanted to stay here and learn some more from the fey before I went out again."

He laid a tender hand on her shoulder. "Well enough. I hope it helps you." He let his hand fall away, uncertain how long to linger. "But to the other matter. I'm leaving you two in charge, but no one will know that. I'll be telling the rest of the camp that Trentin is in charge. Frankly, more than half the people here are from his keep now, and they know and trust him. It's not that I don't think either of you would be able to do it, but... the fey are only seldom seen, and a leader needs to be present to provide reassurance. Dalia, as much as I know you are no concern to us, a lot of the others here still aren't sure of you. That is why as much as I'm leaving Trentin in charge of the camp, you two will be in charge of him. I'll let him know as much as well. If he gets out of line at all, I'm fairly certain the two of you can bring him back swiftly enough."

"As you say, Captain!" Ayneii said.

Col nearly choked on his next breath. "You've never called me captain before."

"It's what some of the others call you... what does it mean anyway? I thought it was something like a leader."

"It is, yes. But you know I'm not your leader. I don't think anyone could ever control you Ayneii." He turned to Dalia. "The same could be said for you. Neither of you are my followers; I hope you know that. We're all equals here."

"I'm a captain too?" Ayneii asked.

Col chuckled again. "Yes."

"I'm a captain," Ayneii said, straightening a little. "We captains need to get back to work!" She zipped off to help with the cabin again but was back a moment later. "Oh, and you can count on me to keep things safe here and watch the big human." Then, she was gone again.

Dalia was laughing a little, quietly. "Myself as well." She put a hand on his shoulder then stepped in on her toes to give him a peck on the cheek. "Keep safe out there," she whispered, before stepping back.

"I will." He reached for her again and squeezed her arm reassuringly. They gazed at each other for a moment, then he nodded. She nodded as well, and he left.

Now to go find Trentin and tell him he was in charge... sort of.

14

ZATHARYN WAS GROWING CONCERNED.

He'd done a blood-seeking as Lord Gariast had asked. He hadn't thought there would be much of interest to find... and he had been so very wrong. He'd found the man Lord Gariast had been seeking, but immediately, his attention had been drawn to something else. Some source of great power near the man. So, he'd performed a scrying, using a looking glass to actually see the man as he rode through a forest at the head of a great trail of people.

It had been clear what the source of power was, or more precisely... who. There was a girl at the end of the trail of people. If his unwitting spies in Gariast's estate were to be believed, this was the daughter of a nobleman. The same one who was to have come here but had been waylaid by bandits. He hadn't thought much of the tales of this girl... until now.

Through the mirror, he'd seen the great halo of power around her. He couldn't fathom how she'd come to be so strong in the fey spirit. Had she somehow managed to dominate fey as he had? It seemed unlikely.

It had taken him decades to learn the intricacies of the fey power he'd been imbued with, and longer still to fashion his phylactery to ensure his power would never be taken from him. He'd been unstoppable then... well, by the fey anyway. Any who tried to come for him were added to his collection, trapped within the phylactery, increasing his power. He'd been little more than a boy when he'd first sought the assistance of the fey, but by the time he was powerful enough to stop his aging entirely, he'd been as he appeared now, an old man. A lifetime spent building the power needed to take his revenge.

Yet this girl was still so young. He couldn't imagine she'd have already done what it had taken him decades to do.

He'd used more power to listen in on her conversation. He'd heard her say that she had no idea what she could do, that she was fey-cursed. It certainly didn't seem that way to him. Curses did not imbue people with such a level of raw magical power. Obviously, she hadn't fully realized what had happened to her. Which was good.

Whatever she was, she was a danger to him. Her level of power rivaled his own, and if she were to come after him, he wasn't sure if he'd be able to stop her. Zatharyn still possessed many advantages. She most likely didn't know he existed. Also, she didn't seem aware of her power and was probably ill trained in it. He'd had hundreds of years to practice and hone his abilities. He was a master of the fey magic now. He doubted she would have anywhere near his knowledge or experience.

But he was soon going to show himself to the world. He couldn't risk that she might find training and challenge him once he did.

He had to find her first and destroy her.

But then as he'd prepared a spell to take himself to her... she'd simply vanished from his senses and disappeared from his scrying along with the man Gariast wanted.

Zatharyn had no idea how this had happened, hence his growing concern and frustration.

He needed to find her, but nothing he tried now worked.

He feared that somehow he was too late, that she'd realized her power and hidden herself from him. He knew of no other way she might have disappeared so completely.

He would keep his senses out, searching for her. That level of power would not be hard to sense.

But he feared that he had lost her for good and his plans for domination of this kingdom were in jeopardy.

He could not allow that.

DALIA WAS UP BEFORE DAWN. A PART OF HER WONDERED IF SHE didn't need as much rest being... what she was now. She still didn't have a good word for it other than perhaps 'half-fey.' It didn't seem like the sprites ever rested. Perhaps she didn't need to sleep at all. She certainly felt awake and refreshed enough for only having had a short rest.

It was a vastly different feeling from her extreme exhaustion after The Fury took her. She wasn't sure why that might be. Why she'd felt so consumed and weary then, yet so full of life now.

She wanted to see Col off. A part of her didn't want him to go, but she knew that was selfish. It wasn't as if they were betrothed or courting or anything. She wasn't even sure how commoners formed such bonds, but she certainly felt that there was... something between them. Yet another thing she didn't have a name for yet.

The forest was still quite dark; the predawn light wasn't strong enough to pierce the armor of leaves above them. Yet Dalia had no trouble seeing her way around. She'd been noticing more and more things that had changed about her. She could see exceptionally well in the dark and hear things others didn't seem to be able to.

She blushed recalling Col's words last night. Despite Ayneii speaking at the same time, she'd heard him say clear enough that she was beautiful. That remembrance warmed her on this cool morning.

There was a small group gathered around four horses. She recognized Jaff from their trip to Trentin's keep and approached him.

"Do you know where Col is?"

"In there, packing up some things," the man said, pointing to a cave mouth in the tall cliff that bordered one side of their new camp. The sheer rock face rose about fifty feet from the forest floor and atop it the forest continued. It was as if some great calamity had caused the earth to jut up in times long past. There was a slit of a cave, which Dalia approached. Within, there seemed to be near complete darkness, but after a moment of looking into the depths, she thought she could make out some light within. Deep in the cave, she could see flickering torchlight cascading along one of the rock walls. Voices also echoed out to her.

"Take only what's lightest and most valuable. We have only the room on our horses and we'll want to keep them as unencumbered as we can." It was Col's voice.

She made her way gingerly into the cave. Again, with barely any light but that far off faint reflection off a wall, she was able to see the cave around her and navigate the uneven floor.

She wondered what this place was.

She came around a bend in the cave and her eyes grew wide.

"Oh my," she gasped.

Her comment was loud enough that the three men in the cave turned to her.

Dalia ignored them for a moment as she took in the treasure

around her. The light from their three torches was magnified ten times, reflecting off gold, jewels, and other valuables. It was piled high on bejeweled boxes or on shelves, either natural or cut into the wall. There was enough wealth in this small room to match many of the balls she'd been to as a child. There were even glittering dresses and decorative armor, not to mention weapons with jewels glittering from hilts. It was a bit over-whelming and she stood stunned for a moment.

"Dalia, welcome to the treasure trove of the Black Bandit."

His words sunk in slowly. Of course. He'd been robbing the caravans of nobility and the wealthy for two years or more now. He had to have done something with that wealth... and here it was.

Before that fateful day with the bogey, living as a young noblewoman, she'd heard the tales of the Black Bandit's raids. Her father had alternated between furious and faintly amused. Some of the wealth in this room would have come from her father's estates, but not much. Mostly this was Gariast's and that of his bannermen, who continued to use the road through the Sandren Forest to move their goods as it was far quicker than going around the forest.

She recalled her father mentioning a particularly wealth-laden caravan headed for Gariast's estates, which had disap-peared. After that, Gariast and his knights had been trying to catch the Black Bandit, sending in more and more men around their caches of loot—only to have those taken as well. They had been trying for over a year to catch or kill him. That had never quite worked in their favor. Her father had shaken his head and muttered on about how they should have simply stopped using the forest. If the bandit was that insatiable for wealth, he'd even-tually come out from hiding to rob an estate, and that's when he'd be much more likely to be caught.

If Dalia was honest with herself, she'd heard the tales and

had thought the man part scoundrel and part dashing rogue. The bandit never killed unless provoked and never robbed commoners or women travelling alone... only those wealthy lords.

She knew now this was all... revenge. Col was seeking to hurt the man who'd hurt him. It was petty perhaps, but Gariast had certainly been very upset at his losses. She was sure the lord would give much to find this cave.

She found words. "It seems highway robbery is a lucrative profession."

"Some days." He nodded. "But it's also very dangerous. I don't recommend it for most. You need certain qualifications."

She laughed, but it died off quickly, replaced by her amazement at the wealth around her. "What are you going to use this for?"

"For now? We'll use some of it to buy supplies as well as information, some at the capital, some before we get there to help get us in."

She nodded, watching him empty a small chest of diamonds into a pouch.

She wasn't quite sure what to say now that she'd found him. Especially with the other two men around. Luckily, the two had quickly finished packing their own bags full of precious things. She saw Tom nudge Nik and bob his head toward the door. They left. Tom winked on the way by.

She nodded and smiled, thankful for the man's thoughtfulness.

"Col," she said once the others had gone. She stepped carefully over the jagged floor and clutter of small crates to him.

He looked up from examining a string of pearls in one hand and a thick gold chain with a pendant in the other. "I don't know as much as you probably do," he said. "Which of these is worth more?"

She drew close to him. "Neither is worth as much as this." She reached past him, her body brushing his, as she plucked up a silver necklace inlaid with tiny gems, each a deep blue and radiating its own faint light. She laid it on his palm. "Those are sun sapphires. They are very rare."

"Oh." He looked up from it to her, then back to it. "Thank you." He dropped the other two items then lifted the necklace until it was beside her face. "They're like your eyes. Are you sure you don't want it? It suits you."

They were close, very close. His words and his offer had set her heart to pounding. "No. You use it to make things right." The next words took a moment and when they did come, they weren't as they'd been in her head. She wanted to say, 'I don't need anything but you.'

"I don't need anything but..." She choked up a little. "But a good friend."

He stood there gazing into her eyes for a long moment before breaking the contact with a deep breath letting it out with a huff. "I've only just started to get to know you," he said softly. "But I'm hoping we can be more than friends, someday."

She felt a surge of courage and reached up to touch his face softly. "I'd like that." Her heart was thundering.

Perhaps encouraged by her touch, he leaned in. The hand with the necklace held her neck and he brought his lips to hers. She didn't flinch away but leaned into the kiss.

Only once before in her life had she kissed a man in passion and that had been the minstrel who'd whisked her away from her family. His kisses had been hard and deep and a very new thing to Dalia. This was new too, soft and tender, yet lingering as their lips adjusted and pressed repeatedly.

Her breath was gone when he finally drew back. His voice was faint but ever so earnest when he said, "Something to remember me by. Just as I will most surely remember you."

She could only nod as she tried to regain her breath and rein in her stampeding heart.

He sighed reluctantly. "But I must go."

He slid the necklace into a pouch.

They stayed there for a moment as well, eyes locked, hands gently touching. She knew she was flushed and didn't care. She needed to say something.

"Come back soon," she breathed. He nodded and began to lead her out of the cave. But just before they reached the bend, which would take them out of the treasure room, she squeezed his hand and pulled him back.

He stopped, turning to merge gazes with her again.

"Yes?"

"Come back to *me* soon," she said softly.

He smiled.

"I will." He leaned in then and kissed her again, only briefly, but still enough to make her—only just steadied—heart pound, once again.

He led her out of the cave. He didn't drop her hand as they approached the other men but held it firm. He wasn't ashamed of her, and that act alone meant more than anything.

He squeezed her hand before letting it go and swinging up into his saddle.

With a wave, he was off into the morning mists.

Dalia sighed heavily. "Come back to me soon," she repeated at a whisper.

15

Colric stared at the battlements that surrounded Roval, the capital city, and tried to hold back the flood of memories and emotions, which came to him at the awesome sight.

This city had been his home for nine years. Three of those had been in the royal barracks within the palace itself. He knew these walls, had trained in the fields beyond them, stood atop them on guard. This is where he'd risen to the rank of captain and had five hundred men, most of them older than he, under his command. This is where he'd expected to spend his life, until Gariast had taken that all away from him.

Now he was going to sneak into the city, lurking like some villain. It seemed wrong, but that was where his life had led him. He only hoped that one day he'd be able to return to this city with honor.

For now, he flipped his hood up over his head and sank down into a slightly shrunken posture. His clothes were rough, homespun, and ill fitting. Today he was not himself. He was Yerris, servant to Tom Willow.

Nik and Jaff were similarly attired, and the three of them all walked as Tom rode. Their horses were laden with baggage, mostly fine pelts they'd purchased from a hunter at a village not far from the edge of the Sandren Forest. Tom was playing the part of a minor merchant coming to sell his wares at the capital with his three laborers. He shouldn't provoke much curiosity entering the city, and his three followers would be even less of a concern for the city guards.

They waited in a long line of others entering the city and when it came time for the city guards to question Tom, they didn't look twice at the three scruffy servants. They questioned Tom a little, but Col had given him all the answers he'd need.

When the guards asked him to, 'state his name and business.' Tom answered quickly with, "Tom Forester, with hides for Master Grunston." Grunston was a well-known and respected furrier in the capital. The guards would know his name.

The only other question they had was, "Is that all you're selling, no other wares?"

Tom shook his head. "Nothing else, feel free to check." He motioned to the three horses he was leading, heavy with furs.

They waved him through.

That had gone well enough.

They found a disreputable tavern in the Brown District of the city. This part of the capital was known by the locals by a variety of much more colorful names including the 'dung' district and worse. The air was foul, tainted by tanneries and knackers. This was where all of the less savory businesses had to put up their signs and as such, it was home for many of the city's less than legal citizens as well.

A perfect place for Col and his men.

Once they were safely in their cramped room, Jaff asked, "What now boss?"

"It's getting on to evening, so for now we rest. And yes, I do expect you to rest. No carousing tonight even though we're in the capital. Tomorrow I'll expect you to be out all day and all night, so you might as well sleep while you can."

"What are we to do tomorrow?" Tom asked.

"Tom, you've got the best manners and a bearing which might pass for noble." Col tossed him a bag of gems. "Get yourself some new clothes, very nice clothes, and then go mingle in the Gardens."

"The Gardens?"

"The Green District, on the other side of the city."

The man nodded.

"That's where most of the visiting nobles and well-to-do's stay when they're in town. Pretend you're a minor lord from somewhere far to the west; no one should question you as long as you don't question it yourself. Just assume everyone is beneath you and get offended at anyone who suggests otherwise. Essentially, act like a noble."

"I can do that." He grinned.

"Good. Try to get into whatever function is happening that evening. There is something nearly every night. Ask around and grease some palms until you have an invitation to the most prestigious thing. Once there, see what people are talking about, what's the big news of the day. Get as much information as you can, even if it seems trivial. When it comes to nobles, the trivial stuff is probably going to end up being the most important to us."

"Got it, Captain."

"And don't call me captain in the city. 'Boss' will do if you have to say anything. Arron is better." It was a common enough name and one he was used to responding to.

The three nodded at that. Tom was really the only one who used Col's old rank anyway, so it shouldn't be too much of an issue.

Col turned to the other two. He would never say it, but these two would never pass as nobles. Of the two, Jaff was the worst looking and the better fighter. Sometimes, Col wondered how the man could be related to Lily. Her features were smooth and pleasant. His were lumpy and... not. That made it easy to choose where he went.

Col pressed a few silvers into the man's hand. "You do the same thing in the Gray District, just to the west of us here. Find out what you can. Listen at the bars and see what the commoners are saying. It's not the greatest part of town, so don't spend too much in one place or you'll probably get jumped. I trust you to handle yourself if that happens."

Jaff flashed a gap-toothed smile and a well-tended blade, which he'd drawn with alacrity. "Aye, boss."

Col turned to Nik. "Sorry Nik, but you get to do the same thing here in the Brown District." He gave the man a handful of copper coins. "People here will be much more secretive and standoffish. I'm trusting you to use your stealth and guile to listen where no one will see you. Use the coins to get yourself some darker clothing if you need to. Understood?"

The man nodded. Nik was far from the strongest or brightest of the three, but he had a quiet way about him and the ability to walk softly which meant that of the three he was generally the least noticeable. He'd do fine.

"What about you?" Jaff asked.

"Me? Don't worry too much about me. I get the easy job. All I have to do is sneak into the palace dungeons and escape with two prisoners."

Jaff's mouth hung agape.

Col put on a big confident grin. "Now, like I said, let's get some sleep."

≈

THE NEXT DAY, THEY ALL WENT THEIR SEPARATE WAYS. COL HEADED out of the Brown District to the Silver District where the streets were filled with markets, tradesmen, and merchants. He wore the hood of his tattered cloak low over his face and led the three horses laden with furs.

He knew his destination by heart and quickly arrived at 'Grunston's Leather and Furs.' He left the horses outside and stepped through the door of the shop, which caused a bell above the entranceway to jingle.

A booming voice greeted him, though not in the politest of manners. "Shoo, you scamp! We don't need any of your kind in here. We have only the best here and serve a higher clientele. Go over to Romdol's. He'll sell ya some flea-infested finery."

Col knew that voice well enough and couldn't blame Grunston for mistaking him for a vagabond. He was a vagabond.

He made a quick check to ensure the shop was otherwise empty then pushed back his hood. "Is that any way to treat an old friend?" he asked with a smile. He had to hope this ploy would work. Albior Grunston had been one of two main merchants who had purchased items from his family when they'd been hunters not so long ago. Grunston had bought their furs and leather. The other man, Uthden Jarek, had purchased the meat, but he was based out of the town of Haverstal. Grunston was his best contact in the capital, but it was a risk. Col was a wanted man. He had to hope Grunston would help him and not turn him in.

"By the Eight High and Holy Gods!" The man breathed the words, his voice leaving him. "Col? You're alive?" Grunston was a big man in all aspects, taller than most men Col knew and built like a bear with a thick chest and even thicker gut. He wore a great dark beard, which, for the sake of his clientele, was well trimmed, if still a little bushy.

Col stepped in closer, his voice low. "Yes, and I need your help. Is there somewhere more private we can talk?"

Grunston nodded and ushered him into a small room where the walls were hung with several sample coats and stoles of fine fur. "Wait here," the large man said and left.

Col could hear Grunston then calling out for someone named Elline. After a moment, the big man returned.

"Oliria's gone now and Elline's all I have. She's old enough to run the shop for a bit," Grunston said as if Col should know what this meant. Vague memories returned to Col, an older woman, Grunston's wife, had her name been Oliria? That could be it. Then there had been a waif of a girl always hiding behind her mother's skirts, Elline perhaps?

"I'm sorry for your loss," Col said, somber.

"It was the Sweating Sickness, came through here in a wave, two years ago, not long after you... what did happen to you, boy?"

There was a small table in the room with four chairs. Col sat and sighed heavily. "I made a mistake and it cost me everything."

"You killed that prince?"

"Yes, but that wasn't really the mistake. I was set up to kill the Santhine Prince and didn't know who he was at the time. It's a long story, which I don't have time to tell." He paused to look Grunston in the eye. "Can I count on you for a little assistance?"

The big man looked a little concerned. He took a moment and sat across from Col, the wooden chair creaking under his weight.

"They say you committed treason. You and your family were killed for it. I don't think they needed to go that far, but... I can't help if what you're doing is going against the king."

Col nodded. "I understand. Well, let me tell you what I plan and why, and you let me know if you can help."

The other man nodded.

"The tales of my death, as you can see, were lies. I have only recently learned that apparently the death of my family was also a lie."

"What!" Grunston roared.

"I know. But my parents are in the royal dungeons right now and I am here to free them. As you say, they do not deserve such a fate."

Grunston considered for a moment, and then reluctantly said, "Agreed."

"What I need from you is a way into the palace, and only that, nothing more."

"You'll get yourself killed in there," he said, eyeing Col.

"Perhaps, but I must try."

Grunston heaved out a long breath. "How would you propose I get you into the palace?"

"Do you still have a contract with the royal furrier?"

"Aye, I do."

"Perhaps you'd like to take him some furs to examine... today."

The big man grimaced through his beard. "I usually only come when he asks..."

Col said nothing as the man's voice trailed off. Was there more to come?

Grunston began nodding slowly. "But... I have been known to go see him on occasion when I have something special, on which he might want first bid."

"Do you have anything like that today?"

Grunston seemed to hold his breath for a long moment, tapping his fingers on the table. "I do." He shook his head now. "But Col, I don't know if I can... What you ask, what you're doing... by the Cursed Caves, boy!"

Col let the man sit and stew as his plan hung in the balance.

"For the sake of your father, I'll help you, boy, but on one condition. You sit here and tell me that long story of what happened all those years ago."

Colric nodded. If that was what it took to get the man's help, he'd do it. So, he told Grunston the tale of Lord Gariast's invitation and the death of the Prince of Santhine. "There you go. Yes, I killed the man, but it was not as everyone thinks. It was revenge by a petty lord, a punishment for beating him at a tournament."

Grunston nodded. "Nobles can be a fickle and petty sort. I know this Gariast. He is as cruel as you say. Alright, boy, I'll take you in. Wait here for a moment while I tell Elline I'm going out for a while."

By the next call of the watch, Col was hidden under a pile of furs—sweating like a pig—and through the palace gates.

Grunston let him out from his hiding spot once they were out of sight of the gate guards and before he reached the palace furrier. "Best of luck, my boy," the man whispered, and Col nodded, disappearing into a nearby shadow. From here things became a lot easier... he hoped.

Most palace guards would only know the usual ways to get around the palace and its surrounding fortifications. It was a calculated move by the king to ensure that if any average guard was ever captured and interrogated by an enemy, they would not give any of the palace secrets away. But captains of the guard were privy to a more detailed layout of the grounds including the hidden servants' corridors within the walls. There were hidden entrances all over the palace so that servants could get in and out of rooms without being seen in the regular halls.

Col slipped into one such secret entrance and then moved quickly and purposefully to his destination. Any servants who saw him thought him simply another new servant. He might arouse some suspicion, but with luck that wouldn't amount to anything until after he was gone from the palace.

And he wouldn't be travelling the servants' corridors for long.

His first stop was the guards' barracks.

The men of the King's Army, tasked with protecting the capital, were stationed in the Black District of the city, a section dedicated to the military. Only the King's Guard specifically were stationed, and had barracks, within the palace itself.

Col listened at the secret entrance that would take him into the barracks until he'd heard nothing for some time. As he slipped in, he glanced around. Anyone who was in here was unmoving on a bunk, hopefully well asleep from a night shift. No one seemed to take notice of him, so he quickly went to the first wardrobe he could find next to an abandoned bunk. As he had expected, there was a secondary uniform hanging there. Most guards kept a couple of uniforms with them in case anything happened to one. He stole the uniform and slipped it on.

Now came the hard part. The uniform did not come with armor. Most soldiers only had one set of armor. And if he really wanted to pass as a guardsman, he'd need armor. Also, since he was dressed as a guardsman now, he couldn't use the servant corridors anymore, so from here had to use straight bravado and walk, in the open, from the barracks to the armory.

He knew well enough that most people wouldn't be paying much attention to him. He just needed to make sure he didn't draw any undue attention to himself. Also, he had to be careful about being recognized by someone who might know him. It had been two years, but that was still a very distinct possibility.

He drew himself up, making sure he looked like he belonged here instead of looking like he was trying to avoid being noticed. Then he left the barracks.

He kept a brisk pace, hoping that any who saw him would think him on a mission, and not interrupt him.

He made it to the armory without incident, but as he reached for the door to slip inside he heard a voice within... a voice he knew.

It was Kellan of Yorst, a man who'd been one of his lieutenants when Col was captain. If anyone would know him on sight, it would be Kellan.

Time slowed as Col's mind whirled for what to do. The latch of the door was pulled from his hand and opened inward revealing Kellan speaking to someone behind him, head turned away.

Col took that extra moment to cover his face and cough, turning away from the door.

He felt a light pat on his back. "You feeling well, soldier?" Kellan asked.

Col nodded. "Fine," he said in a voice he hoped was not his own.

"Good."

Footfalls could be heard leaving.

Col risked a look and Kellan was on his way toward the outer wall. Col sighed out his relief and entered the armory.

The man Kellan had been talking to was still inside, but it wasn't anyone Col recognized. So, he went about his business outfitting himself as if that were exactly what he was supposed to be doing, just like the other man here. The guard left without even acknowledging Col, which was a godsend.

Now he had armor and a sword and looked like a true guardsman. The added benefit of the armor was the helm, which covered most of his face. The guardsmen helms were made to provide significant protection without sacrificing vision. There was a single cutout from the steel of the helm, one inch wide and stretching far to the sides. This allowed for near perfect sight, including peripheral vision. It was uncommon, but not unheard of, for guardsmen who were not actually on the walls, to be wearing their helms around the palace. So, Col wore his helm and began the trek through the palace toward the dungeons.

His best chance to free his parents would be during a changing of the guard, which took place every eight hours, the next of which would take place at the fourth call of the watch after noon. That was still several hours away. But there was something else he needed to do first.

In order to get in and out as quickly as possible, he'd need to know exactly which cell, of the dozens in the palace, held his parents. To find that out, he'd need the dungeon-keeper's ledger. The problem was, that was with the jailer himself.

He'd met the jailer a few times in his time as a captain of the King's Guard. When he marched purposefully into the man's small office deep beneath the palace, he was relieved to see this wasn't the man he'd known. This man was younger, a new dungeon-keeper.

"I need to see your ledger."

There must have been something menacing in his voice, for the jailer was practically trembling as he handed the logbook over to Col.

Col leafed through the thick tome searching for the names of his parents. He found the period when he thought they would have been admitted but couldn't find them. He grew more and more worried as he searched through the ledger.

Then he found it.

Two entries from about three weeks after Gariast had betrayed him several years ago. His parents' names and beside them was marked 'traitor.' But that wasn't what inflamed him the most. Next to both names was a large 'X,' which meant they were both dead.

He couldn't make sense of this for a long moment. Trentin had told him they were alive, but... it wasn't like the knight had been here. He didn't know what happened in these dungeons. It was clear enough that his parents had been alive when Gariast was telling the world they were dead, but... what had happened to them after that? How and why were they dead now?

His anger built as he turned slowly back to the dungeon-keeper.

He slammed the ledger back down onto the jailer's desk and pointed to the entry. There was rage in his voice when he spoke. His voice was not loud, but a menacing whisper. "These two, the traitors, what happened to them?"

The man was a coward, that was plain as day. He shrank back, falling off his chair. His shrill voice quavered when he answered. "They're dead," the man said, scurrying back against the wall of his small office.

"I can see that!" Col bellowed. Then he steadied himself and, through clenched teeth, asked, "How did they die."

Panic played over the man's face. It occurred to Col then that the dungeon-keeper looked like nothing so much as a rat, with a long, pointed nose and tight fidgeting mouth, not to mention the small darting eyes.

"I can't—"

Col stalked around the desk and lifted the man from where he half-crouched against the wall. Col had never been the strongest of men, but he found the strength to lift the man clean off his feet, pinning him against the wall.

"Tell me, or you'll die." This was a flat even tone. Col meant every word. At the moment, he'd kill anyone who got in his way. This man meant nothing to him.

"Lord Gariast!" the man shrieked. "He would visit them from time to time and beat them. Eventually, they refused to eat. It was as if they wanted to die. They almost did early on, that's what got my predecessor dismissed. When I came, Lord Gariast had me force-feed them, but..." The man shook his head apparently uncomfortable with the memory. He must have seen something in Col's eyes, for he continued with, "It wasn't my fault, Lord Gariast tortured them too hard one day! But they were traitors. It was his right to—"

"They were good people and no more a traitor than you are."

The man shut his mouth and froze.

Col let him down slowly. He desperately wanted to strike the man or throttle the life out of him, but some shred of common sense stopped him. A dead, or even unconscious, jailer would be noticed, and he didn't want that. He simply turned and left. He didn't need to silence the man. He'd been just another guard seeking information on a couple random prisoners. That jailer didn't seem the sort to raise much of a ruckus anyway.

But once he was outside of the man's office, the door slammed shut behind him, he suddenly didn't know where to go.

He felt adrift, torn apart. Just a few days ago, he'd thought his parents dead and now... they actually were. Nothing had changed and yet everything had changed. He'd had hope for the first time in a long time. He'd dared to believe his family was alive, but it had all been a terrible lie.

As he stood there, his anger grew. At first, he was angry with Trentin. The knight was the one who'd told him his parents were alive, had given him hope. But it wasn't Trentin at all. It was Lord Gariast who had orchestrated this ghastly series of events designed to hurt him at every turn. Even now, years later, the man's actions still stung Col. Gariast would pay for what he had done, but the scum of a lord wasn't here, and at that moment Col needed some outlet for his anger.

There was someone in this palace who had also betrayed him, who had allowed all of Gariast's vile behavior and never lifted a finger to stop the man despite being the most powerful man in the kingdom: King Halviar himself.

Col had a direction now. He began to make his way out of the bowels of the palace up to the royal chambers. Tonight, the king would know the wrath of the righteous!

16

Tom had had a busy day.

It had taken him a while that morning to plan his very careful movements around the city. He'd set off to the Silver District, where he'd discreetly asked around for the best tailor. He could have gone directly to the gardens and done the same thing, but in his current attire, he'd never pass for a nobleman. No, he needed to look the part of a noble before he even entered that district.

It had taken a while—and a few gems—to convince the tailor to take him in so urgently, then to find and fit an outfit that a noble would wear in the latest fashion. That had taken him almost until noon.

His next destination was the library in the gardens. He walked in ignoring everyone, hoping that's what nobles did. Indeed no one tried to speak to him or stop him. He asked one librarian where he might find the noble's registry, with a story about wanting to validate that his family's connection to the royal line was closer than the Athernons'—that was the only noble name he knew off hand, that and Gariast.

The man had pointed him in the right direction, and he'd

spent a short while in that area finding a suitably obscure family from the far west coast. He'd decided that would be safest. It was unlikely that any west coast families were currently in the capital. He decided he would be Jared Breakwater of Throvanhold. The Breakwaters were an ancient line, but apparently small and insignificant. So, he'd be noble, but not worth anyone's scrutiny, which was perfect since he didn't want to draw too much attention.

From the library, he'd gone to the best rooming house in the gardens. Most nobles with estates near the capital would probably have a house in the city, but a family from far away would have to book a room or suite to stay in. The Golden Gardens was the pinnacle of such places. He bought a whole floor—the gems from their treasure horde were quite valuable it seemed—and set himself up as a visiting noble. Then he sought another tailor, this time in the gardens. He told the man a story of having his chest of clothes fall from his carriage and spill all over a rain-soaked road, ruined. He'd need a whole new wardrobe for his time in the capital. Most importantly though, he'd need the man's finest suit for the evening's entertainment.

That's when he'd hit a stroke of luck. The tailor had innocently asked, "You're going to Lady Tandor's Ball?"

Now Tom knew the place to be that night. "Yes!" he'd proclaimed and once again outlaying a large amount of their ill-gotten wealth, he'd had a lavish suit made as hastily as possible and left a retainer for the rest of the "wardrobe" the man was to make for him and send to the Golden Gardens. It was a huge waste of their funds because Tom knew he'd never be there to receive the rest of the clothes, but he had to keep up his appearances.

The rest of the afternoon and evening had been spent securing entrance to Lady Tandor's Ball.

That's how he'd come to find himself dancing with a stunningly gorgeous woman. She wore a dress that was the epitome of daring, a plunging neckline exposing a round bosom, and a high cut slit on one side showing a long stretch of leg.

He hadn't known this was to be an 'eligibility' ball.

As a commoner, he'd heard of such things, where young unwed noblewomen were paraded around before potential suitors in hopes of finding a good match. He'd thought it sounded more like selling off cattle. Being in the middle of one, however, he was finding himself rethinking that opinion. Oh, it was still a cattle auction, but these women were far lovelier than any cattle he'd ever seen.

This particular ball was hosted by Lady Tandor. Her daughter Valeesa, yet to be seen, was the talk of the local lords. She was the highest-ranking noblewoman who'd be shown around tonight. The other available women here were all from families of lesser knights from around the capital region. There were five other girls, all in dresses meant to show them off.

Tom wasn't dancing with any of them. They were all young things and had enough attention already. Tom had chosen to target the ineligible women, some of the mothers of the girls or others who had come just for the party.

Lady Sonserra, with whom he danced at the moment, was far from an old hag. Apparently she had two small children, if she was to be believed. Tom had trouble picturing the woman with children around her. Also, if she was to be believed, her husband was out of town and her estates were feeling cold and empty. She'd invited Tom to stay with her three times as they danced, saying that it was common courtesy to host a visiting noble. He was quite certain she had other intentions. Any other day, he might have taken her up on those intentions. But he was here to find out what the nobles were chatting about and learning about Lady Sonserra's loneliness did not seem of peak importance.

When the dance was finished he flattered her and said he'd think about her offer, then quickly moved on.

He sat out the next dance, choosing instead to visit the buffet and linger around the lords chatting there.

This is where he finally got some decent information.

Sidling up near one group, he listened in.

"... from Lord Tandor himself."

"He's in town? I thought he'd be licking the boots of Lord Gariast. Did you hear about Lord Edwir's betrayal? All of Gariast's knights and bannermen will have to be on the lookout so as not to poke that dragon."

"No, he's here. He said he wouldn't miss his daughter's party, but he seemed... I don't know, scared?"

"That doesn't surprise me at all. And you say you heard it directly from him, that that upstart commoner is still alive?"

"Yes, Colric of Haverstal. I'll never forget that name. He humiliated me in the archery contest that year. I'm nearly always a close second to Gariast, but that commoner showed us both up. He hit the dead center of the target at three hundred paces! And it's not just him either. You'd heard how Gariast had killed the man's family, well..." the man laughed, "I'd always thought he'd kept them to torture. Now I find out I'm right! They're still alive, though I'd assume by now they wished they were dead. Tandor was telling Lord Oster to tell as many people as he could that the family was still alive. I'm betting they want to set a trap for this Colric!"

"And I'll bet the man is long gone from these lands," another said dismissively.

"But if he isn't, I hope Gariast knows what he's doing. The man's already bested him once. What's to say he won't do it again?"

"A world without Gariast? Whatsoever would we do?" The

man sounded happy at the thought and indeed the rest of them laughed.

Tom moved away after that.

So, Lord Gariast was planning a trap for Col? That was useful information indeed.

The music stopped, and a booming voice echoed through the large hall. "Ladies and gentlemen. May I have your fullest attention, please! It's now time for the pinnacle of tonight's ball, the only child of Lady Erissa and Lord Kerrik Tandor!"

Tom made his way to one of the large support pillars that kept the lofty arched ceiling in place and leaned against it. He was some distance off but standing a step up from the lowered dance floor, so he could see over the heads of most of those in front of him.

"May I joyously present the jewel of the south! Lady Valeesa Tandor!"

Double doors opened at the far end of the hall and a girl stepped through.

Tom's breath caught.

She was some distance off, but even so, he could see her beauty and poise. She walked slowly to the top of the grand stairs and stopped. A hush fell over the assembled men and women as she was simply taken in. The silence was quickly followed by a low murmur as people began whispering among themselves. Tom caught a few of the comments from those close by.

"She certainly has filled out this last year," one man said.

A young woman sighed and let out a dejected comment of, "There go my chances with Lord Mirnal. She'll win his heart for sure."

Tom didn't know or care who Lord Mirnal was, but his own heart was certainly captivated.

He crept forward along the edge of the dance floor, wanting

a closer look. She wore a long, flowing gown of deepest blue, highlighted with purple. Something in the fabric made it sparkle, like the stars in the night sky. It hugged her figure, clinging to hips and bosom. The front of the dress arched up toward her neck in a graceful curve then came down under her arms, leaving her shoulders exposed. Her skin was pale and flawless. Raven-hued hair flowed pristinely down to fall over shoulders and back. Some of those silken locks had been carefully piled atop her head in a delicate pattern with flowers of brightest blue. As he drew closer, he saw large dark pools for eyes, perhaps deep brown. A heady flush covered her high cheeks. She was the most perfect woman Tom had ever seen.

Another wave of murmurs washed through the crowd as she began to descend the steps to the floor of the hall. As she did, a shadow seemed to loom over her. Looking back up to the top of the stairs, a tall, broad-shouldered, barrel-chested man stood there looking rather dour. Lord Tandor.

Tom turned away as a flood of men approached the stunning young woman. He knew he wasn't anyone she'd ever consider. Even if he had been the noble he pretended to be, his family was small and distant and probably no match for a family as powerful as the Tandors. Though in truth he had no clue how powerful anyone here really was.

So, he made his rounds and danced with a few other spoken-for ladies as he gathered what intelligence he could. He didn't expect to be seeing much of Valeesa that night. That was until a new wave of gossip hit his ears.

He was passing by a middle-aged lord dressed in so much finery he seemed more peacock than man. The lord seemed rather put out. "I couldn't believe it! I'm the highest-ranking lord here! But Tandor told me I could dance with his daughter and nothing more. She was off-limits to every man here. This whole event was a formality, a charade!"

Tom stopped dead.

He couldn't help but intervene. "A charade you say?"

The lord didn't know Tom from a bramble-bush, but he seemed happy to continue his rant. "Aye! And when I pressed him, for there is no man who can withstand my gaze, do you know what he told me?"

"No." Tom wanted to keep the man talking.

"He said the girl was spoken for." He lowered his voice. "By none other than Lord Gariast himself!"

Tom had no words for that.

Lord Peacock continued in his conspiratorial tone. "He told me she would be taken away directly after this ball and sent to Gariast's estates. I wasn't about to argue with that. Tandor I may be able to bully, but there is no way I would go against Lord Gariast himself. I pity the fate that girl will find with such a man."

Yes, so did Tom.

He gave his thanks and left the peacock to his tales. His thoughts were tumbling, falling inexorably toward a single conclusion: that perfect woman could not end up with Lord Gariast.

Which meant only one thing.

He had to get her out of here before her father did.

17

DALIA MARVELED AT THE LIGHTSHOW BEFORE HER.

As a child, she'd snuck out onto her balcony some nights in high summer. She'd lay on the stones looking up at the play of the stars above. This was so much more intense than that. Dozens of sprites danced around the small clearing, each with its own unique glow, bobbing and floating over the lush grasses and scattered flowers. It was late at night, but still she could see easily by the light of the fey.

"Go ahead," Ayneii said at Dalia's shoulder. "Out to the center and we'll see if we can't unlock a little of what's trapped inside you."

"Will it be safe?" Safe for whom she wasn't sure. The fey didn't seem concerned about who she was or what she could do, but she didn't know if she might hurt them. If that was even possible. Luckily, they were far from the camp and other people. If The Fury—or whatever it actually was—took her here, she wouldn't be putting people in danger. But a part of her wondered if this was safe for her. She didn't know what the fey were going to do. What did it mean to 'unlock' her abilities? Might it possibly be unsafe for her?

"Yes, of course," Ayneii said, seeming perfectly fine with what was about to happen. Certainly, the fey didn't seem to be experiencing any of the tension Dalia was.

Dalia drew in a long breath and marched to the center of the clearing. The dancing fey moved around her, circling and swaying, moving like flotsam caught up in a slow-spinning whirlpool.

Then the song began. It was stirring and powerful if a little discordant. It was like no song Dalia had ever heard... no, it was like every song, every noise she'd ever heard. Those nights as a child laying outside and hearing the crickets chirp and cicadas buzz, it was that, but mixed with the sound of horses in the field, of wind rushing through leaves. It combined every natural sound in some miraculously joined music.

It touched her soul.

It seeped into her being and began to pull out what lay hidden there.

She felt The Fury come, but instead of needing to fight, to run, to attack, she was held still as it took her. The world seemed to turn red and grow brighter, if that was possible. Every noise was amplified, every detail of everything she saw was analyzed and remembered, every scent discerned. She became aware of so much more than just the fey.

There were animals out in the forest around her, a deer intrigued by the lightshow watched not far away. A family of rabbits also observed, as their usual nightly feeding ground was overtaken by the fey. And there was so much more than this. She was aware of every gnat and insect in the air around her, those burrowed in the trees around the clearing, even the ones in the dirt beneath her feet.

She knew them. It went beyond her enhanced senses now. She was... feeling them with her very soul and spirit. And this awareness only grew as the song of the fey intensified. Slowly, the red-tinted rage of The Fury faded, but the heightened sensations stayed. She stretched beyond herself and connected with the forest and all beings within it.

She floated out on wings of a thought and found the forest camp where Trentin and the others lay sleeping. Not all were sleeping; several men were on watch. She floated past one and he didn't see her, his gaze passing through her as she ghosted through the area.

"Oh!" she said softly, letting the word out more as a breath than anything else.

She felt more at peace than any time before in her life, even before the bogey had 'cursed' her. Then she slipped into a place of silence and peace; stillness and harmony; joy and union and music and even sorrow. She felt all possible emotions exquisitely defined but so conjoined as to cancel each other out into a single moment of pure existence.

Dalia hadn't realized she'd closed her eyes until she opened them once again. Though in truth, perhaps they hadn't been closed at all, she'd just been seeing with... other eyes. She was quite surprised to find herself floating, several feet off the ground. She spun slowly, lazily in a semi-reclined position. She had a moment of panic, which quickly faded. This was far from normal, but it was certainly comfortable. It was an odd sensation. She felt like there was some great bubble within her that helped her simply lift from the ground.

No, not one bubble, but many. They slowly percolated up within her, floating up to the surface, then popped. With each pop, some new awakening came. More than just her senses and awareness of everything around her, she now felt fully connected to her body. She felt every hair keenly, knew every ache. Even stranger, was knowing her own inner workings. She didn't have words for the understanding, well for most of it. She knew she was hungry, but now she knew why, how her stomach dealt with food and turned it into energy or waste. She felt the air in her lungs, knew each muscle and bone.

She finally understood how she was capable of what she did when The Fury took her. She understood how her body could move in certain ways and use such a small frame to throw larger men around or hit with incredible strength. She also knew that The Fury was more than just her body. There was magic woven into it as well. It wasn't natural to become lighter than a feather or hit with more force than her muscles should allow. It was a perfect combining of her body and magic to create an ideal warrior.

More and more of these bubbles of knowing popped within her.

...But they began to blur. She would understand something only to have that knowledge fade.

A great exhaustion took her then and...

She woke to darkness.

She started and sat up not knowing how she'd come to be where she was, laying in a clearing filled with moonlight. She blinked.

The fey were gone.

"Ayneii?" she called, and the sprite appeared.

"Hello, you fell asleep." The sprite's green glow added light to the darkness. "I think we unlocked too much. You couldn't handle any more. This would be the human side of you limiting your progress."

Fuzzy memories came to her. There was so much she recalled, but she felt like there was a vast amount she didn't. "That was amazing." She wiped a stray hair from her face. Her hand was wet. All of her was wet. She'd been laying in dew-covered grasses. She sighed. After the ecstasy of revelation she'd undergone, now she just felt cold, damp, and tired.

"I should get back to the camp." She rose and began walking.

Even in the dark of night in a place she'd never been, she knew the way back to camp. How did she know?

She stopped.

Not everything of that moment of knowing had left her. Her senses were still extremely keen and she... she just knew where people were. She could sense them.

"Hunh."

"What?" Ayneii asked.

"Well, something stuck," Dalia said as she continued walking.

"What did you learn? What was unlocked?" Ayneii asked, her glow intensifying with curiosity.

"You don't know?"

"No. We only perform the ritual. We don't know what you experience."

"It was amazing," Dalia said softly. "Thank you for helping." And as she walked, she relayed what she could recall.

18

Despite the burning ire of his rage, Col had taken his time. He knew the best place and time to catch the king alone would be in his bedchambers after he'd retired for the night.

He'd bided his time by sneaking down to the kitchens for a bite to eat, then eating his small supper slowly while he dreamed of what he would do to Gariast and how best to deal with the king.

Several ideas blazed hot through his mind. He quickly decided he could not kill the king. The man had no heirs yet. The first queen had birthed only stillborn children on the rare occasions she'd carried a child to term. The new queen had had three daughters so far. With no heir, that left the throne open to men like Gariast, and the last thing Col wanted was for such a man to have the power of a king. And in truth, Col had no desire to kill or even harm the king. He just needed justice for what the man had allowed to happen to him and his family. No, the king must live, but if that was the case, he'd be able to identify Col as his assailant.

Col had not brought his Black Bandit mask, so he'd made a trip to the royal tailors and 'borrowed' a piece of dark cloth. He'd cut two eyeholes into it and tied it around his head then put his helm back on. He'd also found a storeroom and stole a length of rope to finalize his preparations. Then he'd returned to fantasizing about his escapade with the king.

Night came far too slowly for Col's liking, but once full dark was upon the palace and the second call of the watch past midnight had been called, he began his trek to the king's chambers.

Then, still disguised as a king's guard, he strode purposefully to the king's audience chamber. It was dark and empty this time of night, which made it easy for him to cross the large room easily and exit out the doors on the far side to a wide balcony. The audience chamber was on the second floor of the palace and the king's chambers, conveniently, were directly above with a similarly wide balcony.

Col tied one end of his rope firmly around the marble railing of the audience chamber balcony, then he stripped off most of his armor including the helm, anything that restricted his movement. He tied the other end of the rope around his waist so that if he did fall in the upcoming climb, the rope would hopefully swing him under the balcony and just above the ground.

The palace walls were made of fitted stone, more precise than most buildings, but it was also older than many as well. There were enough cracks in the mortar or rough bits of stone for Col to climb. He was an accomplished climber, having scaled the trees in the forest as a child. This was different and far more difficult, but he took his time climbing the twenty feet up to the king's balcony and though he was sweating and breathing hard, made it without a slip. He then tied off the rope to the railing of this balcony, so that all he had to do was swing down to the balcony below when he fled.

With his black mask in place and sword ready, he snuck into the king's chambers.

A wide and tall bank of windows formed the wall that looked out onto the balcony. The glass was hazy but not transparent. It would let in light, but there would be little view from inside. In the center of this wall were two doors made of the same glass. There were great curtains, which could be drawn across the span of windows on the inside, but tonight they were not drawn, bunched at the sides. Apparently, the king preferred to sleep in a well moonlit room.

Once Col was inside, there was enough light that he could easily see the great bed and the small form of a man within it. Luckily, the queen was not with him tonight. She would have her own rooms elsewhere in the palace. It was known to most who worked in and around the palace that she rarely spent a full night with the king

Col crept onto the bed and next to the king. Then in one swift motion, he straddled the sheets overtop of the man, ensuring the king's arms were pinned whilst also clamping a hand down on the man's mouth.

The king's eyes flew open in a panic to find Col's sword under his chin.

Col lowered his voice and whispered, "Make a single sound, and you die. Do you understand, my king?" To reinforce his point, he pressed the flat of his blade tight against the bottomside of the king's chin. If the man moved his jaw at all, Col would feel it and be able to cut down into his throat. He wasn't going to kill the king, but he also had to make sure the other man knew Col was in control.

The king nodded carefully.

For now, Col kept his hand over the king's mouth, just in case.

"You are a weak and futile king," Col began, all his pent-up frustration and anger pouring out. "You do not protect your people but sacrifice them to power-hungry noblemen who use them up, then discard them when they have no more use for them. You demand loyalty but have no idea what that word even means. You let innocent men and women die at the hands of tyrants in your own palace and are powerless to stop it. Give me one good reason why I shouldn't kill you now."

Before he removed his hand to let the king speak, Col reiterated, "Call for help, and you will die. I don't care if I die, do you?" It was a hollow threat. He had to live to free his siblings still trapped with Gariast. Hopefully the king wouldn't sense that. Then again...he'd thought his parents were alive and found they weren't. Who was to say if his siblings still lived? It seemed likely though. Trentin had lived at Gariast's estates. His information about Col's siblings would be a lot more reliable and current than what the man had known of Col's parents, trapped away in the capital.

The king did not call out when the hand was removed from his lips; he didn't speak either. There was something odd in his face as he stared up at Col.

"Do I...?"

"Answer my question," Col bit out the words in a harsh whisper.

The king grimaced and there was no mirth in it. "I do deserve to die. Is that what you want to hear?"

It was. It was also the last thing Col expected the man to say.

The king went on. "You are right. I cannot deny any accusation you just made against me. I am a weak and useless king." Something hard entered the other man's gaze then. "But I am not ready to give up my life just yet." That piercing gaze drilled into Col. The king had the clearest of blue eyes and right now, they were starting to make Col uncomfortable. "I don't think you are either... Colric of Haverstal."

Col's heart nearly jumped from his chest.

"How...?"

"You can hide your face, but I had to stare into those eyes of yours when I betrayed you to Gariast... and that is something I will never forget. So yes, I know who you are. To be honest though, I thought Gariast had killed you."

"The reports of my death are a little exaggerated. The same cannot be said for my parents."

The king drew in a breath and let it out slowly. "That was a tragedy and I am sorry, Col. They did not deserve to die like that. Would you believe me if I said I tried to protect them? But Gariast has a long reach and a lot of gold. Once he'd bought off the new jailer, I heard no more reports of his comings and goings in my own dungeons."

That, unfortunately, Col could believe.

"So, what now, then?" Col asked.

"Perhaps if you remove that sword we can talk like civilized people?"

Col wasn't sure he could trust this man, but he was fairly certain that if it came to it, he could escape the palace even if the King's Guard was searching for him. He took the sword from the king's neck and slipped off the bed, putting the sword away.

The king sat up, propped by many pillows. "Do not worry. I will not call for the guards." After a long moment, the king said, "I think perhaps we can help each other."

Col removed his mask and raised an eyebrow. "How might we do that?" He found his anger at this man draining away. He'd known all along that the king was not the true source of evil in this realm; he was just apparently powerless to stop it. It reminded Col of his own impotence. He wanted to storm Gariast's estates but couldn't. Not yet.

"I know what you think of me," the king began slowly. He let out a clipped, harsh laugh. "You made your opinion abundantly clear a moment ago. And as I said, I agree with you... for the most part." He looked away for a moment, his eyes distant, and

Col wondered what the man was thinking. "Do you want to know why things are the way they are?"

"Please enlighten me." Col was pacing around the room now. His anger was gone, but it had been replaced by restlessness. He felt uncertain, like he had after he'd learned his parents were dead for the second time earlier that night. Without his rage however, he simply felt directionless.

"It was my father. If you think I am a weak king, you should have met him. He didn't care for the kingdom one whit. At least I care, but unfortunately now I can't do anything about it because my father gave away most of our power to the high nobles."

"You're a king, can't you take it back?" Col asked.

"I wish it were that easy. My grandfather, King Alharon, would have done just that. I did not know much of him; he died when I was quite young, but he was a hard man. From what I've heard, he was a fair man as well, but he wouldn't let anyone get away with anything untoward. The problem is that my father didn't want to rule the kingdom. He didn't want any responsibility at all. He wanted to drink and wench and eat, and that was it. So he gave the lords independent power to rule their lands as they wished as long as they paid taxes and kept fealty to him. He even created the Council of Lords, those with the greatest lands and the oldest families, to rule the kingdom in his place. The nobles have been living with this power for almost thirty years now, and if I tried to abolish the council and take back the power given to them, they'd simply rise up and overthrow me. I have some limited power now, but for all intents and purposes, I am a puppet. I have to play their game and play it well, to eek back slivers of power here and there, so they don't notice I'm trying to take back what should be mine. But at this pace, it will take me three lifetimes to reclaim what should be mine by birth."

The king's voice had risen to a heated tone; his face flushed.

Col had stopped his pacing and stood staring at the king. He'd known none of this.

"So even if you had wanted to stop Gariast from hanging me..."

"He was well within his own right to do so, given that what you did was on his lands. I couldn't stop him."

Col was confused. "Then why... why did he bring me to you for sentencing?"

The king's smile was sardonic. "In part because this was a capital crime, but you know Gariast, why do you think?"

What did he think?

Gariast was a cruel man, petty and power-hungry. It sunk in slowly. "He... wanted to play it out..." The fullness of Gariast's depravity and vileness hit him then. "He knew I was your man. He wanted... to see you condemn me. He wanted to hurt me... hurt us!"

"Yes."

"He humiliated both of us! Gods, does that man's villainy know no bounds?"

"Not that I am aware."

Col began pacing once more. He had a direction now, and as it had been before, it was pointed directly at Gariast. "You said we could help each other. I'm an outlaw, how can I help you?"

A cunning grin spread over the king's face mixed with a mischievous glint in his eye. "You are perhaps the only person who can help me."

That caught Col's attention, and he stopped his pacing again. "Go on."

"The King's Army is the largest army in the realm. Fully twice the size of any other lord's personal force, even including levies and bannermen. But..." he pressed his lips together. "But, there are several reasons why I could never use my army against any lord. First, the King's Army is spread all over the realm, supplementing forces for all nobles. If I wanted to throw the full force of the King's Army at anyone, I'd have to recall them first, so chances are the nobles would know something was brewing. Second, if I did manage to gather the army and take out any one noble, the others would band against me and their combined forces would outnumber the King's Army at least ten to one. Third, I have no doubt at all that some nobles, Gariast being the foremost of which, have already bribed or otherwise turned some of my captains or generals. They'll serve me right up until I try to take back power from the nobles, then they'll abandon me, taking their troops with them."

"The only men I can trust are in the King's Guard, but they are a small force—only a couple thousand, and I couldn't take them away from defending the palace." The king sighed heavily. "And... in recent days, I've come to question if I can trust even them. Some of them sure, but as a whole..."

Col shook his head. "I can't imagine any of the King's Guard would betray you."

"That's because you're a loyal and trusting man. I've learned that most men are not like you."

Col continued to shake his head, nothing to add.

"Here is where you come in, my... friend?" The last word was clearly a question.

Col met the king's intense gaze. He still wasn't sure. "We'll see." That was as far as he was willing to venture at the moment. The king nodded to that and went on.

"As an outlaw, you are outside of all of these machinations, and no one would suspect that you were secretly working for me. You are also a brilliant soldier and commander. If you had even a small group of men working with you, you could begin to pick away at the nobles' forces. I know you want Gariast gone as much as I do. Without him, the Council of Lords loses its most powerful member. If we can bring down Gariast together, it serves us both."

Col nodded. The idea had merit except... "I have no force to work with." Well, he had Dalia, as well as Trentin and his score or so of men, but that wasn't a 'force' of any means.

The king smiled the same mischievous grin. "What if some of the King's Guard or the King's Army were to 'disappear'? I can spin the loss to make it work for us. Most likely, the lords will just think me even weaker than they'd thought. Perhaps some of my commanders lost faith in me and headed south to Forsea to create their own kingdom. It's not completely implausible. Or even better, I can say the Forsean are pushing northwards, and I've sent a force to deal with them, but alas, the whole force was lost. Those Forsean are excellent horse-archers after all."

"The lords would know if there was any activity in the south," Col pointed out.

The king shrugged. "Perhaps." There was a glint in the man's eyes.

"What?"

"I am not completely without allies. Lord Athernon still supports the crown, and I know he hates Gariast almost as much as I do."

Athernon? Dalia's father?

Colric said only, "Oh?"

"Yes, despite Athernon's lands being more expansive, and his heritage even older than Gariast, he was not chosen as the head of the council. That, of course, went to Gariast. Athernon was not pleased about that."

"Ah."

"Athernon's lands extend far to the south. I'll send some troops in that direction and a bird to Athernon. He can tell the other lords that there had been raids into his lands and that's what the troops were for. In fact, if the report of the loss of the troops came from him, that would work even better. Perhaps, some of his own forces might be 'lost' as well if he's willing. Though, I am uncertain if he'd donate many men as his fighting force is much smaller than most other lords in the area and spread thin over his larger realm.

Col nodded. "Who from the King's Guard would you give me?"

"Whomsoever you choose."

"Kellan was the finest of my lieutenants; he'd probably come."

"He's a captain now. He was indeed fine, so I promoted him to your post."

Col nodded. "As a captain, he commands a full cohort, five hundred men. That should be a sufficient start. I don't think the lords would believe any more than that going missing at one time." Col considered this plan for a long moment before finally nodding to himself. "So, I take down Gariast, help you restore your power, and in return I get my name cleared and my position back?"

The king nodded. "Yes."

"Done."

Col turned away for a moment. This was a lot to take in. The king wanted to give him five hundred men to fight in secret on his behalf. The fact that the king seemed to despise Gariast as much as he did also came as a surprise. Col had always thought the king to be a good man up until that day when the king had betrayed him. Yet even that made sense now. All of it made sense and behind all of it was lord Gariast. That man needed to be stopped, and he was being given the tools to do just that.

Something occurred to Col then. "What If I need to get ahold of you, or you me?"

The king considered this for a moment. "How did you get into the palace today?"

Col smiled. "An old friend."

"And do you think this old friend might be willing to carry messages back and forth?"

Col thought about it. "For me, maybe, but for the king, almost definitely. His name is Grunston; he's a furrier with a contract to supply the palace."

"I know the name," the king said with a nod.

"If you give me a writ to give to him to explain all this, I'm sure he'll understand. For that matter, I think I'll need one to give to Kellan as well if you don't mind."

The king nodded and rose from his bed. He strode over to the large desk on the other side of the large chamber and unstoppered a vial of ink. He then put quill to paper and wrote two notices.

"Where should I tell Kellan to meet you?" The king asked as he wrote.

"Follow the king's road south into the Sandren Forest, I'll find him there."

"Given the time it will take to arrange this, don't expect him for at least five days, probably closer to a week."

That seemed fair to Colric, despite his desperate need to free his family as soon as possible.

The king finished his notes, which he then dusted with sand before rolling them carefully into two small message cases. These he brought over to Colric.

"So, we have a deal? I give you five hundred men, more later if I can, and you fight Gariast for me?"

Colric took the message cases, ensuring he knew which was which, then shook the king's hand. "We have a deal."

19

TOM HAD A WILD PLAN.

He didn't know if it would work, but it had to. He'd make it work.

Gods, was he nervous.

"A drink, m'lady?" He offered the delicate and slender wine glass to the delicate and slender Valeesa Tandor.

He was next to her now and her beauty was even more stunning up close. Blushing cheeks set off pale skin, soft and smooth. Her perfect features were set in pristine relief on that idyllic face. Large, dark brown eyes, deep and alluring, turned to him.

"I fear I may have had too much already," she said softly. Her voice was music.

Tom knew that every eye in the room must be on him as he conversed with her and probably a few of those nearby were listening in. It was growing quite late and most of the other eligible girls had retired for the night. So too had many of the lords. It was clear that word had gotten around that Valeesa wasn't available. She'd actually been on her own or speaking only with other ladies for some time now.

"For courage," Tom urged, and downed the wine in his glass for that very reason.

"Courage?" Those large eyes blinked.

He lowered his voice. "Do you know what lies in store for you after this?"

She nodded. "I'm to be sent south."

"To Lord Gariast."

Shock widened her eyes, but only barely, she hid it well. She hadn't known that much. "Oh!"

"Exactly." He had to speak quickly and quietly before anyone might step closer and overhear. "If you want to avoid that fate then take this glass and drink it all, then be waiting by the door directly behind you across the hall just after the next call of the watch. I'll be there."

"Where will you—?"

Someone was drawing close, Tom heard the footfalls behind him. Tom spoke up saying. "Are you sure you will not take this drink?"

She eyed him, and in that moment, his heart truly fell for her, because he saw in those eyes intelligence and wit. She knew enough not to speak further on this, but gave him the barest of nods then said, "Why thank you, I believe I will." She took the wine and sipped it.

He nodded. "It is my pleasure to serve one as beautiful as you." He bowed to her and turned away.

And nearly ran into her father.

"Who are you?" Lord Tandor said menacingly. A meaty hand fell on Tom's shoulder. Tom wasn't tall, perhaps a hair past average in height. Tandor wasn't truly tall either, but he was taller than Tom and built thick and wide. He seemed to loom over Tom in that moment.

Tom stepped back a pace, edging out of the man's grip, heart pounding as he bowed. "Lord Jared Breakwater of Throvanhold at your service, Lord Tandor."

"Never heard of you."

Tom gave a grimace and nodded. "That wouldn't surprise me, my Lord. My family is small, and our holdings are on the west coast. I am the first to visit the capital in ten years." Before Tandor could speak again, Tom pushed onward, "I do so hope you do not mind my words with your daughter. She is truly enchanting, and alas, I know a man of my station with a tiny estate far from here could never hope to win her. I sought only to pass on my regards."

Tandor eyed him for a long moment, then nodded, dismissing him easily. "Don't approach her again."

"I wouldn't dream of it." Well, he'd been dreaming of getting close to her since he'd first laid eyes on her, and he was going to be close to her again soon, but it was an easy lie.

Tandor swept by him to speak with his daughter.

Tom took his time moving away. He stopped at the buffet table, which wasn't far away. He hoped to overhear what her father said to her.

The man's voice was quiet, but the rumbling tones carried well enough. "You have until the next call of the watch," Tandor said gruffly. "Then we must leave."

Tom peered back over his shoulder. She glanced his way for the barest of moments before her eyes darted back to her father. "Yes, Father. I'll be ready. I wish only a little more time to enjoy the evening."

Oddly Tandor's broad shoulders slumped with a sigh as the man whispered, "I wish I could give you a lifetime."

Did the lord himself not want her to go off to Gariast? Was Tandor not so loyal to his liege lord? Certainly, he'd have to know what Gariast was like.

Perhaps Lord Tandor didn't want his daughter going.

Perhaps the man wouldn't hunt him down after Tom stole away his daughter. Then again, Tandor's other option was to disappoint Lord Gariast, which would not go well for him, Tom was sure. So there would be hunting, almost certainly.

Well, that just made things all the more interesting.

Tom bided his time and watched discreetly as Valeesa expertly moved from group to group around the hall, making her way to the door he'd indicated.

The call of the watch came.

Tom's heartbeat slowed as the moment arrived. He made a show of stumbling into the buffet near where the wine and spirits were being served. He hit the table hard with a mumbled, "Sorry!"

But he'd had the intended effect. Two bottles fell over and began disgorging their contents. He reached out clumsily, as if drunk, to pick them up, but instead knocked over a candle-tree into the alcohol.

Flames erupted.

He screamed and staggered away, shouting, "Fire!"

That had people's attention. He moved further away as others noticed the quickly spreading flames. He hoped he wasn't about to burn down the whole of the gardens and the capital, but if he did... it'd be worth it to save Valeesa.

After a few other shouts to make sure everyone's attention was on the fire, he quickly skirted the hall and removed his jacket. It was a jolly yellow in hue and would mark him easily. He dumped it in a potted plant, and with his more muted cream-colored shirt and blue pants, he hoped he was less conspicuous.

He caught sight of Lord Tandor scanning the hall. The large man was thankfully at the far end, shouting for Valeesa, but apparently not seeing her.

Where was she?

Tom had lost sight of her too.

Tom came around the edge of the hall toward the door he'd indicated and found her pressed against a column hiding from the rest of the room. Gods, she was quick. He opened the door and caught her eye. She rushed over and the next instant they were alone in a long hallway.

The last thing he heard before he shut the door was Tandor's bellowing voice shouting over the growing commotion in the room, "Valeesa!"

She looked at him then, expectant.

He grinned and held out his hand.

She took it.

"This way," he said, and led her away from a horrid destiny. He just hoped she would understand when he told her... he wasn't a noble.

COL, NOW BACK IN HIS ARMOR AND HELM, MARCHED ATOP THE curtain wall of the palace. It was even easier moving among the King's Guard in the dark.

"Captain Kellan?" he asked as he approached a group of three figures talking quietly. This is where he had been directed to find the captain of the watch.

One of the men turned.

Col handed him the message case.

"Soldier, bring over that torch," Kellan demanded. One of the other two drew nearer.

Just to be safe, Col said, "This is for your eyes only, Captain."

Kellan nodded and made sure his back was to the man with the torch as he read. When he finished, he looked up at Col and seemed for the first time to look past the helm, through the small eye slit.

"Old friend?" Kellan ventured.

Col extended his hand. "Still friends," he replied.

Kellan nodded, betraying little of his emotions except a faint smile. "I shall see you again soon then. Are you staying long?"

"No, I must be gone before morning."

Kellan nodded then called down from the wall. They were near enough to the gate that he shouted to the watchmen there. "I'm sending someone down, let them through the gate!"

There was a reply of 'yes, Captain.'

Kellan then took the torch from the man nearby and burned the note. Looking back to Colric, he said, "Take care."

"And you." Colric saluted, bringing the fist of his right hand to his right shoulder, bent arm parallel with the ground. Kellan returned the salute, then Colric was gone and soon enough through the gate and back into the city.

His next stop was Grunston's shop. It was closed, of course, as it was now well into night. He considered his options for how to get the message to the furrier and decided on the least invasive method. He sat himself down in the yard around the back of the shop and promptly fell asleep, waiting for morning.

"WE CAN'T STAY HERE LONG. I'M SURE YOUR FATHER WILL TEAR apart the entire gardens looking for you." Tom was stripping away his finery. He needed to look like a commoner now, not a lord.

He'd brought Valeesa back to his room at the Golden Gardens, but they needed to be gone from here quickly. He wanted to be out of the gardens and back safely in the Brown District by morning. Lord Tandor would have half the city looking for his daughter soon enough. Tom just hoped he wouldn't expect two nobles to be hiding in the worst part of town. It seemed obvious to him, but nobles didn't think that way. At least he hoped they didn't.

"Jared?" The voice spun him around. He was half-dressed, and Valeesa was looking a little shocked. For a moment, the name didn't register with him. Then he recalled his alter ego. Though he hadn't thought he'd ever told her... but he had told her father when she wasn't far away. Perhaps she'd overheard.

"My name isn't Jared. It's Tom. Tom Willow."

"Tom?" The shock turned to confusion. "Willow isn't a noble house."

"That's right. I'm a commoner. Sorry m'lady. But that doesn't change the fact that you were headed off to Gariast's estates for who knows what purpose. Don't worry. You're safe with me." He pulled on his rough-spun shirt, and then turned away again to remove his pants and change them as well.

"My apologies for the lack of privacy, but as I said, we're in a hurry." When he turned back, now fully attired as a commoner, there was a blush on her cheeks.

"You are a very forward man, Tom Willow." That glint of intelligence in those dark eyes returned. "But only one of us looks like a commoner now. This dress—"

He finished her thought. "Is very identifiable, yes, I know."

The corner of her mouth quirked into a faint mischievous grin. "Shall I strip too? Do you have a dress for me?"

As much as Tom might have liked that, he said, "No, I don't. I didn't know I'd be rescuing you when I started the night. But you can't keep it on, either." He tried frantically to think of how to make such a stunning woman look... normal.

The hint of a smile on her face grew. "I have heard tales," she began slowly. "Of lords bringing ladies of ill repute to this establishment for... entertainment."

Tom had no idea where she was going with that comment

but listened for the moment as he searched for some solution to her dress.

She continued. "Some of these lords are particularly mean and keep the poor women's clothes, hiding them away, a humiliation to add to whatever else transpired. Such women have come to be known as sheet girls as they often leave wrapped only in..."

"Bed sheets?" Tom finished.

She nodded.

He glanced at the bed, then back to her, then back at the bed.

"Do you have a knife?" she prompted, holding out a hand. He nodded and pulled a small knife out from a hiding spot in his boot. She took it and sat, proceeding to cut away the bottom of her dress just above the knees. Then she made her way over to the bed, plopping his knife back in his hands as she passed.

"Are you going to help me or just watch?"

Watching had been working quite well for him so far. Those pale legs, so well formed and slender.

He snapped himself out of the reverie and helped her pull off the blankets and sheets on the bed. They took one sheet and figured a way to wrap her in it such that the sheet covered what remained of her dress entirely. It was not inconvenient that her dress had no sleeves or straps. Once done, he surveyed their work and smiled.

She looked like she was wearing a sheet and no more. That thought got him a little hot and flushed. As much as he knew she was still wearing her dress, the thought of her actually only being dressed in a sheet was just a little too much for him.

She turned to a long looking glass, and harrumphed. "No, it's not quite..."

Tom thought it was more than adequate.

"It's my hair," she said after a moment.

"Oh, yes," he agreed, now that it had been brought to his attention. If she was a 'sheet girl' then the previous activities of the night probably wouldn't leave her with immaculate hair.

"Help me with the pins," she said as she began pulling out long pins and the flowers.

He came up behind her. He was tall enough that he could just see over her head. That meant that as he drew close, he could smell her hair. It had the scent of roses. His heart quickened as he reached up to touch the thick locks, searching for more pins and drawing them out.

At first, he was quite distracted by each fall of hair, how silken and beautiful it was. Then he became distracted by searching for the last few pins. He couldn't find any more, but she insisted there had been fifteen pins and there were only thirteen they'd removed so far. But once they found those last two and the distractions faded, only then did he notice how close he was to her, his body brushing against hers. For a moment, their eyes caught in the looking glass and those deep dark orbs held him.

She released him from the moment as she reached up and further tousled her hair, teasing and playing with it until it was quite disheveled. He had to step back as she did, for fear of getting whipped in the face with a stray strand.

She turned when done and smiled. "Do I look like a sheet girl now?"

"You could never be a sheet girl," he said softly. But regained himself after a moment and added. "But you will play the part convincingly enough."

He looked at her feet.

She followed his gaze. "My slippers would be a giveaway. I'll have to go barefoot."

He nodded.

"Tom..."

He looked back up from her feet to her eyes, enjoying what he saw as his gaze made the trip. "Yes?"

"Why are you doing this?"

Before he could answer, she spoke again. "Why am I doing this? I barely know you. And yet..." She trailed off.

He prompted her. "And yet?"

She grimaced. "And yet..." she sighed out heavily. "Any man there could have helped me. I presume they all knew my fate was to be sent to Lord Gariast, and that's why none had any interest in me. I was fine with that. I was not so fond of the idea of me being shown about like a prized mare to be sold to the highest bidder."

Tom recalled his thought from earlier that night about the ball being a glorified cattle auction. She'd apparently had similar thoughts... only with horses.

"Any man could have rescued me, but they are all too afraid of Gariast." She'd been looking away, thinking through her words, but her gaze turned to him now. "But not you."

"I'm not afraid of that man." Tom felt a hardness in his gut. He had his own feud with Gariast, of which very few people were aware.

"You should be."

"So I'm told." He shrugged. "Lady Valeesa—"

"I'm not a lady anymore. Not dressed like this."

She'd always be a lady to him. "True. Valeesa then?"

She nodded.

"We do not have a lot of time. We need to get out of the gardens. You don't need to trust me very far, but for now... trust me a little further? I have a place in the Brown District we can go. I doubt your father will be looking for you there anytime soon."

She crinkled her nose at the mention of the smellier part of town but nodded. "You are a strange man Tom Willow." She pursed her lips for a brief moment before adding, "But I'll trust you that far."

"Good." He smiled and gave a single nod.

And so, they snuck out the back entrance of the Golden Gardens with him dressed as no more than a commoner and her as a whore.

Tom could only marvel at the woman's resolve and ingenuity. She hadn't batted an eyelash at the thought of disguising herself in such a way. She was extraordinary, and he was certain that whatever she did next would only ensnare him more in her spell. At this point, if she'd asked him to run away with her he just might have. Col was a great man and had taken him in when the world had not, but Valeesa was... a force of nature.

It only occurred to him then that he'd be taking her back to Col, Nik, and Jaff. He wondered what they'd think of her. Then he shrugged. It didn't matter what they thought. He was going to help her, with or without them.

Valeesa was a tough woman. That much became clear to Tom as they ran through the streets with her bare feet slapping the paving stones. She didn't complain and tried her best to keep pace in her concealed dress.

In the Silver District, Tom stopped and told her he was going to get her some shoes. They found a cobbler's shop, and he broke the window and stole her a comfortable pair of boots. He had been helping Col rob noblemen for a while, but he felt bad about stealing from a merchant. He left a quickly scrawled note apologizing for the theft and the broken window and left the man several gems to repay him—it was far more than enough.

After a similar not-quite-theft to get Valeesa some new clothes, and a stop in an alley so she could change, they made for the Gray District, then the Brown. By that point, the sky in the east was starting to lighten.

Morning was coming to the capital.

20

"Ho, there!" A bellowing voice woke Col.

Eye's snapping open, Col looked around frantically, trying to recall where he was. It was still dark, but faint light brushed the horizon to the east. He was in a yard and a large man loomed over him. "This is an odd spot for a king's guard to be sleeping. I should report you to the king himself. I've met the man you know, I—"

"It's me, Albior," Col hissed. Now he recalled where he was, out back of Grunston's Furs.

"Colric?"

Col stood and stretched stiff muscles, then removed his helm.

"How...?" Grunston asked bewildered.

"A long story. I wasn't able to save my parents; they died in there." The words burned a little to say. Again, he found it odd that he was so worked up about his parents' deaths. Not long ago he'd thought them dead and had come to terms with that. But now, even though nothing had changed, he still felt all upside-down emotionally about it all.

Col handed over the scrollcase. "I am sorry if this inconveniences your life, but trust that it is for a good purpose."

Grunston's face darkened as he took the case and removed the message. He'd brought out a candle-tree with him, which he set on a barrel next to the rear door of his shop. He read by that light then seemed to read the message a few more times.

"This is the king's seal. This is a king's order. I... What happened last night?"

"I am the king's man again, just not officially. We'll need your help to communicate."

Grunston nodded. "I believe the king is a good man and I know your father was. I will do this for you." Then he smiled, though the only way Col could tell was by how the man's beard shifted. His voice changed to a more sardonic tone. "Not that I have much choice." He laughed then.

"Good, thank you. Don't forget to burn that note. The king will be in touch or I will when needed. Take care, old friend."

They shook hands.

"I think you'll need more care than I, but I'll keep safe, never worry about that," Grunston said gruffly.

Then Col was gone into the dawning day.

He arrived at the tavern in the Brown District to find Nik and Jaff sitting eating and talking quietly in the common room.

"Tom not back yet?" he asked, strolling in, still dressed as a king's guard.

They took a moment before answering. Nik glanced at him twice before recognition set in.

"Boss?"

Col came to stand next to them. He didn't mind the title. There wasn't anyone else in the common room but the tavern keeper anyway.

Jaff was quicker to adapt. "Tom's here," he said, going back to his food. After a few chews, he added, "with a special guest."

"He brought a lady friend back with him." Nik shook his head. "Leave it to Tom to find a girl when he's supposed to be working."

A woman?

"Did he say why or who she is?" Col didn't like this disruption to his plans, but he trusted Tom. He hoped the man had a good reason for whatever it was he'd done.

Jaff shook his head. "Didn't tell us, but she's sure pretty."

Col nodded. "When you're finished here, get the horses saddled and be ready to leave shortly. I don't want to linger. You can report when we're on the road."

They both nodded, and Col went upstairs.

Just in case Tom was up to something more intimate with the woman, Col knocked before he entered.

Tom's voice came through the door. "Col? Come in."

He entered and found Tom standing by the small window in the room. The woman was dressed in a brown dress with a gray apron, but something wasn't right about her look. Her hair looked like it had been hastily hand-combed from some disarray and... her dark eyes were steely, hard, assessing him.

"Col," Tom said, taking a step toward him. "Might I introduce, Lady Valeesa Tandor. She'll be coming with us."

"Will she?" Col was a bit taken aback.

Tandor, he'd heard that name before. Tom had said, 'lady' as if it were a title, not just an honorific. Did he know a Lord Tandor? Yes, he did. The knight had been one of the last in the sword-sparring competition that Col had won three years ago. A bannerman of Lord Gariast. This was most likely that man's daughter. But why would Tom have her and—more intriguingly —why had she come with him?

"Tom, what did you do?" He couldn't stop his gaze from moving between the two of them.

"The quick version is: her father was sending her to be with

Gariast, so I rescued her from that fate. But if you want the long version, perhaps we should be on the road first? Half the city is probably looking for her by now."

Col turned to the girl... no, not a girl. She may have been young, but there was a sense about her. She wasn't being dragged along here. She knew what she was doing.

"You're well and good with all this, m'lady? This life... it's not an easy one; not a noble's life."

She considered for a moment before responding. "If you were me, would you rather have a noble's life living with Lord Gariast, or that of a free commoner?"

He half grinned. "Just wanted to make sure you knew what you were getting into."

She glanced at Tom. "I didn't at first... but I understand now. We should go."

Col nodded. Apparently, they were going to abscond with a noblewoman. He couldn't fault Tom. Col had been telling the man over and over that 'we help who we can.' It seemed the man had finally taken that to heart.

To Tom he said, "I can't wait to hear your full report." He turned to the woman. "Welcome to our merry little band, Lady Tandor."

It was only much later, once they were out of the capital and on the road, that Tom told him the entire tale, including the trap Gariast was setting for him.

Col took it all in stoically. He'd be ready enough for Gariast. He'd have five hundred men soon enough... then the lord would pay for his crimes.

~

"HIT ME," DALIA SAID.

She stood with Trentin in a small pool of light in a large

cleared area. It might be considered a village green for their new small camp, as it was situated in the center of the circle of houses. It wasn't green, mostly dirt and fallen leaves, but it was fairly level and open.

The day had dawned clear and crisp, and Dalia had awoken rested despite her late night. There was still so much she felt like she didn't know, even after everything she'd learned. But she thought she knew enough to start taking control of her abilities. She'd gone to Trentin's newly grown small house and asked him for a favor. He'd agreed, not knowing the favor was to attack her.

Trentin seemed taken aback, surprise clear on his face, mouth hanging open. His daughter Sahras giggled from somewhere off behind the large man.

"I don't think that's a great idea," Trentin said, though he seemed to be scrambling for some reason as to why.

"Because I'm a woman?" She put her hands on her hips and glared at him. "I've fought off twelve mounted soldiers; I don't think my womanhood should count against me now."

"It's not because you're a woman, it's..."

Sahras had snuck up next to her father now. The girl still seemed a bit shy around any new person, but she was slowly warming to Dalia. "Daddy's scared of you," Sahras whispered far too loudly.

"I am not!" He knelt next to his daughter. "Why don't you run along and play now."

Sahras gave a shrug and grimaced. "But, Daddy!"

"Run along."

She huffed and stalked away.

Trentin turned back to Dalia. His voice was hushed when he said, "I lied. I am scared of you. After what you did to those knights... frankly, I never want to go against you. You terrify me."

Sahras giggled from not too far away. "I heard that, Daddy!"

Dalia smiled. Her smile quickly faded though. She couldn't practice without someone trying to attack her.

"Please. I've learned about my abilities. I should be able to control them enough not to hurt you." She paused. In truth, she hadn't tried anything since last night and wasn't sure if she could control The Fury yet. She really did not want to hurt Trentin, but desperately needed to see if she had gained any control. She knew she was asking a lot of him. "Put on your armor if you like. Trentin, I need to learn more about how this works, and that means I need someone to fight me. I can't ask any of the villagers. They have no training at all, and I'd be afraid I'd… break one of them. But you are a trained knight. You know how to take a hit and you have armor you can wear."

She could see the thought behind his eyes. Those mounted men had been well trained and wearing armor too, and they were still dead.

Hana came up behind her husband, laying her hands on his shoulders. "She needs help, Trentin," his wife said. "You'll be fine, but please do wear your armor."

Trentin seemed about to resist, but sighed out a long breath, his shoulders slumping, and nodded. He went to get his armor.

Hana came over to Dalia. "Please be careful with him. I only have the one husband and I'd hate to lose him."

Dalia nodded. "I'll do my best."

Not long later, Trentin stood before her on the village green in full armor, looking more than a little concerned.

"Go on then. Hit me," she said.

He set himself as if there were some great bull charging him, and then swung at her. The punch was aimed for her shoulder. She could tell that quickly enough as time seemed to stretch.

The Fury kicked in. Only, it wasn't really The Fury this time around. There was no haze, no instant counterattack. For the briefest of moments, she was in control, then…

She reached up and took his wrist as she spun out of the way of the blow and in closer to him. She crouched and pulled his arm down, using his upper body weight against him and throwing him over onto his back. She still had a grip on his arm and twisted it, while at the same time bringing a foot down onto his neck. He was pinned through the combination of the angle of his arm and the placement of her foot.

That was where the true difference came. The Fury might well have kept going and made her crush his throat, but she managed to stop at that point. Even so, she didn't seem to be fully in control, as she couldn't release him yet.

He groaned.

That seemed to snap her out of her haze. She released him, stepping away.

He coughed a few times, rolling away, massaging his arm. He came to his knees after a moment, still rubbing his arm.

"Well," he said slowly. "I'm still alive; that seems like progress."

It was. She'd been able to keep herself from using lethal force on his neck. It wasn't the first time she'd been able to keep herself from killing while in The Fury, but this time had been vastly different from any other. She'd seen what she was doing; known the moves and how to do them and had been in control for most of it.

She nodded. "I'm hoping I can get to a point when I can just let you hit me."

"Really? Why would you ever want anyone to hit you?"

"I don't want to be hit. But if I am, then that means I have full control over these... abilities." She was still getting used to not thinking of all of this as a curse.

He shrugged. "I suppose that makes sense."

"Are you willing to try again?" she asked, trying to add a bit of a hopeful and cheery tone into her voice.

He groaned. "Yeah, sure. But I'll tell you now if you keep wrenching my arm like that, I won't be able to do this more than a few times." He rose and blew out a breath, then set himself again.

"Give me a moment," she said. She calmed herself, closing her eyes and taking long breaths. She tried to clear her mind, then thought really hard about not attacking, not reacting. She recalled a bit of that peace she'd felt last night and the deep knowing and connection with her body.

"Okay, now," she said.

"Aren't you going to look at me?"

She hadn't realized she still had her eyes closed. She knew he was there. She could 'see' him in her mind. She shrugged, curious about her abilities.

"No. Go ahead I'll be fine."

There was a hesitation, then she heard him blow out a sigh. "If you insist." He sounded even more scared to be attacking her with her eyes closed than he had before.

She heard the soft padding of Trentin's foot stepping forward; she could even picture his swing in her mind. She felt the brush of wind as his fist drew close and heard the metallic scrape and jangle of his armor moving.

Once again, she spun away from the attack and into him. This time though, she did not grab his wrist but brought her elbow up as she drew near. She had enough foresight to know this was going to hurt him and pull the attack. Her elbow still hit his jaw, knocking him over with a grunt, but she hadn't continued with the attack. She could envision the entire rest of the move: follow through on the elbow, spin and bring her foot up into his chin, snapping his head back as he fell. She'd stopped herself, which good, but still not quite enough control.

"Did you do that with your eyes closed?" Trentin's incredulous voice snapped her out of her reverie. She opened her eyes.

"Maybe," she said defensively. She looked to see him lying on his side, rubbing his jaw.

"And you're sure you're not possessed?"

Dalia flinched as if struck, cringing back. Gods, she hated that term. The trouble was, she couldn't entirely deny it. Perhaps that's where her loathing for the word came from. She'd learned enough now to know there was something that wasn't human within her. And it was true that her actions had been controlled by that inhuman thing at times. But she had to believe that she was still herself at her core.

She sighed heavily. "I don't know," she breathed. "I don't feel like it most of the time, but..."

"I'm sorry, Dalia. I didn't mean..." He grunted. "I'm an oaf, forgive me." He stood, still rubbing his jaw. "I'm sure this can't be easy for you."

No, it wasn't. She changed the topic.

"How are you feeling?" she asked. "Up for more?"

He shrugged. "I'm not dead yet, so... that's probably a good sign."

She smiled. "Once more then?"

They squared off.

She quieted her mind to focus on her body. She dug deep into her recollections of the previous night. The knowing she'd felt around The Fury and how it worked, enhancing her body with a touch of magic. In her mind, she repeated the phrase *I'm in control*.

Trentin swung, and again time seemed to slow. This time, unlike all the others when she'd just acted, she had a flash of insight, which lasted no more than the blink of an eye. She saw all of the ways she could use the attack against him, all of the countermoves, all of the evasions, all possible outcomes, all possible victories. The knowledge filled her and overwhelmed her for a moment.

Then a fist struck her shoulder, and she was knocked back. She began to fall. Even as she did, the thinking part of her brain shut off and the reaction of her abilities kicked in. She did a nimble back flip and landed once again on her feet in a crouch. She knew she could spring at him, surprise him, attack him, but she didn't. She simply stayed where she was.

Trentin's face was a mask of confusion. He seemed sorry and triumphant all at the same time. He opened his mouth a few times to speak but said nothing. He just kept blinking and shaking his head.

It was her turn to rub her shoulder.

She let her reflexes go and walked back to him. "That was new."

He nodded. "You controlled it."

She grimaced. "Actually, no."

His brow furrowed. "But...?"

"That wasn't control, that was... distraction. Instead of just reacting, my mind gave me every possible action and outcome. It threw me off. So, as I said, it's new. I think it's progress."

Trentin grinned. "I'm not on the ground, so it seems like progress to me."

She laughed. "Let's try again tomorrow. How's that sound? Give you some time to heal."

"Sounds good," he said, looking relieved.

They went their separate ways and she returned to her hut. Of all of the new structures the sprites had grown for the people here, she was the only person to have one to herself. It was small, like Col's had been back in the previous camp. She returned to find a fire already burning in the pit at the center of the hut. A structure of wood held a pot suspended over the fire, and it was giving off a pleasant smell.

Ayneii appeared. "Hi, Dalia. Analla stopped by to make you a meal."

"Oh?" Dalia hardly knew Analla. She'd seen the matronly woman around the camp but had spoken no more than a few words to her.

"I like Analla," Ayneii said, settling herself on one of the shelves in the room, legs dangling and swinging over the edge. "She's kind and tends to plants and people alike. She's sort of like a sprite, but much bigger."

"You'll have to introduce us some time." Dalia picked up a bowl from a shelf, along with a spoon and began portioning out some of the soup.

"Oh, she doesn't know me at all."

Dalia stopped. It occurred to her that she'd become fairly familiar with this tiny being, but She'd forgotten that sprites usually didn't allow themselves to be seen by humans. "Who have you shown yourself to?" she asked, returning to her soup.

"You, and Col, and a couple other men who have sprites, and... that's it."

"Other men have sprites too?"

Ayneii nodded. "Tom has Riiku, and Jaff has Kiiva. Nik keeps asking for one, but he's much more fun to tease. It takes a special sprite to want to be so close to a human, and a special human too."

"Oh."

Dalia sat and ate, thinking this over for a moment. The soup was hot. There were chunks of parsnip along with a bit of meat, soft and tender. There was a spice she couldn't identify, which gave the whole dish a bit of life. All in all, not bad and quite filling.

A question came to Dalia. "So, all those fey that helped me... has Col or anyone else seen them?"

"No. You're a very special case. I think eventually when you come to your full awareness, you'll be able to see us fey whether we want you to see us or not. It is very rare that we let humans see one of our rituals, even rarer to have a human participate in one."

Dalia smiled. "I'm honored."

Ayneii nodded. "You should be."

Dalia laughed. "Shall I go back tonight?"

"No. Perhaps later we'll do another such ritual, but for now, you need to be patient and let your human side catch up with the rest of you. We unlocked what we could last night, but in truth, we don't know how much that was. It might be everything. We'll need to wait and see what you grow into in the next few days to know for sure. Once your body has caught up to where your spirit is, then perhaps we can do another ritual."

Dalia nodded. That made sense. Now it was just up to her to remember and adapt to what she apparently already knew on some level. She drew in a long breath and let it out slowly. This was going to take a lot of work and a lot of time, but it seemed like it was the only way.

Unfortunately, patience had never been one of her virtues.

21

Tom took Valeesa for a walk.

It would be another day before they returned to the forest camp. They had been riding hard for three days and had reached a village at the outskirts of the Sandren Forest. At Tom's request, they'd stopped for the night despite it being only midafternoon. There was a small common house here, and the rooms might not be much, but they'd be better than sleeping on the ground with only a few blankets. He was thinking of Valeesa, though she hadn't complained once during their trip so far.

To facilitate her riding and help disguise her further, Col had suggested Tom purchase some men's clothes for her, pants and a shirt. Col had also suggested Valeesa cut off her long tresses. If she wore a cap, she might pass for a boy, if her shirt was baggy enough to hide her more feminine features. Tom had balked at that. It seemed a travesty to cut that beautiful hair, but Valeesa had agreed with Col. She knew if she was going to hide from her previous life, it would require sacrifices. Tom knew it too; he'd just not wanted her to have to make those sacrifices.

It was one of the reasons he wanted to get away from the others now, while they had some time before dinner. She'd been quiet for much of their travels, and he wanted to know how she was doing. She was still wearing her 'boys' outfit which hid her well enough, but once they were away from the town and walking through the forest, she removed her cap. Tom sighed at her roughly cut hair. What had been long flowing locks was now a jagged fringe around her head, no lower than her ears.

"Thank you," she said softly.

He wasn't sure what that was for, so he asked. "For what?"

"Everything." She looked over at him then, those large dark eyes seeking comfort. He put an arm around her shoulders, drawing her close. It seemed natural and she didn't resist. Her body nestled in next to his. "This..." She looked around at the forest. "This is not the life I'd imagined for myself."

He nodded. She should be living luxuriously, not hiding in a forest.

"But," she went on. "I can't imagine what the alternative would be." He felt her body tremble. "I don't want to imagine. I've heard far too many rumors about Lord Gariast. I can tell my father is terrified of the man and he's not scared of anything else in this world." She stopped suddenly. They were far from the town now; no one would see or hear them. The sounds of the forest, birds and wind through the leaves, were all that remained around them. "I know I don't want to be there." She hummed and hawed for a moment. "Not long ago I wouldn't have wanted to be here either, but..." She turned toward him, standing in front of him, her body brushing his. He was reminded of that moment in front of the looking glass back at the Golden Gardens. "With you here, I think I can do this." She laughed a little then. "I hardly know you and yet I feel like I know you. Does that make any sense?"

It made perfect sense. "I'd love to get to know you better," he whispered.

"As would I." She stepped closer, arms wrapping around

him, her head resting on his shoulder. His arms enfolded her as well, holding her close. He turned his head toward her. Jagged, flyaway wisps of her short hair tickled his nose.

She stayed there for some time, not making any move to leave his embrace.

If she wanted to know more about him, he'd tell her.

"I was born in the town of Kilian's Hollow." Kilian's Hollow should be known to her. It was the town that supported Gariast's estates. "My childhood was one of freedom. My mother didn't know what to do with me once I was old enough to run off on my own. I got into all manner of trouble but was rarely scolded. I saw other kids getting paddled, or worse, for less than what I had done, but I... was never touched.

"I had my own little gang after a while. We were terrors. Yet still, if we did something bad, they'd all get a whipping, but I'd be told to 'not do it again' in stern words and no more. Not that I minded, but I began to wonder why I was being treated differently.

"Then there were the looks. All the villagers looked at me strangely. As a kid, I didn't notice, but as I grew older, I noticed it more and more. I finally asked my mother why everyone seemed... afraid of me. She broke into tears and couldn't tell me. I didn't understand that. It made me feel like I'd done something wrong, but nobody would tell me what I'd done.

"And so the trend continued. I would ask and get no answer. This only made me angry. One day I got fed up. I pulled a knife on the elderly tavernkeeper. My mother had worked for him for years as a barmaid in the small common room. I figured if anyone would know what it was that she couldn't tell me, it was he. I'd had a growth spurt, and though I wasn't filled out yet, I was as tall as the other man, and my anger made me strong enough to pin him against a wall, knife to his throat. I demanded he tell me why everyone treated me so differently.

"He did." Tom couldn't help a bitter note seeping into his voice. This part of the tale was not easy to tell. In truth, this would be the first time he'd told it to anyone. Even Col didn't know. No one knew, but he wanted to tell Valeesa.

"He told me of a day before I was born." Tom had to swallow hard to keep going, his voice was strained as he went on. Valeesa must have noticed as she pulled away slightly to gaze into his eyes. Her look was concerned. His hand lingered on her shoulders. He needed the contact and reassurance to go on.

"He told me that... that a nobleman had come to our village one day. He'd been passing through and had stopped for a midday meal." Tom's heart was beating furiously, tears in his eyes which he refused to let fall. "My mother had caught his eye. She'd been young then. The noble had asked the tavern keeper how much it would be for her; for a quick trip up to one of his rooms. The tavern keeper had tried to explain to the noble that she wasn't available in that way. The noble had grown angry. He'd grabbed my mother and..." Tom's voice cracked. "He'd taken her there, in the common room, with the villagers watching. And after, he'd slapped a gold coin down next to her and had said that everything was available for the right price. Then he'd left."

"Tom, that's horrible!"

Tom could only nod for a moment as he brought his emotions under control. He hadn't told her the worst part yet. "That nobleman was my father." He was trembling, partly with shame for what had happened, but mostly with anger. "That nobleman was Lord Gariast."

Valeesa flinched as if struck.

That was the reaction Tom had been expecting. He'd been holding her shoulders, but he dropped his arms to his sides. He would understand if she didn't want to be close to him now. For a moment, there was a look in her eyes like the villagers had had so long ago: fear and repulsion. That stung his soul. Yet it lasted only a heartbeat before it was replaced with compassion and sorrow. She stepped into embrace him again.

"Tom, you're not him. You're nothing like him, if that's what you're worried about." Her words were a healing salve on the open wound that burned within him. That was exactly what haunted him every moment of his life. Her grace and acceptance were too much.

Tears fell.

He blubbered as he said, "I'm his son, how could I not...?" He was too choked to go on for a moment.

"Because you had a loving mother. You're her son too. Always remember that." She stepped back to look him in the eye again but kept herself close, arms still on his chest. "Perhaps, if you'd been raised by the man, you might be like him, but you weren't. Those villagers didn't know what to make of you, that's all. But it's plain as day to anyone with eyes to see that you are kind and caring and compassionate. You helped me without knowing who I was."

He wiped away the wetness on his cheeks, sniffing back any further tears. After a couple deep breaths, he felt better. Her words had helped so much.

"I went to work for him."

She quirked a brow in question. "For Gariast?"

Tom nodded. "I was always good with horses and got myself a job in his stables. I needed to see the man, to meet him." He shook his head as the memory resurfaced. "It only took one meeting. That was enough. I'd failed to brush down one of his stallions just right, and for my mistake, the head stableman was beaten severely. It was so bad the man had to retire, not able to do his job. Then I knew why those villagers had looked at me the way they had. They were expecting that... in me. So, I didn't feel too bad the day I took five of Gariast's prized mounts out to graze... and never came back. I rode to the nearest town that wouldn't know the horses and sold them for half of what they were worth."

"I knew I could never go home after that." He sighed heavily. He hadn't seen his mother since, and she'd died a couple years ago.

After a moment, he went on. "I wandered for a bit, getting into more trouble. I became a great horse thief... but eventually I'd made myself too well known. I knew I couldn't stay in these lands anymore." He grinned. "I have wanted posters in a score of towns and villages."

"I sought refuge in the Sandren Forest and that's where I found Col. Even though he's of a similar age, he's been more of a father to me than any man. Well, perhaps a brother. It's hard to define."

She nodded. "I can see how you look at him. It's clear enough to me. Just as it's clear how much he cares for you." She drew in close once again. "Other than these past few days, my life has been... charmed. I can't and shouldn't complain. I have no right. I've been through nothing like that."

Tom pressed her close to him, the bonding of their touch soothing the ache in his soul. "Thank you," he said softly. "I should tell you, I've never told Col about my father, just... that I was a horse thief."

She nodded, her head moving against his chest.

"So," he said. "Tell me about this charmed life of yours."

And after a while, she did.

They continued their walk, talking until it grew dark. They picked their way carefully out of the forest and returned to the common house for a long sought-after bed, even if it wasn't together.

There had been one thing Tom had not told her. The gold coin Gariast had given his mother, she had never spent it. It had become a symbol for her, something to give her strength. As long as she kept it, then that meant she hadn't been 'bought.' She'd passed the coin on to him before he went to work for his father. Only then had she been able to tell him the story, as hard as it had been for her. Tom still had that coin tucked away in a pocket. He'd made it his vow to return it to Gariast... when he killed the man.

22

DALIA NEEDED TIME TO THINK.

Or maybe she didn't need to think at all, but to do something. She was so conflicted.

She was desperately trying to remember all of those possible moves that had blinked into her mind when Trentin had attacked her and she'd been hit, but there were so many, and the memory was fading quickly. She tried focusing on just a few of them, which seemed to work. She studied the moves, going over them in her head. Next, she tried stepping through them, inside her small hut. Each made sense, and she could see the value of the different options. She was certain she understood these moves, but even as she congratulated herself on that, she felt a sense of overwhelm returning to her.

She now felt comfortable with a handful of moves meant to deal with one, basic type of attack. Yet there had been what seemed like thousands that had come to her for that one attack. That meant the total sum of things she could do against all possible attacks must be almost innumerable. She could see a way to mastery through this slow process of understanding a few moves at a time, but it would take her years, more likely

decades to get through them all. And that was just understanding her ability with fighting. There was so much more the
fey had shown her. How long would it take to fully understand
what she was and what she could do?

She sat heavily on the pad of blankets, disheartened.

Ayneii popped into existence in front of her, startling her.

"Hi!" came the high-pitched and all-too-chipper voice of the
sprite.

"Hello Ayneii, what would you like?"

Ayneii set herself down on what had become "her" spot on
the shelf. Once again, her legs swayed carefree beneath her,
hands on the shelf as she leaned forward. Yet there was a difference in her movement this time. Not as loose, more tense. Her
gossamer wings moved, seemingly of their own accord adjusting
slightly, swaying, and keeping her in balance.

"I'm worried about Col," Ayneii said after a moment.

"Me too," Dalia agreed. He'd been away for nearly a week
now. She knew it would be several days to reach the capital, and
she had no idea how long he planned to be there, but it still
seemed far too long for him to be away... from her.

Ayneii looked up at her with a look of terror. "Do you think
he got eaten by a dragon too?"

Dalia stifled a laugh; the sprite's concern was as sincere as it
was absurd. "Why would you think that?" Something occurred
to Dalia then which prompted a second question. "Dragons
aren't real, are they?" Dragons were tales, myths, or so she
thought, but she'd thought the same of fey until just a little
while ago, and now she was talking to one.

Ayneii scrunched up her face in a look of reproach. "Of
course dragons are real, even though you humans hunted them
to near extinction. To this day, dragons are near impossible to
find. And why wouldn't I think that some dragon had eaten Col.
I don't know all that much about what happens beyond this

forest." Her shoulders slumped in dismay. "Most sprites don't travel far from their given realms."

Dragons? Real? That was a scary thought. No wonder people had hunted them.

"Oh, really? Don't sprites talk to each other?"

Ayneii squirmed at the question. "We do yes, but most sprites don't take as much mind of what humans are doing as we do here. It's hard to get those farther away to tell me anything. They just don't know. They can't tell one human from another!"

"Oh." Dalia nodded. That made sense.

"That's why I'm so worried that Col might have been eaten by dragons!"

"I'm sure he wasn't. He's on a dangerous mission, yes, but I don't think there have been any dragons around here in a very long time. If, as you say, dragons are real—"

"They are."

"Then I'm sure they're staying away from us humans. We did hunt them to near extinction as you say. Besides, no human I know has ever seen a dragon."

"And lived to tell about it."

Dalia had no response to that.

Ayneii kept rocking back and forth for a moment, then she asked. "Well, if not dragons, then why are you worried about him?"

"We humans can be pretty dangerous and scary too."

Ayneii nodded. "That's true." She sighed forlornly. "Now, I have to worry about Col around dragons *and* humans."

Dalia's heart went out to the poor sprite who seemed to feel everything so very deeply.

Ayneii perked up suddenly. "He's here!"

"Who? Col?"

Ayneii nodded. "Yes! I just got a message from one of the other sprites that he and the others are returning... with a woman... who looks like a boy." Ayneii shrugged. "Some of these messages don't make much sense."

Dalia was up in a flash. "What are we waiting for?" She headed for the door.

Ayneii flew off the shelf and joined her as she left the hut. "Well, they're not *here* here. They're still a few miles off, but they'll be here shortly. We have lookouts."

Dalia paused just outside of her hut. Perhaps a short walk would do her good and Ayneii might be able to help her with her problem. "I'm going to walk a bit. Can I ask you something?"

"Sure!"

Dalia thought for a moment. She really wasn't sure what she wanted to ask. She already knew that the sprites had no idea about what she'd experienced during the ritual. So how could she try to get some useful information about what was happening to her?

She started with something simple. "As a sprite, what can you do?" She realized that was a little vague and quickly modified the question. "What makes a sprite a sprite? What magic do you have? That sort of thing."

Ayneii bobbed along beside her for a moment before answering. "We tend to nature, to all things living. We make sure that seeds find root, well those ones that are meant to. There are a lot of seeds out there, you know."

Dalia nodded.

"We make sure things grow as they are supposed to. Humans tend to think that means that trees should be straight and tall, but we see a larger pattern. Not all trees can be straight. Some are meant to be twisted and small. Some are not meant to live for long at all. So, we also tend to death. When it is a thing's time, we usher its spirit back to nature. There is a great chaotic cycle out there, of life and death and living and waiting to be alive. More than just plants, we ensure the cycle for all animals as well. We used to for humans, but that was a long time ago. You try to take too much control now, it's not as nature intended; you kill each other and have medicine to stop illness. We've given up on you. Well, most of you."

This wasn't helping Dalia. It was interesting, but not useful. "But what... what powers do you have?"

"Powers?" Ayneii shrugged. "I have no special powers. I just do what I can do."

Dalia had expected an answer like that.

"But I have 'powers' that are fey, correct?"

Ayneii nodded. "Yes."

"And the powers I have, do fey have abilities like that?"

"To fight like that? No, well not sprites anyway. Your healing ability. We do have something like that."

"Healing?" She had a healing ability?

"Have you not noticed you heal far quicker than most others?"

She had, that's right. She'd forgotten how quickly her wounds seemed to close.

A wild idea struck her. She stopped walking and drew her knife from her belt and, before she could think too much about it, poked it into her palm. It wasn't a big cut, but it bled well. She closed her eyes concentrating on her hand, the pain, the blood... but what else? She was more intimately connected with her body now. She felt not only the blood leaving her, but all of the blood pulsing within her. She felt how it changed around the wound, clotting and closing, trying to stop her body from losing more of the precious fluid. She tried to help the process, quicken it. She wasn't sure what she did exactly, it could best be described as just pushing energy. She focused on the wound and tried to move the latent healing ability within her muscles to the cut. It closed in a matter of heartbeats, but afterward a great wave of fatigue washed over her, and she had to steady herself against a tree.

"Why did you do that?" Ayneii asked.

It seemed obvious why people would want to heal themselves.

"You used far too much energy for that small cut. It was like you were trying to stop a trickling stream with a massive boulder."

Dalia's head was spinning a little, but she got Ayneii's point.

"I could have used less... power?"

"Much less."

"Oh." She really needed to work on this.

"Why are you trying so hard?" Ayneii asked. She sounded concerned.

"I need to understand what's happening to me," Dalia said. She drew in a long breath then tried walking again. She wobbled for the first few steps but managed fine. She felt like she hadn't slept in days.

"Yes, I know, but you're working far too hard. Understanding comes in part from doing, but mostly from reflection. Once you let yourself simply 'be' what you are meant to be, I think that will go a long way to understanding who you are."

"What about my humanness getting in the way?"

"That's pretty much what I'm talking about. Stop trying to 'do' understanding. You humans are far too focused on action. Just be."

Dalia wasn't sure she understood what Ayneii was saying exactly, but the clop of hooves nearby distracted her.

Col was returning.

Perhaps it was her lightheadedness that made Dalia a bit brazen, but when Col had dismounted, she threw herself on him in an embrace. He laughed and returned it quickly enough.

"It's good to see you too, Dalia," he said.

"Dalia? Dalia Athernon?"

The voice was familiar, but Dalia couldn't place it. She untangled herself from Col.

Walking toward her was... someone. The face seemed familiar, but somehow out of place.

"Dalia? That is you," said... the girl? Yes, Ayneii had said there was a woman dressed as a boy with those returning. "It's me, Valeesa Tandor."

Valeesa?

Dalia looked a bit closer, and indeed the face was right, but with the baggy clothing and cap, the cropped hair, she wouldn't have otherwise recognized the girl who was always properly dressed and presentable. They hadn't met that many times, but they were of an age and had seen each other and spoken at a few balls and events. Though Dalia supposed she'd been just as prim and presentable at those times and must look a shambles now.

Valeesa smiled slowly. "It's good to see a familiar face. What are you doing here?"

Dalia's voice was a little sour as she said, "Did word of the demon-girl not reach you?"

"Demon-girl?" Valeesa blinked. "I... I'd heard something, but I didn't think? Was that you?"

Dalia let out a sigh. "It still is, but that's a long story we can catch up on later."

Valeesa didn't seem to care. She still approached her and embraced her softly. "Well, no matter, as I said, it's good to see someone from that life here."

"What are you doing here?" Dalia asked, curious.

"That is a bit of a story as well."

Tom came up behind Valeesa and the way he laid his hand on her shoulder and her comfortable reaction to it spoke volumes.

"I'd love to hear it. For now, welcome to our home. It's... special."

Col laughed at that. "It certainly is."

As Valeesa marveled at the huts and the trees around them, Col pulled Dalia aside. "I've missed you," he whispered, and it warmed her heart to hear it.

"I've missed you as well. You haven't had a chance to sleep a night at the new camp and..." Would it be too forward? The words sort of tumbled out: "I thought, since there was a hut made for you, but with Valeesa here, she might want that, and maybe you could stay... with me?"

He held her close.

"I'd like that."

She held him in return squeezing tight.

And much later that night, that was how they slept, wrapped in each other's arms, easing each other's pains.

23

AFTER FOUR DAYS HAD GONE BY, COL MADE TRIPS OUT TO THE king's road every day, wanting to make sure he caught Kellan and the troops when they passed through the Sandren Forest.

It was on the sixth day after he'd left the capital that they marched through. He dropped down from his hidden perch in a tree, where he'd been watching the road, and landed lightly in front of the column, next to Kellan.

Kellan dismounted, and they shook hands.

"Well met, Col," Kellan said.

"Well met," Col said, and embraced the man.

Kellan asked, "Where to from here?"

"There is no road to get to where you're going, and the forest is fairly thick. Riding will be hard. The men will have to dismount and lead their horses through the forest. It's about two hours to get to my camp."

In preparation for this group, the sprites had been working all hours to grow several long bunking houses and a stable. Their camp was growing significantly.

Kellan nodded and quickly communicated this to the men who dismounted and followed them.

Col led them through the forest back to the camp. It was nearly evening by the time they arrived and full dark before they were organized and settled.

Col was growing excited, impatient. He couldn't sleep well that night and left Dalia's warm embrace to wander the camp.

Plans needed to be made.

His next target was Lord Gariast's estates. He had just over five hundred men, but would that be enough? From Trentin's report of Gariast's army, there would be at least double that stationed at the estate at any given time. If Gariast was planning a trap for Col, there might be even more, as much as four times the numbers Col had.

A frontal assault wouldn't be possible.

Col walked the forest camp and planned. He'd used guile to fool greater numbers before... but never on this scale. He had to make some hard decisions.

He found Tom with Valeesa. That didn't surprise him. "Might I have a moment?" he asked the other man, and Tom nodded, stepping away from his newfound love.

Col made sure they were away from everyone else in the camp before starting. "There are some things you need to know if I don't make it through what is to come."

"WE'RE OUTNUMBERED AT LEAST TWO TO ONE, IF NOT FOUR OR five to one," Kellan confirmed what Trentin had said. He frowned, lips pressed together.

The ex-knight nodded.

Dalia stood away from the others in the meeting room of the command cabin. This structure was new, erected for Kellan and his lieutenants. It also had a large room where gatherings like this could take place. Trentin had described Gariast's estate, and one of Kellan's men, a talented artist, had used a large piece of parchment to sketch out the area. It, and many other papers, were scattered over a large table in the center of the space.

Trentin said, "It's hard to know how many men will be at the estate at any one time. Gariast has two cohorts he keeps at his estates. But he controls at least two more, which are always close by, patrolling in his territory. However, there could be even more than that. He could call levies from his vassal lords and bannermen to swell his number to over six thousand strong. But the only way he'd have that many men at his estates was if he knew we were coming."

"Which he does," Col said coldly. "He just doesn't know when."

No one at the table looked happy.

Dalia wasn't particularly happy either. She was here because she would be going with them when they went to raid the estates, but she wasn't able to contribute anything useful to the plans since she knew nothing about warfare. So, she kept her mouth shut and brooded.

Valeesa hadn't joined the meeting. She knew she would be of no use in such matters and wouldn't be going so there was no point for her to be here. That made Dalia the only woman in the room and quite aware of that fact.

For some time now, she'd forgotten the way men treated women out there, in her old life. Col had always been so open with her and accepted her for who she was and what she could do. She wondered why more men couldn't be like that. She was certain women could do nearly anything men could do if given the chance. She'd heard of far-off places were women ruled instead of men. She knew it was possible. She could easily best any man in this room in a fight, probably two or three or more at a time. Men always claimed they were stronger and thus meant to be in charge, but by that logic, she should be in charge of this group. She was realizing more and more, that the rules men imposed were rather ridiculous. She promised herself that if she ever had the chance, she'd do something about that.

But first, she had to understand who and what she was, and that was taking much longer than she liked.

So, for now, she brooded.

Col was speaking. "We don't have the numbers for a frontal assault. We knew we'd be outnumbered, what's the problem? We'll defeat them using guile instead." He stepped in closer to the map. "We know that if we bring our full force against them in an open fight, we lose. So, we won't do that. Our goal is to get in and capture or kill Gariast, correct?" He waited for their mutters and nods. Dalia knew that Col had another goal as well, but this wasn't the time to bring it up. "Well, a small force can sneak in and do that, perhaps even easier than a large force can. In fact, even if we had more men than he, chances are he'd flee, and we'd lose him anyway. "

"I propose we bring the army up onto this ridge here." He pointed to a hill drawn on the map. Gariast's estate was in the middle of an open plain. The only place an army might be able to approach without being seen was to the east behind that ridgeline. There was a small wooded area to the north as well, but it wouldn't be able to hide an army of any significant size.

Colric continued, "If we do it at night and have each man carrying two torches we might be able to fool them into thinking we have double our numbers."

"But when they come out to engage they'll still crush us," Kellan said, disheartened.

"Will they come out?" Colric asked rhetorically. "They have an eight-foot outer wall. They don't need to do anything."

"And there is no way we can get close and scale that wall without—"

"You won't have to." Colric held up his hand. "Let me finish.

All you have to do is stand on that ridge and look menacing. You're the distraction. We want them to be looking that way while I, and a small force, sneak in and over the wall."

Kellan nodded for Colric to go on.

"With any luck, we'll be in and out before dawn. Your force can retreat without a fight. If they do come out, you simply run away. Hopefully, that will still buy us time to do what we need to on the inside."

Everyone let that plan sink in for a moment.

Finally, Kellan said, "That might work. When do you want to head out?"

"As soon as possible. Tomorrow, if we can. Gariast's estate is about a day and a half from here. If we leave before midday, we can be there before dark the day after."

"WHAT DO YOU MEAN YOU CAN'T FIND HIM!" SPITTLE FLEW FROM Lord Gariast's mouth as his frothing rage intensified. "First Tandor fails me, now you!"

Zatharyn remained calm. He was not in the least intimidated by this man. He knew he could use his magic to restrain Vandar if he needed to.

"They must be using magic. They are hidden from my magical sight," Zatharyn explained evenly.

"I am the only one with magic! I have you! What could they possibly have?" That was an excellent question, which Zatharyn could not answer. Could it be that the Athernon girl had grown powerful enough to hide herself and her allies from him?

They were in Vandar's dungeon office with a map of the region spread on the man's desk. Lord Gariast was so agitated he kicked out at a suit of armor mounted on a metal frame knocking it over with a loud clatter. He picked up a pauldron that had come loose and threw it at Zatharyn. The wizard made a motion with his hand, and the offending object was sent on a different course.

"How dare you! I am your master and if I say you should be punished—"

"There is nothing you can do to me," Zatharyn said, still calm.

"I can do whatever I want to you! You're mine!"

This was a misconception, which Zatharyn had been happy to let the lord sustain. Gariast thought everything was his, but that was far from the case. Perhaps it was time to dispel that myth.

Zatharyn whispered commands to his slaved fey minions and made a grasping motion with his hand. Even though the man was across the room, Gariast's shirt collar bunched in front as if Zatharyn had grabbed it. When the wizard lifted his hand, Gariast was swept off the floor, surprised and gasping. Zatharyn released his fist, but Gariast remained suspended, the motion had been an activation only, and the magic could easily be sustained with a thought. Instead, with that same hand, Zatharyn made a beckoning motion and again whispered in the secret language of the fey. Gariast was carried ungraciously across the room. His shins hit his desk and his writhing legs kicked most of what was on the surface off as he was dragged across it.

Zatharyn stopped him just far enough away so the man wouldn't be able to lash out at him then lowered him until his feet were only just off the floor. Zatharyn then levitated himself up until he was eye to eye with Gariast.

"Understand this, petty mortal." Though speaking softly, he laced his words with venom and power. "You may control trade and other lords and thousands of peasants. But never be mistaken about me. I serve you only because it furthers my agenda, and when you are of no more use to me, I shall abandon you. In truth, I am no servant at all. You are my servant and it would behoove you to act as such. I could end you here and now, but I am not done with you yet." His next words he said slowly as if to a child. "Do you understand?"

Gariast nodded, frantic.

Zatharyn released him, but not before weaving a special magic into the man's mind. The effects of which were readily apparent when Gariast tried to punch him the moment the lord hit the floor.

Zatharyn did not flinch as Vandar's fist stopped inches from his face.

"Try as you might. You cannot hurt me. It is futile," Zatharyn said softly. He shook his head. "But for being so insolent as to try, perhaps a second demonstration of your impotence is in order." He made a flicking motion with his fingers. Gariast was thrown back, into and over his desk, then into the wall behind that. There were several cracks and screams as bones were broken.

Zatharyn moved slowly around the desk to the whimpering lord. Kneeling next to him, he put a hand over the man's mouth to stop the pitiful sounds.

His voice was just a whisper. "Understand, I heal you now not out of remorse, but necessity. I do require you for a while longer. Blink once if you understand and are done with your tantrum."

The lord blinked once.

Zatharyn whispered to his minions and used their power to fill the lord with healing energies. He stood slowly and moved away. Gariast would recover in a moment.

He stopped at the door to the study. "I will notify you when I sense something. I believe hiding as many men as your foe has, requires only a single location to be hidden. Once they are on the move, you will know, and you can make your preparations." He paused for emphasis of his last words. "Just remember. The Athernon girl, she must live. She intrigues me. That is all I need from you for now."

He left and returned to his study.

Such use of magic had drained him a little and he would need a rejuvenation from his phylactery.

As he did, he mulled over the problem of not being able to sense Colric and the Athernon girl. He couldn't believe she'd grown accustomed to her power so quickly. There must be another explanation, but nothing came to him.

Hopefully, this was only a temporary setback and his foes would reveal themselves soon enough.

Yet he was plagued by thoughts of what might happen if the Athernon girl had somehow grown fully into the power she carried.

She might then be a threat, and he could not allow that. Not when he was so close to dominating this kingdom and making it pay for its cruelty against him.

24

DALIA STOOD IN THE SAME CLEARING WHERE THE FEY RITUAL HAD been performed. There were no sprites to light up the night, only the faint stars above.

In the stillness, she tried to let herself just 'be.' She cleared her mind and tried not to think of how badly she wanted to control her powers. She instead tried to recall the night of the ritual. It was one of the reasons she'd returned here. Maybe the location would help her remember. But she couldn't force it. That's what she'd taken from Ayneii's words earlier.

The words returned to her then, floating like falling leaves through her stilled mind.

...you're working far too hard...

...let yourself simply 'be' what you are meant to be...

...stop trying to 'do' understanding...

...just be...

...that will go a long way to understanding who you are...

Just be.

She closed her eyes, drew in a long breath through her nose, and picked up a thousand scents from around her. Each tree had its own flavor, each flower a perfume, every insect, every... person?

Someone was coming.

Her 'life sense' as she'd come to call it—allowing her to sense people and other living things around her—caught a person heading her way. She tested the air again and identified the person through his own unique scent.

With her eyes still closed she said, "Hello Col."

He stopped, still several feet away behind her. He was quite adept at stalking through the night. Her ears could only barely hear his footfalls.

"I..." There was hesitation in his voice. "I didn't mean to disturb you. I hadn't thought I'd been that loud."

She shook her head. "You weren't." She lied a little when she said, "And you aren't disturbing me."

She opened her eyes and turned to him.

The night was alive around her. Even just from that brief moment without her sight, using her other senses, she'd picked up so much and now she could see so much as well. Even with only the starlight, she could pick out details at the edge of the clearing. She could see the quirk of a smile playing at the edges of Col's lips.

"Good," he said softly. "It's late." He glanced back over his shoulder in the direction of the camp. "Are you well? You should be sleeping."

"So should you," she chided. She crossed the distance to him and took up one of his hands. "But this is something I need to do." She hoped her eyes conveyed her urgency and desire. She grimaced. "Besides, I don't need so much sleep these days anyway."

"Oh," he said, then looked away from her eyes to the clearing. "What was it you were doing?"

She laughed at his words. She hadn't been trying to 'do'

anything. "Nothing actually. I was trying to be. It's a long story, ask Ayneii."

At the sound of the sprite's name, as if summoned, she appeared.

"Hello you two."

Dalia spoke first. "Hello, Ayneii. You need to explain to Col the difference between being and doing."

"Do I?"

Col laughed. "Apparently, yes."

"And while she does that—" Dalia levered herself up to kiss him lightly. "—I'm going to go back to being." She smiled and turned at Col's slightly confused expression.

She'd made it only a few steps when a thought occurred to her and she turned back. "Ayneii?"

The sprite had only just started launching into an explanation of 'doing and being' and stopped in mid-sentence.

"Yes?"

"Can someone just be... with others around?" She didn't mind Col being there, but perhaps that would somehow disturb the process.

"You humans are silly. You can 'be' when you're alone or with others. It doesn't matter."

Dalia nodded, then addressed her next words to Col. "I'm going to... commune with nature a little. You can stay if you want, but I'm going to be... a little..." Her heart was pounding, but she knew that if she was going to do this, Col was the only one she would be comfortable doing it around. "I'm not going to let anything restrict me," she said finally. Her own modesty prevented her from saying much more.

"I understand?" Col said, clearly not understanding.

"Do you?" She demonstrated as she began stripping away her clothes. She wasn't sure why she needed to do this, but it felt right. It had been her plan all along to expose herself like this once she was here.

She heard Col's hushed. "Oh." After a moment, he added in a louder tone. "Are you certain you want me here?"

Dalia didn't hesitate. "You are welcome to stay. But I leave that up to you. If it were anyone else, I would send them away. But you..." She let the last of her garments fall away, and she stood before him naked. A shiver ran through her in that moment. "I don't want any secrets between us."

His gaze took her in with another breathy, "Oh." Then he nodded. "No secrets."

All of her senses were enhanced, even the brush of wind on her arm, the tickle of the grass on the soles of her feet.

She could feel his heartbeat through her life sense, the pounding rush of his blood. She could almost hear it. His scent changed, she smelled fear and excitement and longing.

She nodded to him then turned away and closed her eyes again.

Ayneii was droning on now about doing and being, but she tuned that out. She relaxed and cleared her mind once again.

"Just be," she whispered, and let her senses wander.

She focused on her sensations, to help herself experience this moment fully. The breath of a faint cool breeze on her skin made her hairs stand and gooseflesh rise. The earth was soft, yielding under her feet, the grasses wet. In the stillness of the night, there were so many sounds to her exceptional ears: the distant hoot of an owl, the chirp and hum of insects. One of those insects was circling her... a gnat, small and curious. It landed on her arm, and she could feel each of its tiny legs as it crawled around for a moment. The small thing was disturbing her calm. Yet she didn't want to raise an arm to swat at it or shoo it away. She wanted only to be still. So, she used her life sense to target it.

Go away, she said though the words were not spoken or even fully formed in her mind. They were a... feeling.

The small bug lifted off and meandered away.

Had she done that, or had it left on its own?

She tried an experiment.

Targeting the same gnat with her life sense, she sent it the message to... *return*. It had been on a direct course away from her, but it turned and a moment later was resting on her arm again.

She had done that. She was sure of it.

You can stay as long as you don't bite me, little gnat. It crawled around for a few moments longer then flew away. Perhaps with no food here it sought sustenance elsewhere?

She reached out to Col.

Can you hear this? she sent to him.

She sensed his reaction; shock and fear. A moment later he said aloud, "Dalia? Was that you?"

Yes, Col. I'm finding this 'being' very useful. It's so peaceful, I seem to be able to do anything!

She heard and sensed his breath of a laugh. "I'm glad."

She felt empowered. She let her senses seep farther out into the world as they had the night of the ritual. She could feel the camp and the other animals of the forest. She heard the whisper of wind through the leaves far away and could smell the fear of a rabbit diving for its hole to escape a fox.

She felt... open. During the ritual, she recalled now there had been something that felt like bubbles within her, welling up, each popping and revealing more of herself. There wasn't that same feeling now, but she did feel lighter, and with every breath, she drew in more awareness, not only of herself, but everything around her.

"Oh!" It was a surprised whisper from Col.

She wondered at the reason, then...

Everything changed.

She was connected to everything around her and, for a moment, she saw through Col's eyes. She saw her body, glowing faintly and floating, arching up onto her back, arms and legs relaxed, as if she were floating in water.

'Oh,' indeed.

For that moment of connection, she caught a thought in Col's mind: *she is the most wondrous and beautiful thing I've ever seen!*

Her heart opened to him, and through her connection, she let him know how she felt as well. All her admiration and affection for him poured out. There were no words, only the purity of her emotions.

"Dalia? Oh... Dalia," he whispered.

She drew in a long breath and forced her awareness to contract, back into her body, breaking her connection with the world.

It was a sudden thing, and she hadn't really mastered how to control her floating, which resulted in her falling several feet to land on her back with a grunt and huff of air.

"Very graceful," she muttered to herself as she levered herself up. Col was at her side a moment later.

"Are you well?" His brown eyes met hers, and for a moment, they looked into each other's souls.

While their gazes were still locked, she became quite aware of his hands... on her skin... and nothing else covering her. She was blushing furiously, she knew that, but she didn't care, not with him.

His gaze never wavered. He didn't care that she was unclothed, he just cared... for her. His next words were tender. "Did you find what you were looking for?" he whispered. "Were you able to... be?"

"Yes," she responded just as softly. "And I think... if I can keep doing this, I'll learn so much more."

"What you did tonight was rather intense." A wondering smile spread over his lips, and his eyes widened. "I could... feel you. I knew how you felt. It was amazing."

"You're amazing," she said, and pulled him close, holding him tight to her. There were tears in her eyes, emotion choking her hushed words as she said, "I don't think I could ever thank you enough for everything you've done for me."

His whispered reply soothed her aching heart. "You'll never need to."

She drew back, needing to see him. "I'm..." What words could describe how she felt? There were no words. She rose up and kissed him. They were both breathless some while later when they drew apart.

"All these nights," she said in a whisper. "That you've just held me. You have been so tender, so kind, so wonderful. I love you, Col."

"I love you too, Dalia." He drew her close, warm arms encircling her, holding her as he'd done so many times. She was still faintly connected to him and could sense in his heart only caring and warmth.

~

Zatharyn hurried to his study. He'd spent a significant amount of energy yesterday placing a general locating spell in the wide area around which he'd last sensed Colric and the Athernon girl. That had just sounded, a bell clanging within his own mind. He rushed to the looking glass to scry on his foes.

He had thought initially that if he did sense the girl again, he'd simply go to her, eliminate her, but he hadn't survived all these years and advanced to his position by being reckless. His caution won out. He would spy on them first. Then see if he needed to eliminate her now or not.

The scrying spell slipped from his lips once he was safely locked inside his room, and the looking glass blazed to life with a forested scene.

The two he sought were walking, hand in hand, with many others around them.

He needed to know what the girl knew, if she was at full potential yet. He wove a delicate spell, a powerful and invasive mind-bonding. He drew more power from his phylactery to do so, wanting to ensure that, if she was as powerful as he feared, she didn't sense him.

The spell pierced her thoughts and he began sifting through them.

He breathed a heavy sigh of relief. Then he nearly laughed.

He had nothing to worry about. She had advanced in her abilities but was still so very far from understanding all of it. Most of her thoughts were consumed with her love for the man with her. She was weak and distracted. He would have no trouble defeating her.

The question now became: should he claim her now or later? Her thoughts had told him that she was coming to him, so he could wait. That would give her another day to possibly unlock her full potential, but he did not believe she would be able to do it in such a time.

He decided to wait.

He'd also learned from her that the king was actively working against Lord Gariast now, using this Col to do so. That was a worry. Zatharyn doubted the king knew about him specifically, but he didn't want his powerbase to be undermined. Yet he could work with this. He would first make sure this upstart force was eliminated. If Gariast died in the process, Zatharyn was close enough to taking power that he could seize that moment and do so. If the lord didn't die in the fight… he could make use of the man a little longer. All outcomes favored him.

He dispelled the scrying and rubbed his ancient hands together with an excitement he hadn't felt in ages. He would truly enjoy dissecting Dalia's power and stripping it from her. It would be something new, taking power from someone other than a fey. He was quite happy, grinning as he made his way up to Gariast's formal study to tell his 'master' that their foes were on their way here and would soon be in their grasp.

25

DALIA CROUCHED, HEART RACING, HIDING IN A WOODED AREA TO the north of Gariast's estates. With her were Col, Tom, Nik, Jaff, and the ex-knight Trentin. Six of them against whatever resistance they might come up against.

She was sure that the pounding in her chest must have been heard, if not somehow felt, by the others in the group, but they all seemed calm. She knew they weren't. Her life sense told her of the pent-up tension within all of them, but they were controlling themselves and their composure much better than she.

In truth, she was less concerned about the upcoming raid than she was about whether or not The Fury would take control of her. She knew she'd learned so much since the last time it had, at Trentin's keep, but did that mean she had full control?

She'd been doing more sparring with Trentin over the last few days. The man had been quite helpful, working with her consistently. Col and Kellan had joined the previous day as well. Kellan had been dubious about her ability to fight. After the fourth time ending up on his rump, with her quivering to restrain herself from killing him, he admitted she was good. As it was, she was at a point now where she could evade an attack without automatically counterattacking, just getting out of the way. But she hadn't been in a situation where The Fury would be truly tested—where men were trying to kill her—until tonight.

Certainly, there were many other aspects of her abilities she was more comfortable with. The enhanced senses were second nature to her now and with them, the life sense. She could expand them out or contract them at will. But she was certain there was still so much she had yet to understand and that left her with a taste of doubt about how the raid might go tonight.

Her heart was also racing for Col. He kept his emotions tightly concealed, but she was closer with him than any other, and she knew how much was at stake for him. He was a mess of fear, determination, vengeance, hope, and strife inside. She hoped he found some peace after tonight. He'd done so much to help her find peace that she wanted the same for him.

"There they are," Col whispered.

She looked out into the night. The estate was to the south and could be made out in the darkness by a series of torches at regular intervals. According to Trentin, the eight-foot wall around the estate had guard platforms built at spots behind the wall where two men would keep watch. Over to the east, she saw what Col had pointed out. Their force had arrived, a line of torches in the night, across a tall ridge.

So far, everything was going as planned, though really, not much had happened yet.

"When do we go?" Nik asked.

"Soon," Col said. "Let's give the guards a moment or two to see that force and, hopefully, redeploy their troops to the eastern end of the compound."

They waited. It seemed like an eternity before Col finally said, "Let's go."

They ran through the night, slow enough to remain silent

and not trip on any uneven ground, which turned out to be not that fast, more of a jog.

Yet soon enough they reached the wall. Col had made sure they reached the center point between two guard posts, the darkest spot along the wall. Here they paused.

No alarm had sounded. No men were calling out. No one had challenged them. They'd remained unseen... for now.

Next, they had to get over the wall. Trentin was tall enough to reach the top with just a little jump and haul himself over, so he waited until last, giving everyone else a boost before clambering over himself. Then the six of them crouched in the shadow of the wall and waited.

Again, no alarm was sounded.

Peering across the vast expanse of the estate's grounds between them and the manor itself, Dalia's heart fell. On the map yesterday, it hadn't looked that far, but there was most of a mile to cross on level ground. There were no guards in their way currently, but that was a long way to go and not be seen.

The next step of the plan was to incapacitate the guards at the towers closest to them. This would hopefully give them a greater chance of crossing the open expanse ahead of them for two reasons. First, the guards on those towers might be looking in more than out, which was a risk they couldn't take. Second, if they subdued the guards and took their uniforms, they would have disguises when moving through the estate. Also, if there was no changing of these guards before they left, this would be their best place to leave the estates without being seen.

Col, Jaff, and Dalia went one way, slinking along in the shadows of the wall. Nik, Tom, and Trentin went the other. Her small group approached the base of their tower. Looking back through the darkness, her owl-like eyes could pick up the shadows of the other three men in the distance, also ready. Dalia was the means by which they would coordinate their twin attacks. The other three would go, and she was the only one who'd be able to see them and tap Col to let him know to go as well.

Tom's team began moving toward the ladder.

She tapped Col and he moved as well. She would go up last, Jaff would be first; the man seemed to have a thick skin and could take a punch or two without noticing. That, and his own fists were heavy things, meant for brawling.

Jaff ascended the ladder, Col right behind him. Dalia alternated between watching them and keeping an eye out around them.

Jaff threw himself onto the tower's platform and Col quickly followed. There was a clipped cry, not that loud and that was the only sound. Dalia took that as a good sign. If the guards had done well, they'd be making more noise than this.

Soon enough, Col and Jaff came down, now roughly dressed as guardsmen.

They had until the next changing of the watch, however long that might be. Trentin had told them the schedule as he'd known it, but it could have changed since he'd left.

The six of them met back at the spot between the watchtowers.

From there they set off, walking calmly toward the manor. It seemed to take forever. She and Trentin were the ones without guardsmen's uniforms. She'd have been too small for any of them and he'd have been too large.

Finally, the estate drew near. Nik and Jaff ran ahead to the guardsman at the side entrance they approached.

Jaff got close enough to grab the man and break his neck before he could challenge them.

Trentin tried to take what bits of this guard's uniform might fit him, but it was a motley look, which wouldn't pass any significant scrutiny.

They slipped inside through a servant's entrance that led almost immediately into a large chamber with several cots and chests, where servants would stay and sleep between shifts. There were a few confused looking men and women in this room who stared at them as they passed. None of the servants said a word, however. Dalia knew they would never question the actions of those above them, as odd as those actions might be.

Col chose one of the men in this room and approached him. Dalia's astute ears caught his quick conversation with the man.

"Hello, what's your name?" Col asked.

"Jasob, sir."

Col whispered intently to him. She heard the emotion rise in Col's hushed voice. "I'm told Gariast has a maid. Her name is Rissa. Do you know where she is?"

The man nodded. "She's in his suite."

Col just nodded to that and returned to the group. "Trentin, show us the way."

The once knight knew the estates well and led them through the corridors. They stalked through the estate, up a flight of stairs, to the second floor.

As they reached the top of the stairs, a group of guards met them, headed down.

Dalia tried to hide behind the larger form of Trentin, but it didn't matter. Their mismatched group drew too much attention.

One of the men in the oncoming group stopped and demanded, "Which of you is in charge? Who is your commander?"

"Lord Tandor," Trentin said quickly.

"Tandor's been missing for days now." The man was quite clearly very suspicious of them.

Trentin shrugged. "It was worth a try." Then he stepped

forward and punched the man in the face so hard the guard collapsed in a heap.

After that, it was chaos.

There were shouts, and an alarm was raised. The fighting was so quick that Dalia never even had a chance to push past the press of bodies and join. Her only moment of action came when a man raised a crossbow and fired at her. She spun out of the way of the bolt. That man had fallen to Col's sword before she could get closer.

That was it. If anyone had heard the fight their surprise was blown.

That's when she heard the curse from Nik behind her. She turned to see the man crouching next to the limp form of Jaff. The butt end of a crossbow bolt stuck out of Jaff's chest, the red feathers used for fletching were an odd match with the bloom of blood soaking through the man's clothes.

Only one bolt had been fired by the other men. The one meant for her. The one she'd dodged... had hit Jaff.

Dalia's emotions spun and squirmed within her. Her hands were over her mouth, tears in her eyes. Her body trembled as the immensity of this moment dropped onto her. Gods, this was horrible!

Was this her fault? She didn't want to die, but she hadn't wanted any of the rest of them to die either. She wouldn't have changed what she'd done, but... somehow, she still felt as if she could have done something different to have avoided this. She even saw it, a flash in her mind's eye. The Fury hadn't kicked in. She'd avoided it, but she knew how she might have moved quicker, she could have—with just the right motion at the right time—hit the bolt and sent it on a different path without hurting herself. She hadn't because she hadn't known it was going to hit someone else... but if she had known...

Col's strong arms were around her a moment later, and as

soon as she felt his body, she turned into him and sobbed. "I... I could have... he didn't..." Her words were muffled, and she couldn't seem to form a coherent thought anyway.

"Hush," Col said, rubbing her back. "This is not your fault. Men die in war."

"We don't have time for this. Leave him. We're close." Trentin's voice was hard, and in that moment, she hated the man for his callousness.

"Can you go on?" Col asked, his voice hushed, a breath near her ear.

She didn't have much choice. She nodded, stifling her emotions, and sniffling back her tears. She pushed herself away from him. "I'm well."

He looked like he didn't believe her, but their options were limited. Already, heavy-booted feet could be heard running toward them.

"They're coming," Nik said.

Now, with all her emotions running wild, she felt The Fury rise within her, burning like so much bile in her throat. Her voice was deathly quiet when she said, "Let them come."

26

"THERE, THREE DOORS DOWN ON THE LEFT," TRENTIN SAID, urging Col onward. Then he turned back to keep guard. More and more soldiers were swarming to meet them.

Not that the soldiers were a problem yet. Dalia was being rather frightening in her ability to dispatch whatever came at them. She was behind Col and the others, fending off any and all guardsmen. The remaining four of them were staying out of her way, as it was dangerous to get too close to her.

Col hurried to the indicated door. He kicked it in and was greeted by the sight of several armed men. He took in the room in a glance, even as he spun out of the way of several crossbow bolts shot at him.

"Get ready!" he called out to the others. They stayed back for a moment, waiting for his move.

A moment later, he dove into the room, rolling in low as more crossbow bolts went by overhead. He came up running, skirting around the side of the room as more bolts narrowly missed him. One crashed through the wood of a small sidebar, the other punctured a long couch and thudded into the floor behind him.

He had their attention, good. That would give the others time to get into the room as well.

He took in the situation quickly before diving behind a heavy pedestal supporting a statue. There had been eight men with crossbows firing in two lines, one kneeling, one standing. They were now dropping their ranged weapons and all drawing swords. However, there were more men than that in the room. Another four were already charging toward Col's position with weapons ready.

Another quick glance showed him that the eight covering the door were turning, coming for him. That would give his friends easy access to the room, but he was well outnumbered. Hopefully, he could keep everyone's attention until the others arrived and broke up the soldiers.

Col knew he was one of the best swordsmen in the kingdom, but twelve on one was something he'd never done before. Perhaps, if he could deal with the four charging him quickly, he might have a chance against the remaining eight, but that was still a stretch.

He spun out from behind the statue, leapt atop a small table, and kicked aside the sword of one of the men coming at him while blocking a blow from another. He stepped on one man's blade and quickly relieved the man of his sword hand. That left only three, then the other eight...

Though his friends were already entering. Hopefully they'd distract the eight other men.

He jumped off the table. They would have to come around it to get to him. Parrying a stab from one, he snaked a strike through that man's guard, piercing the man's sword shoulder. That one backed off, but one of the other men scored a hit on Colric's non-sword arm before he could back off and defend again. The wound wasn't deep and the layers of clothes over it would soon staunch the wound, but the pain gave him a boost of adrenaline and alertness. He managed to bind the remaining two attacker's swords together, entangling them, and then strike a deep cut on one of those men's thighs. That left him one-on-one with the last of the four men. He needed to take this man quickly.

Taking a step back, he hit a wall.

With a quick flurry of his blade, he befuddled the other man and was able to disarm him. He ran the man through.

Yet eight men were still charging at him. He couldn't see his friends any more. Why hadn't these men turned to fight the others? He didn't know what was going on and didn't like it. He tried to get away from the wall to give himself some room, but it was too late.

He was trapped, nowhere to go.

The eight pressed their attack, and he moved with the fluid speed of one who had practiced for hours on end and was also fighting for his life. He was a dervish of steel, but only just managing to block all their attacks. His only advantage was that the eight men couldn't all reach him at the same time. Only four attacked at once, but that was also their advantage. He was going to tire quicker than they, and with four of them still fresh, it was only a matter of time before his skill was not enough to fend them off.

A lucky stroke, knocking one of their swords down hard onto the sword hand of the man next to him dropped his opponents down to three, but he felt fatigue creeping into muscles and bones, and a new man stepped into the gap quickly enough.

"Throw down your arms!" the voice boomed over the clash of steel and the din of combat. In the next instant, there was an echoing silence as everyone froze. It was unclear which side had called for the surrender.

Colric couldn't see much until a few of those attacking him turned to see who had called out. His gaze flicked around the room in the brief instant of calm. There seemed to be men everywhere. He found Trentin, the large knight not too hard to find. He was back-to-back with Tom Willow surrounded by a half-dozen of Gariast's men. Apparently more had arrived. Where these new guardsmen had come from Col didn't know. He couldn't see Dalia, but there was still commotion out in the hall, which seemed likely to be her. Finally, his eyes settled on a most disturbing sight. Gariast had entered the room from a door on the far side from Colric—probably where those new guardsmen had come from as well. Gariast held Rissa, one hand around her slender torso, the other holding a dagger to her throat. Around him were ten more guards. He spoke again just as Colric's eyes met his.

"Your little band has failed Colric of Haverstal. Surrender now and I won't kill your sister." Gariast pressed his cheek against Rissa's head, sniffing her hair in a way that made Colric sick.

The other thing he noticed which enraged him was the mottling of yellow and brown over his sister's face which suggested many significant bruises in the process of healing. "I also have your two brothers down in my dungeons, which you will never find on your own. If you want your family to live, you will throw down your sword and surrender. You have lost."

Col's sword arm quivered. He was torn. He knew Gariast would kill his sister without any qualms if he didn't stop fighting. Yet as much as he knew that, he also knew the man would still most likely kill all his siblings even if he did surrender. At the same time, seeing Rissa there next to Gariast—and knowing his brothers were here somewhere, so close—so disturbed him it was a struggle to resist the urge to fight his way through and kill the bastard nobleman. Finally, his hand opened. His sword fell to the ground in a clatter and ring of steel.

At the very least, this might buy them all a little time. There was still a wild card yet to be played.

The men around him rushed in to grab him. One of them, with a vindictive look on his face, slashed him low on his side before putting away his sword and helping the others push him toward their master.

Col let out a yelp of pain and doubled over, but was quickly pulled and prodded to his feet, a few punches adding to his growing list of aches and worse. He gritted his teeth, enduring it all.

He could see Trentin and Tom surrendering as well. Nik was nowhere to be seen, and the commotion in the hall was still going.

Even Gariast noticed not all was calm and ordered his men to go and see what was happening.

One of his men responded after a quick look out into the hall. "There's a woman, my lord, she's fighting off all our troops, keeping them back."

"A woman?" Gariast's face spread with a disbelieving grin. He even laughed at the comment.

"It's true, my lord!" the man said insistently.

"She is mine." The voice came from somewhere behind Gariast, a small, aged man stepped forward and moved toward the door. Col noticed Gariast's reaction to the man. He stopped laughing, and a strange look crossed his face, fear mixed with loathing, and curiosity? It seemed odd, but that one look shifted the balance of power in the room, at least as Col saw it. Whoever this little man was, he was the one with the real power here.

What was happening?

Gariast was distracted, looking at the other man and toward the commotion in the hall, the noise getting louder, nearer. The knife he held to Rissa's throat fell away for just a moment...

Col surged forward, managing to get one hand free, reaching

for his sister... before something hard hit the back of his head, sending him to his knees. He let out a grunt as stars exploded through his vision. He was soon held again, more firmly.

"If you move again, I'll kill her," Gariast said softly. He looked like he was enjoying himself once again.

Rissa's head had been tilted forward, down. Now that Col was on his knees, looking up he finally met Rissa's eyes, and what he saw there drained the life out of him. She'd been such a spirited and joyful girl, but all that remained in her eyes now was a vacant look of resigned despair. She'd been broken. Gariast had done this to her.

Colric's heart tore and he felt hot tears come to his eyes. This was his fault. Sure, Gariast was the one to blame for the horrors that had befallen his family, but if Colric had been more savvy to the ways of the nobility three years ago, none of this would ever have happened.

He looked away ashamed.

He saw the small old man approach the door as a guard came flying, upside down, into the room, landing hard and sliding a few feet.

The wizened man stopped just short of the door.

Gariast muttered, "A woman? My arse!"

Then Dalia made her entrance...

...and any doubt was cleared away for all of them.

27

DALIA COULD FEEL THE DIFFERENCE IN THIS FIGHT.

The Fury was with her, but now she was in full control. She chose every action, every attack. The battle was slowed for her. She could see and hear and feel everything around her and had the time to make each decision. She felt the unity of her mind and body and even knew how to use the bits of magic that would enhance her strength, speed, and endurance. She *was* The Fury as opposed to the other way around. It was an amazing feeling.

So many men had come against her, and she was proud of the fact that none of them were dead. Some she'd left with broken limbs and no more, others wouldn't wake up for a while, but at least they would wake up.

She'd been backed up to the door to the room that Col had entered. A guard charged her. It was easy enough to evade his wild stab and redirect all that energy over top of her, sending him flying behind her into the room.

She didn't know what was happening in the room but figured if there were men still fighting in there, she didn't want the rest of these guards to get in as well. Taking a step that placed her in the doorway, she jumped up and grabbed the tiny ledge of the doorframe inside the room. On her swing back, she kicked out at the two men who thought this might be an opportunity to finally get to her. They both staggered back from blows to the head. She then swung backwards, spinning into the air to catch the top of the door itself and haul herself up.

For the briefest of moments, she perched on the top of the door. Then kicked it backwards, shutting it, as she launched herself into the room head first. She caught the collar of a guard who seemed to be simply standing there, and as her feet found the floor, she flung him back against the just closed door to make sure it had something in front of it to keep it blocked.

She stood, gaze taking in the room. No one was moving. She was used to people seeming as if they were standing still while she was magically enhanced within The Fury, but this was different. Everyone here was like a statue, still. They were all looking at her. Col was on his knees, being held. Trentin and Tom were also restrained. Lord Gariast was near Col holding a girl—Col's sister, perhaps? He had a look of surprised horror on his face. In front of her was an aged man, small, with a long white beard, and eyes which danced with power. She could feel this last one. Her life sense slipped over and around him. He felt strange... enhanced somehow.

In the stillness, while everyone else remained frozen, the old man reached a hand up for her, and she sensed magic building to be thrown her way.

She stepped in, grabbed his wrist, and twisted it, then spun, pulling him off balance and threw him toward the door.

He looked so surprised as he flew the short distance.

Then the others began moving.

One of Gariast's men moved toward Dalia. Her leg snapped out to the side catching the man in the groin. He went down groaning.

"Let them go," Dalia commanded, surprised at the authority in her voice.

"I think not, my dear." Gariast had recovered from his shock and was backing off a step. "And if you so much as twitch, I'll kill this girl."

She could feel The Fury build. She had done well at not killing anyone so far, but she desperately wanted to kill Gariast. After all the evil rumors she'd heard of him, and the even more vile truths she now knew, she did not think it wise to let him live.

"Dalia, please, she's my sister." Col's voice cut through her like a blade of ice, chilling her. Confirming her suspicion from earlier.

Gariast's expression moved through a moment of confusion to a sort of surprised glee.

"Dalia? The Athernon girl?" He laughed, and it was not a pleasant sound. "That is a surprise! I had thought framing you for the deaths of the Rossferol family was a lark. But it seems you could actually have killed them after all! Now I'll have witnesses to your 'possession' who can testify to the king before I hang you."

The words sunk in slowly. 'Framing her?' That meant that... Gariast had been responsible for the deaths of Padran and his family. He'd killed them, then conveniently dumped their deaths on her.

"It was you." She heard her own voice but didn't recall saying the words. Her vision turned red before her, The Fury only now threatening to take control of her once more as her anger flared.

Something rose out of her, a sound, unearthly. It began low, almost too low to hear, a rumbling growl, which grew in intensity until she was howling in pure hatred and rage.

~

So intense was the emotional eruption from Dalia that it seemed to split her mind completely from her body. She was outside herself, floating, looking down at the scene before her. Everyone in the room was caught up, frozen by the outburst of the small girl in their midst. There was a definite fear growing on the faces of some of the men. Gariast had used the word 'possessed,' and in that moment, even he seemed to believe that was exactly the case. His muscles seemed to go slack, the knife falling away from the girl's throat. His grip on the girl loosened. Others backed off, dropping weapons.

The old man was recovering quickly, and another burst of magic was being aimed at her.

Now was the moment to strike.

And with that, she was back in her body, in control.

The scream had cut off abruptly, and she stepped to one side as the magic from the man behind her erupted at her... and hit Gariast. The lord froze, still.

She launched herself forward, a single leap taking her to Gariast as she plucked the trembling young woman from the man's grasp. Yet where could she take the girl that would be safe? Behind Gariast was a clump of guards. There was another group around Col and a few holding Trentin and Tom as well.

Then suddenly the group behind Gariast all tumbled and staggered forward. Some of them fell into the lord who fell over like a statue, unmoving. Her quick senses caught the form behind the guards who had caused the commotion... Nik. Somehow, he must have hidden during all this chaos, sensing now would be the right time to act. She kicked out at two of the guards trying to regain their balance and sent them to the floor, then danced through them carrying Col's sister to Nik.

"Protect her. Get her out of here!" she said, then turned back to the room.

Only now were others in the room starting to react. Col was struggling to free himself, but the three guards on him had a solid hold. Trentin had freed himself and stolen the sword of the man who'd been holding him. He was in the process of freeing Tom Willow. Other guards were moving to help their comrades.

She needed to help Col.

ZATHARYN COULD NOT BELIEVE THIS GIRL. HE KNEW—HIS MAGE-sense not deceiving him—that she wasn't at her full potential. She hadn't come into her full power, and yet, she was still unlike anything he'd ever seen before.

He'd expected magical attacks from her, not physical. He could sense her use of magic, but it was only to enhance her physical abilities. He wasn't used to fighting someone hand-to-hand, let alone someone as quick and strong as she. He'd always used his magic when others threatened him with physical harm, but they'd been normal. She wasn't. He couldn't hit her with any of his attacks. He needed to try something else.

First, he released Gariast from the holding spell that had been meant for Dalia. The man squirmed and cursed, but Zatharyn paid him little mind after that.

Summoning a great surge of power from his phylactery, he shouted a command as a massive wave of magic radiated out from him hitting everyone in the room. She would not be able to avoid that. It should weaken and drain any it touched. It wouldn't hold them as his other spell did, but they would be stunned for a moment. That would give him time to recuperate and trap Dalia.

Yet he saw the wave affect everyone around him... except the

Athernon girl. She stood there, unaffected, head tilted to one side looking at him with curiosity. Then she was off, dashing around once again.

He couldn't believe his eyes. He himself was stunned for a moment. His magic had washed over her—he knew he hadn't missed—and done nothing!

What in all the pits of the cursed caves was this woman?

DALIA DID A FLIP FORWARD. SHE REACHED ONE HAND DOWN AS SHE passed over the form of a soldier and plucked a dagger from his belt. When she landed, righting herself, she threw the dagger. It hit one of the men holding Col in his shoulder, sinking to the hilt. He fell back with a scream.

Whatever the old man had done seemed to be affecting everyone, slowing them down. She wasn't sure why she hadn't been affected, or whether perhaps she had somehow been excluded from the spell. She wasn't going to question it now. The effect on the others, though, was quite beneficial.

She sent a kick to the head of another man holding Col, causing him to stagger back. A third man, directly behind Col was the last one restraining him. He too went down from a kick to the head.

Col was free.

Affected by the wizard's spell and probably still dazed, it took Col a moment to get to his feet. As she helped him up, her skin touched his and her life sense blazed to life anew with a detailed knowledge of his condition. He wasn't doing well. He'd been hit hard in the head and had a deep cut along his abdomen. Without even knowing how, she felt her energy flow into him.

Healing herself the other day with Ayneii had taken a lot of energy for one little cut. This now seemed a lot easier. It drained her, certainly, but not as much as that one tiny cut had. Perhaps she could only heal others? It was a question for later.

Col blinked. "Oh," he breathed, and straightened as his wounds faded.

Dalia made a quick scan of the room to see what was happening.

The old man seemed dazed himself, slowly getting to his feet. Gariast was kneeling next to a dead body, trying to take something from the corpse, Dalia couldn't see what. Trentin and Tom had freed themselves and were battling through guards toward the large glass doors to the balcony. That's where Nik was, helping Col's sister through the doors, letting in a cool night's breeze to the stuffy room. Guards seemed to be every-where, recovering or acting, moving in all directions. The door to the hall was being pushed open, and more guards were flooding in.

They needed to get out of here now.

"We have your sister, we need to flee!" she hissed to Col.

"My brothers!" he said hoarsely.

Another quick look around did not show anyone who looked vaguely like Col. "Where?"

"The dungeons."

She clenched her teeth. There was no way they were going to be able to fight their way down to the dungeons now. What else could they do? She was certain Col wouldn't leave without his family... all of them.

What could she...

A crossbow bolt slammed into her hip. She'd stayed in one spot too long.

She screamed and fell to one knee as a red bloom of blood spread over the side of her pants, seeping down her leg. Always before, during The Fury, if she'd been hit, the pain wouldn't register, those were glances and cuts. This was her hipbone shattering, and this level of pain was something unknown to her. The piercing, throbbing agony was almost too much to bear. She fell forward to her hands and knees, tears in her eyes making it difficult to see.

"Dalia!" She heard Col's cry. Strong arms wrapped around her, helped her. "You're right, we need to go!" he said softly, near her ear. She could hear the anguish in his voice. He didn't want to leave his brothers here. They'd die almost certainly after this.

She managed, with Col's help, to stand and stagger toward the open glass door to the balcony. She didn't know what they would do out there, but it was away... and that was all that mattered for now. The pain eased, The Fury adjusting to compensate, but she could feel the magic draining from her. She was nearing her limits.

Something sped past her arm.

Glass shattered.

Screams.

Another crossbow bolt had blasted through the glass door of the balcony and taken Nik down, passing completely through the man... and into Col's sister.

Dalia screamed, but it seemed like a distant thing. Col cried out as well and nearly dropped Dalia as he tried to hurry to his sister's side.

Col kept repeating, "Oh gods, no!" as they made their way to the heap of flesh that had once been Nik, and the groaning, curled up form of Col's sister. She was alive, for now.

"You healed me," he said to Dalia. "Can you do the same for her?"

Probably. But she hadn't even been able to heal herself. She didn't really know what had happened with Col, how she'd managed to heal him. It had just happened.

He set her down next to his sister, Dalia more collapsed than sat, her right leg was slick and warm with her own blood, and her hip still throbbed like it was on fire, but she put a hand on the young woman's forehead and hoped healing might happen.

Once again, she was connected intimately with the other body, seeing the damage... and it was extensive. Not only from the bolt lodged in her back but the myriad of bruises and cuts and damage in various stages of healing. This woman had been beaten severely... many times. Gods it was a horrid thing to know and feel.

"Can you help her?" Col asked.

"I think so," Dalia said, hissing through clenched teeth.

"We need to go, now!" This was Trentin's voice. Heavy foot-falls approached rapidly. Without looking, she knew it was Trentin and Tom.

Tom added, "There's about to be a whole lot of men out here, Trentin's right."

"I need a moment," Dalia said. Not only could she hardly move, but would take time to heal Rissa; she had no idea how long.

Trentin shook his head. "We don't have—"

"I'll give you what time I can." Col's voice was low, lethal.

She looked up at him.

He was crouched next to her. He rose. Grabbing Tom's sword from the stunned man, he stalked back toward the horde of men trying to get through the double doors onto the balcony. The men were led by Gariast... holding a crossbow.

ZATHARYN WATCHED NOW, CONFUSED, AND ASTOUNDED. IN THE chaos of the fighting, it had been easy enough to make himself unseen, though he was using more power at one time than ever he had before. He'd made his way onto the balcony before the doorway became jammed with men. Again and again, he'd tried to hold Dalia, to use his magic to restrain her... but nothing worked. She didn't even seem to be doing anything to actively resist. It was as if she was immune to his magic, at least anything he was using to try to capture her.

His next thought was to simply kill her, a great gout of fire should do the trick, but something within him hesitated.

He watched her, seeing the look on her face as the one man took up a sword and headed toward the oncoming wave of Gariast's guards. He knew that look well enough.

Perhaps he could use that.

COL HAD NEVER FELT THIS WAY BEFORE, SO FULL OF RIGHTEOUS wrath. He felt fresh, rejuvenated after Dalia's healing. He didn't know how or what she'd done, but he appreciated the result.

He reached Gariast, who led a group of guards out onto the large balcony. Ducking under a shot from the crossbow, he came up swinging, knocking the crossbow aside and lashing out with all the fury he felt at the two women he loved being targeted by this man. Gariast backed off. He could do nothing else with no melee weapon drawn.

Col scored a long gash across the man's torso from right shoulder to left hip as Gariast hit the wall of men behind him and could retreat no further. Col drew back to skewer the hated foe. As he struck however, one guard knocked his sword down such that his stab glanced along the inside of one of Gariast's legs, no more. Then men were filling in around him and he was quickly on the defensive.

"Kill him!" Gariast shouted, pushing back into the crowd, stealing another man's sword.

Good, as long as they were all focused on him, he was giving Dalia and the others time.

He fought as if possessed. Part of his training in the King's Guard had been fighting multiple men at a time, usually four, but as many as six. The advantages a single swordsman had against a group were limited. The main one being that often, if the group wasn't coordinated, men were more likely to get in each other's way then help each other when all attacking at once. Also, there was only limited space around the single opponent for those men to use.

As the guards crowded around him, the ones behind pushed those in front too close. They couldn't use their swords effectively. Col took a couple out while they were otherwise useless, but the circle around him quickly widened, men jabbing and lunging in at intervals. Col was able to evade many of the blows, dancing to one side, hopping, knocking aside their swords, but a variety of cuts began to mar his skin. He had to do something to break this pattern.

He charged one side of the circle. It was less bold and more stupid, but his goal was achieved. He pushed past the men there, bowling a few over, his sword cutting deep into one, then he was past the front lines. But he'd received a deep gash on his leg and another on his non-sword arm for the effort.

And immediately, he realized his mistake.

He was in a crush of men, and their weapons were useless... but so was his. They dropped their weapons and began punching him. And he couldn't avoid as many blows here as he had in the circle where his sword had been in play.

Men piled on around him bare-fisted blows landing hard all over. One had a dagger, which sank into his stomach and was left there. It only cut him up more as he tried to move and block and fight back.

His energy for resistance quickly drained away, and he was

left curled on the ground as kicks fell from all sides. Spots began to blur his vision. Tears streamed from his eyes at the pain.

He heard a call, though not the words. The attacks on him stopped, and he was thankful for that. He sensed, more than saw, men moving away from him, making room. A single pair of booted footfalls drew close, and he knew they would be Gariast's. He turned his head to look at the man. Only one eye was working; the other was swollen shut.

"Will you never learn, peasant? I will always win." Gariast held his sword with both hands, blade down, and drew it back to plunge it into Col.

Col had almost no energy left. He could roll to one side perhaps, but a better plan came to him. Reaching down he pulled the dagger from his gut and with a feral scream pushed himself up and thrust it into Gariast's thigh, twisting it. Blood poured out over his hands.

Gariast let out a pathetic wheeze of a cry as his sword fell from limp hands somewhere behind Col, clattering loudly as the steel hit stone. The man went limp.

The two of them fell together, Col's last energy spent, blood pouring from his own wounded belly. Oddly, he landed in such a way that he was looking out over the balcony. Through the legs of the guards around him, he could see Dalia and Rissa. His sister looked better, starting to rise.

At least he'd done what he'd meant to, given them time to get away. He could live with that... he could die with that.

Dalia was looking at him, her look of concern, worry, more...

He didn't have any breath left in him, but he mouthed the words, "I love you."

Then his eye closed and he was taken by darkness.

28

THE FLIGHT AWAY FROM GARIAST'S KEEP WAS A BLUR TO DALIA.

It had been a single-story drop from the balcony and Trentin's strong arms had caught them all as they jumped away. There had been little resistance as they'd fled to the wall and then beyond. Gariast was dead; his men were in disarray.

Dalia wanted to go back, wanted to cleanse that abominable place with fire after what they'd done to Col. She would have torn the estate down on all of them... if she'd had any energy left.

After healing Rissa, she'd felt empty, nothing left. Nothing but pain in body and soul. She'd been carried most of the way as they fled, and she'd succumbed to unconsciousness somewhere in that time as well. Her spirit had left her when she'd seen Col die. She knew he was dead. She couldn't feel him through her life sense anymore. If he'd lived, she'd have known it. Her bond to him was too strong. She'd be able to sense him no matter how far away he was.

He was gone.

And she was lost, her heart torn asunder.

DALIA WOKE TO DARKNESS AND WHISPERS.

She was laying on something soft if a bit scratchy. The voices nearby were low but clearly audible to her. At first, she thought they were next to her, but no.

She was in a place of complete darkness, or so she thought until she saw the faint lines of light outlining a door. A room? But where? The voices were not in the room, but not far outside.

"... so much blood and the bone is shattered. She'll keep bleeding until she dies. I can see no remedy. She shouldn't be alive now, and I have no idea how she made it this far without losing more blood..." A woman's voice, unknown to Dalia.

"We have to do something." Tom's voice.

"There may not be much we can do." From Trentin.

"We can't just let her die, not after... Col gave his life, so we could..." Tom sounded hoarse.

Dalia registered pain, but it seemed distant. She felt removed from her body. She tried to move, and the pain became immediate, slicing through her thoughts and sending her spiraling back into unconsciousness.

TOM SAT ON A HARD, WOODEN BENCH IN THE QUIET COMMON ROOM of the Dusty Road tavern. His thoughts were a little jumbled. A mix of concern for Dalia, horror at the loss of Col, and added to that, a great confluence of emotions at being back in his hometown... in the tavern where his mother had worked. Where...

He cut himself off from that train of thought. Gariast was dead and shouldn't haunt his thoughts any longer. Yet even in death, the man still plagued him. Valeesa's words from when he'd told her of his heritage came back to him: *you are not him*. It was true, but he couldn't shake the feeling that somehow, he would turn into some monster.

A soft hand on his shoulder startled him from his reverie. He looked up to see Pasira standing next to him. "You worried for your lady upstairs?" the woman asked.

Pasira had been, in many ways, a second mother to him. The daughter of the tavern keeper and a dear friend of his mother's, they had both worked here side by side for many years. She'd taken the place over when her father had grown sick and then passed on. She was in her fifties now, though somehow, despite the daily grind of running this place, she seemed younger than her years. There were only a few streaks of gray in her hair and a pleasant smile on her mostly unlined face. She was a plump woman with round cheeks on a round face and round body to match.

"That's not my lady upstairs," he said softly. "My lady is safe in the Sandren Forest for now."

"Oh?" Pasira said intrigued. "I'm glad you found someone, Tom."

He smiled thinking of Valeesa. "So am I." He gave a harsh laugh. "I doubt her father will give permission for her to marry me though. She's a bit... above my station."

"Love finds a way. A father's permission is only needed if you want to be on speaking terms with her family."

Tom laughed. "You make a good point." He sighed heavily after that.

"If not concern for your lady, what's producing these heavy sighs of yours?" There were no other customers in the tavern. It was still late at night. The force of King's Guards hadn't wanted to go far after the attack on the estate and Tom had brought them here, an hour's ride. They'd settled Dalia in a bed then he'd come down here to think. He couldn't sleep. The main force was camped outside of the town.

"A dear friend died tonight, and frankly it's... odd to be home again. I don't know what I'm feeling."

She sat beside him. "This friend, is that the Col I hear people mentioning?"

"Yes. He was our leader. I'm not sure we'll know what to do without him around."

"There is no one to take his place? Every good leader makes sure there is someone there to take up the mantle if he falls."

Tom sighed. "Col was a good leader, and he did choose someone... me. But I don't feel prepared to lead. There is a captain of the King's Guard around now. He'd make a better leader."

"Codswallop!"

Tom nearly jumped from his seat at the vehemence of her response.

"When you were a boy, you had a whole gang following you. They would have done anything for you, those boys, and did, most of which got them in a heap of trouble if I recall. What's so different now?"

"I..." He'd been about to reply with his rote phrase of 'I'm not a leader,' but stopped himself. He had been the head of a small band when he was a kid...

The memories flooded back to him. He'd been a little terror in his day and those few boys had been willing to do anything for him. So, what had changed?

He grimaced. That had been before he'd known who his father was, before the doubt.

Suddenly everything became clear for him. It wasn't that he didn't think he could lead; it was that he thought he'd be a leader like his father, a brute, not how Col had been.

Yet again Valeesa's words came back to him: *you are not him.*

And Col had been training him for some time. Tom had been in charge of their little band on a few raids and... he'd been the only one Col trusted with the secret details of his agreement with the king. Only he knew all the contacts needed to get a message to the king. It was his responsibility now.

He sighed. "You're right."

"Of course I am." She patted him on the shoulder. "Now get out there and be a leader to those men." She rose and headed back toward the kitchens.

Tom drew a long breath and hoped he'd learned more than he thought from Col.

He had to talk to Kellan and find out what the next move was... or tell him what the next move was.

That meant he had to figure out their next move between here and their camp. That gave him about ten minutes.

Sure, he could do that.

∾

MORE WHISPERS.

"What shall I do with you?" This voice was close, and Dalia's eyes snapped open to a faint light in her room. It came from no earthly source, but some apparition. The shape was familiar... the old man from Gariast's estates. He was looming over her, semi-transparent, a fire burning in his eyes. She knew it was no real man for there was no life sense there. But there was an emanation of magic.

"You're awake. Good, perhaps you can tell me a few things," the apparition said in a high yet gravelly voice.

"Who are you? Why are you here? Are you here?" Speaking hurt, any movement hurt. Her hip was still blazing like all the blackest fires of the cursed caves. She winced.

The image shook its head. "I do not know how you were injured by a mere bolt when..." He seemed frustrated, upset. She didn't much care. "I will tell you who I am and why I am here.

My name is Zatharyn. I have no family name nor toponymic surname. I am of nothing. I was abandoned by this world and for that everyone in this world shall suffer." He glared at her a moment longer, and she wondered at his pause. There seemed more he could say, but he refrained. "I am here to offer you a deal."

"There is nothing I want from you," Dalia hissed, not surprised at the venom in her voice.

"I doubt that very much." The apparition waved his hand, and his look at her changed, as if this were some sort of test. He was expecting something...

And she did feel something, but... didn't know what it was at first. It was a familiar sensation, something comforting and yet distant. It took her a moment longer of searching through the sensation to place it, and when she did, she became instantly alert.

Col was alive! She could sense him now.

Zatharyn must have noticed the change in her and nodded. "So, you can sense him? I had wondered if shielding him had had any effect." A smile spread on his face, a devious thing. "Are you ready to make a deal now, for him?"

She knew this was a bad idea, but she couldn't say no. She would do anything for Col. "Yes."

"Good. Then in a day's time, at the call of the midnight watch, be at the gates of Gariast's estates. I will return your man to you, fully healed even. But in return, you must surrender yourself to me. Your life for his. That is the deal." There was an evil glint in the eyes of the apparition.

Dalia was of two minds about this. She didn't like that this man had all the power. She knew she shouldn't surrender herself to him. Yet, he hadn't hurt her with his magic before. Perhaps she could defeat him once Col was safe.

"Agreed."

The apparition nodded. "Do not be late." Then the magic in her room dissipated, and the vision faded with it.

Dalia lay there for a moment in the dark trying to calm herself. She needed to be ready for... anything, but she was still laid up with a broken hip.

What could she do?

"Ayneii!" she whispered into the darkness.

A green glow lit the room as the sprite appeared. Ayneii shivered as her glow dimmed a little. She put her arms around herself as if cold, an unhappy look on her face. "Yes? Oh, Dalia!"

"What's wrong?" Dalia asked concerned. The small sprite was usually so chipper and spry. She seemed very unlike herself, so closed off and miserable.

"I don't like going this far out of the forest. Sprites can go beyond their usual realms, but it affects us. We're... diminished.

"Oh, I'm sorry." But she wasn't that sorry, this was too important.

Ayneii seemed to really look at her for the first time. "You don't look so good... Also, where is Col? I haven't heard from him in a while."

"I am not feeling so good, and Col's been captured."

"No!" Ayneii bobbed and fluttered about the room, agitated. "We need to do something!"

"That's why I called you here, Ayneii, I need your help."

"What can I do?"

"Can you heal me? My hip is..."

Ayneii flew down and landed on Dalia's stomach, kneeling to inspect the wound. "Oh... ow... that must hurt."

"It does, yes,"

The sprite turned her tiny head to look at Dalia. "Why haven't you healed it? Actually, what I mean is, why aren't you healing this quicker? It looks like you've already clotted most of the bleeding and are working to refit the pieces of bone back into place, but it's happening really slowly."

"Is it?" This was news to Dalia... but then something she'd heard earlier that evening from the whispered conversation outside her door came back to her. There had been a woman's voice she didn't know saying: *She shouldn't be alive now and I have no idea how she made it this far without losing more blood.*

"So... I am healing myself?"

Ayneii nodded. "Far quicker than any other human would, but not as fast as you could."

Dalia sighed. "I healed others... it came so naturally, I..." She'd connected with their life sense and it had just happened, fixing what was broken. Yet she was very intimately connected with her own life sense so... why wasn't this happening? It was like there was some block in place preventing her from seeing something... something so simple...

She lifted her head slightly only to slam it back into her pillow. "Why is this so hard?"

She felt the barest brush on her torso and chest, as Ayneii walked up to sit on her shoulder. Dalia wasn't looking, staring up into darkness, but she knew the sprite had moved. "You're resisting something."

"Do you know what?" Dalia asked, frustrated.

"I think so, yes."

"Please enlighten me."

A tiny sigh. "From what you've told me, you have developed a deep connection with your own body and spirit. You can sense things beyond human capabilities and feel connected with other beings. That is good. I think... I think you're resisting not being human anymore."

"Not...?" Dalia thought about that. Not being human? She'd accepted that... hadn't she?

Ayneii went on as Dalia considered this. "It sounds like

you're coming to terms with the part of you that isn't human, the fey in you. You see what it can do, and you accept that there are benefits to that. But you're held back from fully delving into that part of you because you want so strongly to still just be a normal human. That is what you are not willing to give up. You can heal others because that is a gift, something you can do that benefits others. You've accepted that. But if you were to heal yourself the same way... that wouldn't be normal. That wouldn't be human. Your body is already doing it on its own, but you aren't capable of doing it faster because... essentially... you don't want to."

All of this had a ring of truth to it.

She clamped her eyes shut. "Is it so bad to want to be... what I was?" She'd wanted to say, 'what I am.' Even that had been hard.

"I don't think so, no, but you wanted to know what was holding you back. I believe that is it. I can't be certain as you are blocking yourself from me, but from what I've heard you say..." Ayneii shrugged.

It made perfect sense.

Tears leaked from her eyes, clamped shut. They traced quick paths down into her ears, cold and uncomfortable. She wanted to wipe them away, or rise and have them fall normally, but she didn't move to do either. Instead, she found herself gritting her teeth.

I am what I am, she thought firmly. But what did that mean? What did she mean when she thought of 'what' she was? Was it human or something else? The answer was simple. Yes, she still thought of herself as human, not as some... mixed-up thing.

"What am I?" she said through her sniffles. Before Ayneii could answer, she clarified. "If I'm not human, I want a name for what I am, otherwise how am I to accept it?"

There was a pause before Ayneii answered. "Perhaps begin with what you are not. You are not human, no. You are not truly fey either. You are... unique to existence. You are something new. Or perhaps something that was defined long ago but has been forgotten. There is no name for it... so I guess that means you can create one."

Dalia sniffed back more tears. "Any suggestions?"

She could hear the excitement in Ayneii's voice when she responded. "Among the fey, it's always a great privilege to get to name a new thing. I've never had that chance before!"

Silence, yet through her life sense she could feel the sprite's excitement. Ayneii quivered with joy.

"How about... Half-fey? No... that sounds too mundane and is technically incorrect since we really don't know the exact portion of you that's fey. So... maybe Fey-line, Feyline? No sounds too much like feline. What about... Feylish?"

Dalia wasn't sure she liked the name.

Apparently, Ayneii agreed. "No, that's not beautiful enough. You deserve a beautiful name. Personally, I've always liked the human name Miranda, but that wouldn't work." Ayneii seemed to be rambling now. "You can't have a person's name for a classi-fication of something. That's just... weird. But maybe it could be something like that? Mirandara? Or perhaps Mirandoline?"

"Mirandine," Dalia said softly.

"Oh! I really like that! Yes! You can be a mirandine!" A pause. A hushed voice, tentative, "but if anyone asks, can you say that I came up with the name?"

Dalia laughed a little. "Of course. You did provide the inspi-ration for it, after all."

"Yes, I did! Oh, thank you, Dalia!"

"No, Ayneii, thank you." She drew in a long breath. The words came slowly. "I am not human anymore. I am mirandine." It still didn't quite sound right, not... true yet. She repeated. "I am mirandine. I am unique in this world." Which sounded interesting and intriguing... and lonely.

"Yes, mirandine! It's beautiful Dalia!" After a moment, Ayneii added. "Do you feel different?"

Dalia pursed her lips. Letting a long breath out through her nose.

"No." She shook her head. Another quick breath. "But it's a start. I just need a little time to get used to it."

"I understand." Ayneii sounded just the slightest bit disappointed.

"I am also tired and could use some rest." She laughed a little. "Maybe I'll feel more... mirandine after a good sleep." After a moment, she added. "And since I still seem incapable of healing myself without great effort, would you mind...?"

"No, of course, I'll heal you." Ayneii lifted off enough to flutter down to Dalia's hip. She crouched there for a moment, and Dalia felt a surge of... something. It was familiar, if backward. It was like what she'd done for Col and Rissa, but in reverse, being done to her. She knew she should be able to do this, and that only frustrated her more. But as Ayneii finished she calmed herself with several long breaths. She needed rest and getting worked up wouldn't help.

"All done," Ayneii said, taking to flight once more. "I'm going to see if I can find Col."

That didn't sound like a good idea, but Dalia wasn't really sure why. She felt compelled to tell Ayneii: "Be careful. He's being held by a wizard."

"A wizard? You mean a human with magic?"

"Yes."

"Oh." Ayneii sounded scared. It was odd to hear from the tiny being who was usually so excited and full of life. Dalia had the feeling that there wasn't much that scared a sprite. "I'll be careful then. Thank you, Dalia." And Dalia sensed the sprite was gone.

She opened her eyes to the darkness once more.

"I am mirandine," she whispered.

Still nothing.

She shook her head and concentrated on sleeping.

Sleep did not come despite time slipping by. She was exhausted, but her mind would not rest.

She was plagued by strange thoughts and images: a dwindling light, trapped in a dark place trying to get out; the sounds of many voices screaming yet silent; a single terrible form, giant and hideous laughing at their pain... so much pain.

Then Ayneii was back in her room once more, shivering with agitation. "Dalia, I can't find Col!"

29

ZATHARYN PACED THE ROOM THAT HAD ONCE BEEN GARIAST'S study—the one up in the estate, not his secret one in the dungeons. Servants had cleared away the dead that had littered the room and thrown them into a great bonfire that burned out in the yard in the predawn twilight.

He was planning.

He'd already written out missives to the lords who'd served Gariast, ones he'd been courting for a while now, letting them know their liege was dead and to convene a hearing for who should replace him, taking his lands and chattels. He already knew the result of that meeting. It would be him, but he needed them here to convince them all. It would be much easier to mold their minds with his magic if they were all in one place.

But there was a more immediate concern.

Dalia.

He stewed over her.

She still wasn't in control of her full power. Yet somehow, she could easily evade his magic, shrug it off. He wasn't sure if she knew that yet, but if she was smart, she'd figure it out from what had happened earlier that night.

His one advantage was the man in his dungeons. That was how he could control her, but... that was where he came to a crossroads. If he did give the man over as he said he would, he'd have no leverage, and if she decided to fight him she'd be free to do so, and he did not yet know how that would play out. So, he did not want to risk it. But if he didn't hand the man over, that might spark her to challenge him, and again he didn't know how that would play out.

He toyed with the idea of asking her to take her own life and only then would he give up her man, but he doubted she'd be so stupid as to comply, not knowing how things would transpire after her death.

He did have a number of spells he could cast on the man to ensure her cooperation, nasty ways for him to die that could be triggered from a distance if Dalia didn't do as he wished. But he'd have to tell her of his spell, so she'd know the consequences of her defying him, and if he did, would she see that as some trick on his part? Would she risk what might happen to her man by assailing him? He could try to enchant the man to kill her if she did try to flee with him, but that was an iffy plan at best. If she found any way to undo his spell or subdue the man himself, then she wouldn't die and Zatharyn would have given up his leverage.

It was infuriating!

None of this would be an issue if he could simply trap her and study her in peace, but he didn't know how to do that. Everything he'd tried last night had failed.

He could simply kill her... but he wasn't even certain his offensive spells would work on her if his other spells hadn't. He couldn't risk starting a fight.

But it need not be he who killed her.

He'd seen her fighting prowess, but he'd also seen her get hurt from Gariast's crossbow bolt. She could be hit and hurt and potentially killed by mortal weapons. Trying to get her lover to kill her might not work because of the magic compulsion she may or may not be able to undo... but getting others to hurt her...

"Captain!" he called out.

A man entered swiftly, having been waiting outside the door. This man, Hillion by name, had been one of Zatharyn's first contacts. He was the captain of the forces stationed within the estate, commanding five hundred men. He knew he'd need this man to follow him once Gariast was dead, so he'd been molding his mind for some time to make him more... pliable.

"How many men had Gariast gathered here before the attack last night?" Gariast had added several hundred men to his forces here in preparation for the attack, knowing a sizable force was coming at him. The real question was: "And how many of those are still here?"

Hillion snapped to attention. It was good to see one's followers so obedient. "Sire, with the casualties last night, the garrison here is down to four hundred and sixty-three able-bodied men. In addition, two full cohorts are waiting out in the bailey but were never used. Those men remain, a full thousand."

"Fourteen hundred men?"

Hillion nodded.

Zatharyn smiled. Even if Dalia came with the same army that had threatened them last night, he was certain that would be enough to crush both her and her forces.

"Good. Ready them. There may be another force assailing us tonight at the High Call of the watch."

Hillion nodded. "Is there anything else?"

Zatharyn was about to dismiss the man, but a thought occurred to him. "Is there any possibility of getting more men before this evening? Any local lords we can call upon who could make it here in that time?"

Hillion seemed to consider for a moment. "Lords Perid and Hosl are close enough to be here within a half-day, shall I send a bird for them?"

"Yes. Demand they bring all of their forces. How many would that be?"

"Perid has a full cohort, Hosl is a lesser lord with only a few dozen men, perhaps a hundred all told. So, six hundred men perhaps?"

"That would be splendid. Two thousand men should be more than enough. Go and summon them."

Hillion nodded and left.

Now he had a plan. He wouldn't need magic at all. He had people to play with, and he would use those at his disposal to kill Dalia and her allies. Then he wouldn't need the man in his dungeons at all.

Though he couldn't dispose of the man yet. He needed Dalia to sense her lover was alive, so she would come willingly, ready to submit.

Feeling more assured of his plans, he summoned a servant and had his breakfast brought to him. He was the official lord of the manor now, and he was going to take advantage of that station.

~

"WAKE UP, YOU BIG LUG."

Col woke with a start, flashing to consciousness from some dark dream...

Had it been a dream? He'd been certain he'd died. Yet he felt alive now. Though in truth he had no idea what a person felt like after they died. Perhaps he was in the everlasting fields... or cursed caves of the underworld, though he liked to think that he was not the type of man who'd have gone to such a place.

As his eyes became accustomed to the darkness, he picked out bits of his surrounding, and it was no eternal paradise. In fact, he was quite sure it was a dungeon. There was some light, though it was faint, perhaps some torch far down the hall outside his cell. It was enough illumination for his eyes to make sense of at least some of his surroundings. He was in a cave-like room carved from rock all except for one side, which was a line of iron bars. There was a small gate in the bars, but it had a heavy lock on it.

And if he was in a dungeon... he'd have to be in... Gariast's dungeon... or the cursed caves if he was dead.

He didn't feel dead.

But, wasn't Gariast dead? He'd thought he'd killed the man clearly enough. But he too should be dead and apparently wasn't, so anything was possible. He felt where his wounds should have been. They were completely healed... like when Dalia had healed him. It made no sense. Who else could heal like Dalia?

"You can't see me, can you?" The voice startled Col, and he looked around, but saw no other person in the cell. Admittedly, it was quite dark, but he could make out deeper shadows in the cave around him, and none of them seemed human shaped. Before he could say anything, the voice added, "I forget some-times that you mortals need light to see."

Mortals?

Light blossomed around Col, and he squinted and blinked at the sudden brightness.

"Is that better?"

It took a moment of adjustment before Col could see much, but when he looked around again, he understood why he hadn't seen the owner of the voice the first time. He'd been looking for a full-sized man, and this was... not.

Leaning against one of the rough stone walls was a small

man. Instantly, Col recalled Dalia's description of the fey she'd met in the forest, the bogey. *His skin was gray as slate. His body was mostly slender but with a round potbelly. He wore no clothes, but his features were indistinct, so it wasn't that brazen. His ears and nose were both far too long and both ended in sharp points.*

That's who spoke to him now.

"You're a bogey," he said softly, awed and confused. Why was this fey here with him now?

"I am." The silver-skinned fey bowed. "I'd give you my name, as I believe that is polite amongst mortals, but it would serve you little, and I shall not be here long."

"What do you want?"

The bogey laughed. "That is not the question. The question, Colric of Haverstal, is what do you want? Also, please phrase your desire with the word 'wish' before it."

Col didn't understand at first. "What do I want? I want—"

"Wrong word."

Col stopped. Something about this felt wrong. His mind flashed to Dalia's tale of meeting this fey. She'd... she'd wished for adventure and excitement and received all manner of strange abilities. Now this fey wanted him to make a wish as well.

"And if I make a wish? What will be the downside? Dalia did not get what she wished for. Not how she intended it anyway. So, if I make a wish, how am I to know what might befall me?"

"You are a keen one, aren't you?"

Col didn't respond to that.

The bogey sighed. "It's taking far too much of my strength simply to be here, so I'll try to make this quick. I am a creature of chaos, so my... boons come with unpredictable effects at times. But I promise you this. Right now, your goals and mine align. We want the same thing, even if you don't know it yet. Trust that what you receive, whatever it may be, will be exactly what you need to achieve your goal... and help me achieve mine."

Col grimaced. He wasn't going to get a straight answer. Yet he had no other options.

He nodded. "I wish to be free of this place."

The bogey smiled. "That wasn't so hard, was it?" He closed then opened his hand, and a key appeared in his small palm. He tossed it to Col who was too surprised to catch it. It clattered to the stone floor with a high metallic clinking. "It will free you from this cell."

Col reached for the key, but his hand hovered over it. Something stopped him from touching it. What else might it do to him? In the end, it didn't matter; he'd accept the consequences as long as he could be free.

He grabbed the key... and nothing unexpected happened.

"Thank you," he said, looking back toward the bogey, but the small fey was gone. His own words echoed around the stone cell as the ball of light that hung over him began to dim. He scrambled to his feet, then to the door, reaching around the bars to the lock on his gate-door. The key fit perfectly and clicked when turned, the lock opened.

Col slipped out of his cell.

Dawn broke. The sun was creeping up over the horizon far to the east. Dalia knew this despite being in a room with no windows. It was yet another thing she didn't fully understand or yet control.

"Tell me again what happened. This time a little slower, Ayneii." She was sitting on her bed now, having had no luck lying down and trying to rest.

The sprite's first rendition of events had been at such verbal speed as to seem like one long word.

Ayneii took a long breath. "I can sense Col. I know where he is, but when I try to go to him, I... it's the strangest feeling like I'm just being bounced back to where I started. So, I tried travelling to him in the physical world. We sprites can move quite fast if we want to. I got as far as some large house with a great span of land and a wall, but I could go no further no matter how hard I tried." She stopped, her high-pitched voice trembling. There was something in those tremulous tones, a terror?

"What? What happened?"

"Well," Ayneii began slowly, and the fear in her voice became a palpable thing, emanating from the sprite. Even the fey's green glow seemed to shift color, darker, duller. "I... I tried to push through the barrier. I couldn't see it, but I could feel it. But when I did... oh, Dalia, it was horrible! Some... something in the barrier... it grabbed at me. Suddenly, I didn't want to get past it anymore. It was trying to pull me in. It felt like it wanted to... to devour me! I only just managed to pull away and I came right back here! Dalia, if that's where Col is... something terrible is going on there."

"It's probably some spell of that wizard. He is a nasty one. I'm learning that quite quickly. I wonder if we got rid of one monster only to replace him with another." She rose. Her hip was still sore, but more in a remembered-pain kind of way. After a few paces around the small room, it seemed to ease. Speaking her thoughts out loud she muttered, "I have less than a day to either free Col or find a way to beat that same wizard." She didn't really feel capable of doing either at the moment. She sighed heavily. "Any thoughts?"

Ayneii shook her head and fluttered about frantic.

Dalia agreed with that sentiment. She remained still for along moment trying to think, but it came to nothing. Even with all her new abilities, her mind was still hers, and she didn't know how to plan this sort of thing. "I need Col. I've never done anything like this. If only I could speak to him." Yet even as she said the words, an idea came to her. "Ayneii, that wizard, he was able to appear in my room without actually being here. Do you think I could do the same thing? Appear to Col without actually leaving this room?"

Ayneii paused in her agitated flight. "Maybe. We sprites have no need to do anything like that since we can simply be next to someone if we want to talk to them. But... we can also far-speak to other sprites at times as well. We stay where we are, but our voice reaches them wherever they are. It's a bit more efficient than actually going to them. What you're saying sounds like that only you're projecting more than just your voice."

"How would I do it?"

Ayneii made a face. "I wouldn't know how to explain it. It's something we just learn to do on our own."

"I don't have the time!" Dalia was growing frantic. "I know I still have so much to learn, but I need to be ready for whatever happens tonight. I can't spend days learning how to 'be,' not anymore. Whatever I am... whatever I can do... whatever it means to be mirandine... I need to know that now!"

"Maybe I can give you some time!"

"What? How?"

"There is a way. Wait here for a moment." Ayneii vanished.

Dalia paced nervously.

The door to her room opened and a plump woman of middle-years appeared. "You're up?" She seemed quite surprised. "But..."

"I heal quickly," Dalia said by way of explanation, knowing it sounded impossible.

The woman nodded, her surprise quickly fading. Though there was something in her look that told Dalia she didn't really believe what she was seeing. "It's just morning now. Would you like something to eat?" The tone was polite.

"Yes please, I'm famished."

The woman nodded. "I'll bet you are." She turned to leave then turned back. "Apologies for my manners. I'm Pasira, and this is my tavern you're staying in. It's a pleasure to meet you."

"I'm Dalia, and the pleasure is mine. Thank you for your hospitality."

"I don't know you from a hole in the wall," the woman said bluntly, but her tone eased when she said. "But you're a friend of Tom's, and that makes you near as family. I'll bring you something shortly."

Dalia nodded. "Thank you again.

Pasira left, closing the door.

Ayneii reappeared, but she wasn't alone; there were a host of sprites with her. "We're going to do a ritual which distorts time as you feel it. You'll move through this day far slower than everyone else. Time will stretch for you, so you'll have more time to relax and find yourself, your mirandine-ness."

Dalia smiled. "Thank you, Ayneii. Is there anything I need to do?"

"No, just relax; we'll take care of everything. Just focus on finding what you're missing within yourself.

"Understood." Dalia sat cross-legged on the floor as the fey around her began a wild and intricate dance, much like the night of the ritual to find herself. But after a moment, they began to slow, as if moving through the air more like water. Then they grew slower still until they seemed to be stuck in the air, barely moving at all. It was only after long moments if Dalia looked away then back that she could tell the tiniest movement had occurred.

Good. She had time. That helped immensely. She could relax and as Ayneii said 'find what she was missing within herself.'

She closed her eyes and began with what she knew, sinking into her senses and slowly connecting with everything around her.

COL HAD ACQUIRED A TORCH, TAKING IT FROM A SCONCE ON THE wall. It was no normal flame dancing atop the metal shaft. It produced no heat and was burning without any source Col could tell. It was a fey-flame, but he didn't know how or why it was here. He didn't question it too much though, as he needed the light to move through the dungeons.

He was moving slowly. He didn't want to come across any guards or the dungeon-keeper unaware. He'd passed several empty cells before he came to one that was occupied.

He stopped, stunned, as the man inside blinked at the light.

"Col? Is that you?" The voice was hoarse and weak, but so very familiar.

"Jaidan?" Col couldn't quite believe his eyes. He'd known, somewhere in his mind, that his brothers were being held in Gariast's dungeons, but he hadn't recognized Jaidan at first. The man before him, despite wearing his brother's face, looked so different, emaciated and weak.

"Col!" Jaidan scrambled to his feet, but it was a series of jerky, trembling movements. The man could barely stand on his own! He stumbled to the bars. "Can you get me out?"

Col had no words. He brought forth the key the bogey had given him. Setting the torch in a sconce nearby, he moved to the lock on Jaidan's cell. The key slipped in... but it wouldn't turn.

His heart fell, and he looked into his brother's eyes to see hope fade. "You're another illusion, aren't you? You're not real!" The pain in Jaidan's voice was heartbreaking.

"No! I promise you, I am here and I'm real." Col gave up on the key and retrieved the torch. He bashed at the lock with the heavy metal shaft of the torch, even tried prying the lock-free, but only succeeded in denting and bending the torch itself. Whatever these locks were made of, it was stronger than these torches. Despite being in rough-hewn cells and halls, there were no loose stones to try to break the lock with. Col doubted stones would work anyway.

Jaidan had watched with a mix of terrible hope and skepticism.

Col knew he could do nothing at the moment, but he had to

reassure his brother somehow. He reached through the bars and caught his brother by the shoulder. "I don't have the right key, Jaidan. I'll go find a key and come back, I promise."

"Col?" The word was squeaked out in a pathetic voice.

"I'm here, Brother. Don't worry. I will return."

Some glimmer of true hope appeared in the man's eyes. "Bear is in the next cell, I think." Bear was their nickname for his other brother, Berris.

Col nodded. "I'll go see. I promise I'll return as quickly as I can."

Jaidan nodded, his gaze still halfway between hope and despair.

Col tried to embrace his brother as awkward as it was through the bars. Then, with a final, "I'll be back," he took up his torch again and moved on.

Jaidan had been right, Berris was in the next cell. He still had some muscle on him and seemed physically healthy enough, but when Col tried to talk to him, Berris only stared at him with unseeing eyes.

It nearly broke Col to see that lifeless gaze.

Berris had always been the biggest of the three of them, well-muscled, but never as quick of mind as Col and Jaidan had been. It seemed he hadn't coped well with what had happened to him here.

Col moved on with heavy feet and a heavier heart. His key hadn't worked on Berris' cell either. He began to curse that bogey, who'd given him a key that would free only him... and no one else.

The dungeons were extensive, but Col searched through them carefully, looking for any guards, any keys, anything to help free his brothers. But other than other prisoners in cells— which he could not free either—there was no one here. Eventually, passing through the torture chamber, he found what he assumed was the way out. There was a small hallway with three doors; the one straight ahead was heavy wood with iron bands for reinforcement.

But his key wouldn't work on that door either. It hadn't worked on anything other than his own cell. Nearly defeated, he tried the key on the door to his right.

It clicked, revealing a small study.

Before exploring that small study further, he tried the door on the left. The key did nothing there.

Odd. His key only worked on his cell and this one other room? How could that be?

The words of the bogey came back to him: *your goals and mine align. We want the same thing, even if you don't know it yet. Trust that what you receive, whatever it may be, will be exactly what you need to achieve your goal... and help me achieve mine.*

Col wanted to escape and free his brothers, but he couldn't, not with this key as it was. But the key did unlock this one other door. Did the bogey want something from here? What exactly were the fey's goals?

He had too many questions and not enough answers.

But there was something about this room...

Perhaps there were keys in here?

Col set the torch in another sconce and began searching.

DALIA WAS FLOATING.

She was aware of this through her enhanced senses. Her eyes were closed, but she'd felt the floor fall away not long ago, and now her arms and legs were fully relaxed as if she were in some invisible chair of air supporting her. She was fully aware and connected with everything around her. She could 'see' the tavern in which she was staying, feel the many people in the village around her, as well as the army camped not far away.

This level of awareness, this distance of 'seeing' and feeling the world, she'd been able to do before. Now it was time to go further... deeper.

She had a mantra now that she hadn't had before: *I am mirandine; just be mirandine.* When she felt her concentration slipping away, or she felt any resistance to pushing farther, she repeated that to herself internally.

Last night she hadn't fully accepted the new name. There was something about not being human, about being unique which had been hindering, lonesome, distant. But now, in this place, feeling so connected to everyone and everything around her she knew she'd never be alone as a mirandine. More than that, she knew she had Col, who accepted her no matter what. Somewhere in realizing this, she changed her mantra to: *I am mirandine, and I am loved.* Now she felt safe enough to delve into the full depths of this new being.

She didn't really know how to discover things, to search for things in this place. She pictured some of the things the wizard had done, tried to conceptualize how she might do them: throwing her image and voice to another place, holding another person in place, frozen. And the more she simply concentrated on those things in this place, suspended between worlds, she came to know them. This was all it took. Time and the will to learn, to know, to seek what lay within her.

And as she relaxed more and more into this place, she came to know so much.

She knew the world, stretching out to see far off lands. First those she knew of, Forsea and Santhine. She caught a glimpse into a court hearing at the Santhine palace, the king listening to petitions and arguments, judging and settling each. Next to the king was the new queen. Their last queen had died in childbirth, too old perhaps to have another child after their prince had been killed... by Col. The new queen was young and radiant and carried two children, twins in her arms. Even at the same time as she experienced this, she was with the Forsea as well, they were wild horsemen with bronzed skin and a fierce warrior culture. She caught a fight, between two women no less. Both were fit and strong, covered in tattoos, they fought with knives, a duel to the death. The victor, the leader of her tribe, had retained her place of power and returned to her brood of husbands. And beyond this, she saw lands she never knew existed, with vast hills of sand, or people with skin like ebony. She saw oceans covered in islands of ice and the small people who called that home. Farther and farther out and away—even into the heavens and the burning heart of the sun.

At the same time, she delved inward, seeing the world that was her body and all of what lay beneath her flesh, both seen and unseen. Her muscles and bones were just a beginning, she became the sinews and understood how they worked. More than this, she felt the great pulse power laying untapped within her core. This, she knew upon discovering it, was her true self, her potential, what it meant to be mirandine.

She dove into that orb of energy... And with that final link, she felt something unlock within her.

She wasn't just connected to people and the world around her anymore. She was an integral part of all existence. She was energy and form bound into one being.

Everything made sense now. She blossomed with power. It filled her as she put her legs down to touch the floor and broke her trance.

The fey were still in the midst of their ritual, slowing time. She could feel its effects palpably now, how everything beyond the circle of fey was slowed. She stepped out of the affected area and felt a rush as she adapted to the pace and flow of normal time.

"You can stop now, Ayneii. I have what I need."

The sprite flew out from the wild dance and hovered before her. "Oh Dalia, you certainly do! Can you see yourself? You're... beautiful!"

Had she changed? She laughed at that thought. Of course she'd changed, but she'd thought it only an internal transformation, not physical. It would be easy enough to find out.

She closed her eyes and stepped her awareness outside of her body. This would be how she'd go see Col in a moment, but for now, she simply turned to look at her physical form.

"Oh!"

She had changed. She was glowing with a faint golden light and... she had wings! Wings just like Ayneii's. They were long, fragile, gossamer things, shimmering in a rainbow of colors. It was... beautiful, as Ayneii had said. She'd never thought of herself as special or beautiful before, but this was different. It was so much more than just her physical form. She was... mirandine, and it was wonderful!

She pushed herself back into her body, feeling heavy and restrained for a moment before adjusting.

She could feel her wings. They weren't physical, but a projection of her magic, a manifestation of what made her mirandine. She moved them slowly back and forth before dispelling them. She didn't need them now, and they might unduly distress those around her.

"Thank you, Ayneii. I feel... complete now. How much time has passed?"

"I don't know how you think of time, but it is still well before the sun is at its peak. I wouldn't say it was long.

The door to Dalia's room opened and Pasira entered with a steaming bowl of something. So, it hadn't been that long at all, perhaps only a few minutes. The fey around her giggled and tittered as the other woman passed through where they had been. They danced away at the last instant, leaving Pasira's nose twitching.

"Thank you," Dalia said, stepping forward to take the bowl. It looked like some thick stew. Stepping back—with Pasira and Ayneii, and the other sprites all before her, the one of them oblivious to the existence of the others—she smiled and said, "Thank you so much," to all of them, a tear in her eye.

Pasira seemed a little confused at such emotion but nodded. "You're very welcome, dearie." She scratched her nose then nodded and stepped out, closing the door.

The other fey left, vanishing.

Ayneii bobbed happily about the room. "Oh Dalia, I'm so glad you've found what you were looking for!"

"Me too," Dalia said as she sat and began eating. She was halfway through her first spoonful of stew before realizing... she didn't need to eat anymore. Yet she finished the meal because it sure tasted good to do so. "And when I'm done with this... I'll go and see if I can find Col."

COL LEANED AGAINST THE HEAVY DESK IN THE LARGE STUDY, WHICH he assumed belonged to the jailer. There were books on torture as well as other tomes he'd not been able to understand. He'd searched the room as thoroughly as he could without disturbing too much. If there was something he was supposed to find in here, he had no idea what it was. He'd also hoped that if this was the jailer's rooms there'd be keys in here to free his brothers, but he'd found none. He stared at the key the bogey had given him and tried to understand what was happening. He couldn't free his brothers, nor could he actually even free himself from the dungeon area. Perhaps it had been a good thing his brothers hadn't been let out. It would have been cruel to give them hope only to find out they were still ultimately locked down here... wherever here was. But if this key only unlocked this one other door... then what was it he was supposed to find or do here?

And how did getting into this room achieve Col's goals? Col wanted to get out of here to return to his friends and defeat Gariast and his minions, if that hadn't already been achieved. Finding himself having been put down here seemed to indicate it hadn't. Had the bogey lied? That didn't seem out of character from what he'd heard of them from Ayneii.

But...

If he couldn't get out...

Was there something here he could do, or use, to defeat Gariast? That was the only thing he could think of, but what was it?

"Col?"

He jumped, his heart pounding like a hammer on a smith's anvil. He spun around and... saw Dalia in the room with him. Only she was a ghost. He could see through her and she shone with some golden-white aura.

"Are you dead?" he couldn't help but ask. His heart lurched at the thought.

"No, Col. But this is the only way I can speak to you for now."

"How...?"

"How do I do any of the strange things I can do? This is the bogey's magic. I am... different now. I've accepted that."

"I'm just glad you're alive." He didn't know if he could touch her, but he was sure going to try. He strode over to where she was and reached out, but his hand moved through her translucent form.

"Ooh!" Dalia seemed to shiver or shudder. "I could... feel that. It was strange."

He hadn't felt anything other than an odd sensation. He didn't know how to describe it in normal terms. The best approximation was that she felt like... liquid light. Somehow, that seemed appropriate for Dalia.

"I wish I could..." How did he want to end that? He decided now wasn't the time for holding back. "I wish I could hold you, kiss you. I love you, Dalia."

She smiled with such joy; he could see tears in her eyes. "I know, and I love you too." For a moment they just stood there, being close to each other while so far away.

Finally, she looked around. "Where are you?"

"I think this is the jailer's study in Gariast's estates."

"Seems an odd place for them to keep you?"

He laughed. "I was in a cell, but your bogey helped me escape."

Her eyes went wide. "What did he... are you...?"

"I'm fine. He gave me a key and I think that's it. I feel no different, but the problem is the key only got me out of my cell. It doesn't unlock the door out of the dungeons themselves. The only other door it unlocks is to this study, and I don't know why, yet."

"That sounds just about right for the little... fool." She drew a long breath. "Well I'm... coming to get you."

"Oh?" He had to smile.

"One way or another." She made a face.

"What does that mean?"

"I don't know what happened after we left the estates, but it seems... I don't know, but I'm guessing that wizard is now in charge."

"Is Gariast alive?" he interrupted. He needed to know.

"I don't know." She shook her head. "But the wizard, he came to see me, the same way I'm coming to you now. He... we made a deal... for you."

"For me? Dalia...?"

"Don't say anything. I'm not going to do anything stupid. But I'd thought you were dead and when I discovered you were alive... Well, I would have done anything at that point. I'm going to meet him tonight to trade you for me—"

"Dalia, no!"

"Don't worry, I don't plan on going peacefully. I don't think he truly means to hand you over anyway. He wants me. I don't know why, but that's what I sense from him. So, I'll bring along an army and well, I'm feeling a lot better about my abilities now. I think perhaps we can defeat him. Then we'll free you."

He nodded. He wanted to say something, but there was nothing to say. He wished he could help, but there was nothing he could do from here. His friends were coming for him. He didn't want them risking their lives for him, but he couldn't stop them. He'd been willing to risk his life for them, to help them get away, so who was he to keep them from doing the same.

"Thank you, Dalia."

She reached for him then, running a glowing hand over his cheek. The feeling of liquid light soothed him, and he saw her close her eyes, feeling something as well.

"I'm coming for you." She opened her eyes and smiled. Then she was gone.

Col sighed heavily.

Then he turned and looked at the room again. Well, if she was coming, he was going to do whatever he could to help. He didn't know what yet, but the bogey's key told him it was something in this room. And he was going to keep searching until he found it.

Tom held his ground. "Do we know for certain Gariast is dead?"

Kellan and his lieutenants stood opposite him. Trentin was there as well, but since he had no rank among these men, he was keeping mostly to himself.

Kellan spoke, "Whether the man is dead or not, we can't go back there. My scouts report that there are three full cohorts and more arriving. They also have the advantage of a wall. We would have no success in a frontal assault. What would you have us do?"

Tom knew little of troops and strategy. That was one area where Col had a vast knowledge base over him. He gritted his teeth. He was losing this fight.

He needed to prove he could lead.

"Their greater numbers and their wall won't matter if you have me." The voice caused them all to turn. Dalia stood holding aside the tent flap to the command pavilion.

Several of Kellan's men laughed.

Tom looked at Kellan. The other man had fought Dalia and knew her prowess. He wasn't laughing, but he didn't seem happy either.

Kellan's voice was tight when he said, "It's going to take more than even your fighting prowess to get us past that wall and those men, my lady."

Trentin rose from leaning against a small table off to one side and made his way to the war table. He said nothing, but he was obviously more interested in what was going on now.

"Then it's a good thing I have more to offer now." She let fall the canvas and strode toward them.

Tom was supposed to be in charge, but he wasn't a part of this conversation at all and didn't have anything to add. He looked back and forth between Dalia and Kellan as the two squared off. She certainly seemed more assured and confident than he had felt when he'd arrived several hours earlier. He hadn't even been admitted for some time as there had been an 'officers only' meeting.

"What are you offering?" Kellan asked, still stony-faced. "I refuse to commit my men to a lost cause. I won't throw away lives needlessly."

Dalia had reached the large table strewn with maps and reports. "For one, I can tell you Col is alive."

That rocked Tom back on his heels and seemed to have a similar effect on Kellan and Trentin. Both men's eyes grew large with shock.

"What? How do you know this?" Trentin asked, his voice urgent.

"I've talked to him using my magic."

"Magic? I thought you were just a strange warrior?" This from Kellan.

"I'm far more than that."

Tom felt compelled to remind them all, "She was shot with a crossbow last night, lived long enough to heal Col's sister, and is now walking again. I'd say there's more to her."

Trentin nodded with a quick, "Right."

Dalia smiled at Tom with a nod. She turned back to Kellan and launched into some other topic, but Tom wasn't listening anymore. He stepped away from the table and quietly called for, "Riiku?"

The gold-and-red-blended sprite appeared before him, a welcome splash of brilliant color in the otherwise dun-colored tent.

"You know how uncomfortable it is for me to come out of the forest. What do you want?" The sprite sounded bored and pained. She was her usual grumpy self.

"Dalia's different; do you know what happened?" Tom whispered.

"She's special. Ayneii says she's mirandine, something new. Ayneii named her. As for what exactly... none of the sprites seem to know, but she's powerful, we can sense that much." Riiku turned and looked at Dalia, shaking her small head. "I could tell she was here even without looking." The sprite then darted away to hover over the large war table and scan the documents there. Kellan made no sign he was aware Riiku was there. Dalia did shift her head a little but kept on talking.

Riiku flew back. "What are you up to? Looks complicated and really I don't care, but Ayneii seems all worked up about some rescue mission?"

"Rescuing Col probably."

"Your leader?"

Tom nodded. He wasn't a leader anymore. Dalia had clearly taken over here, and Col was alive. He wouldn't be needed. "Yeah."

Riiku must have caught his tone for the sprite floated a little closer. "Are you well?"

Tom cocked an eyebrow as he looked up at the sprite. "You care suddenly?"

Riiku shrugged. "It would be even more boring around here without you."

Tom had to smile just a little. "Was that a compliment?"

"Maybe." Riiku crossed her little arms and looked away. "Don't let it go to your head, you big sack of meat."

Tom grinned fully. "It's good to know you care."

"I don't, not really... it would just be... annoying if you left and I didn't have anyone to pester."

"I understand. Thanks."

"As long as you know where we stand." Riiku zipped over to the table again then skimmed the top quickly, making all the papers go flying.

Laughter, perhaps only Tom could hear, filtered to him as Riiku vanished.

Tom rejoined the discussion, listening.

"I guarantee the wall will be down by the time your troops reach it." Dalia was saying. "You'll be able to ride right in and right over the defenders. They probably won't have horsemen ready if they are expecting the fight to be at the wall."

Kellan nodded. "No, they'd have archers most likely." He

paused gauging Dalia. "You can do this? Summon fire and wind to do your bidding?"

Dalia smiled and held out her hand. A flame leapt to life on her palm, and several of the men around gasped, murmuring among themselves. "I can," she said simply.

Kellan drew in a long breath. "Then we will make the men ready and march before sundown. I know you say we don't need to be there until the midnight call of the watch, but it's much easier to move men in daylight."

Dalia nodded. "I'll be ready when you are."

Kellan looked at Tom. "It looks like you're going to get your fight."

Tom nodded.

If Gariast was still alive, Tom wanted to ensure it wasn't for much longer.

DALIA CROUCHED AT THE TOP OF THE RIDGE OVERLOOKING Gariast's estates. It was near to midnight, but she could see the area before her as if it were day. That, and she had so much more at her disposal to sense with. What she could see matched what she felt with her life sense.

"About two thousand men behind the walls," she said softly to Kellan, Trentin, and Tom, kneeling nearby.

"You can see that?" Kellan said. "How can you be that precise? I can see some men down there, but there sure is a lot of darkness and shadow too."

"Trust me. I don't need to see to know. Many are hiding in the shadow of the wall, waiting for our approach."

"So, they know we're coming?"

"Yes. They have someone with magic on their side too. I can deal with him." She'd neglected to mention that she'd made a deal with that same man to be here at midnight. "In fact, I'm going to go down there alone first and call him out." That would work. If Zatharyn came, she could use her new powers to defeat him. If he didn't come, she'd blast the wall out from under the defenders. "You can charge in on my signal."

"What's the signal?" Kellan asked.

"It'll be...big. You'll know it when you see it."

The problem was, she wasn't sensing Zatharyn among the troops at all. He was in the estate somewhere. He hadn't come out yet. She didn't know what that meant, but something about this felt wrong.

"Stay here, come on my signal," she repeated, then rose and started down the hill.

She was sure of her own power, but suddenly uncertain just how strong her opponent was. Could she defeat him? She'd soon find out.

"How does it feel, being helpless?" Zatharyn asked.

He stood on the balcony outside Gariast's study, now his. Next to him, Gariast leaned on the thick balustrade. The man didn't answer because he couldn't. He couldn't move or speak. Zatharyn had positioned him so he'd have a full view of the fight to come. The one Zatharyn would win, not him. He'd healed the man after the attack the previous night, but only so he could keep him as a pet. Gariast had looked down on him too long and needed to be taught a lesson before he died.

"You can watch me win the war that should have been yours. Then I will kill the man who tormented you for so long, but I don't think I'll let you see it. I think I'll kill you first."

He could sense the other man's emotions, which roiled and seethed inside that inert body.

This was the moment of his revenge, and how very sweet it was. After more than two hundred years he was the one in power and this noble was helpless against him.

So few memories of his young life remained with him, but a few came rushing back now. He'd been so young, barely old enough to understand what was happening. He recalled his mother's hand holding his and a grand castle she was pulling him toward. He remembered the look on his mother's face, the blood on her lips from another coughing fit, as the noble—Zatharyn's father—turned them away, refusing to give his mother any aid. He felt his blood heat at the memory of that same noble coming to their small hut. Zatharyn was sent outside to wait. Then the nobleman emerged and flipped him a single copper coin. The memories were jumbled, out of order.

He knew now that his mother had been an orphan and had made her way by the... kindness of men. One of those men had been a noble from some wealthy estate, and she'd become pregnant by him. Yet despite his frequent visits, he never acknowledged Zatharyn as his son, nor gave the woman any special compensation to help take care of him. When his mother had died from a wasting disease, Zatharyn had had nothing. He'd begged for food, but received precious little. The villagers had told him he was worthless and run him out of town. He'd run into the wild, and nearly starved to death, before a friendly fey had helped him. He'd been so close to death, the fey had had to lend him some of its energy to survive. That had been his first taste of their power, and it had been wonderful. He'd sought more. After a lifetime of seeking, he'd captured and imprisoned enough fey to make him immortal! So had begun his quest to reap vengeance upon the society that had shunned him.

Gariast had reminded him so much of his father he'd been drawn to the man. It had been nearly fifteen years ago when he'd joined the vile lord, deciding that this would be the first man whose power he would take. Now he had it, and Gariast was just as helpless as Zatharyn had been as a boy.

He drew in a long breath of the fresh night air, reveling in his victory. He left Gariast there, helpless and frozen, heading to his study in the dungeons. He wanted to draw as much power as he could from his phylactery before going to fight the Athernon girl.

COL HEARD A CLINKING-JINGLING FROM SOMEWHERE OUTSIDE THE room he was in. He didn't know how much time had passed since Dalia had left, but it felt like hours or days. He'd searched the study from top to bottom and still had no clue why the bogey had sent him here.

Now it seemed he'd have company. Luckily, after hours of investigating this room, he knew it well enough now to know the best place he might be able to hide if someone was coming. There was an alcove with a suit of full-plate on a stand. It was mostly ornamental, but it would be big enough to hide behind, and the corner was dark.

It didn't occur to Col until he was already hidden, and the person approaching was too close, that he'd placed that mystical torch in a sconce and left it there, still burning. Would the visitor notice? He hoped not.

A man swept into the room. Col peeked around the high neck guard on the left pauldron and saw Gariast's wizard. Was this his study? That might explain why the bogey had sent him here, but again, for what?

The man stepped into the room and stopped. He turned and looked at the torch on the wall, then shook his head and moved on.

Col breathed a heavy, if silent, sigh of relief.

The man went to the desk and from it picked up a wooden box, with tracings of silver.

Col had seen the item but dismissed it. From what he could tell, it was a useless ornament. It was a low long box, perhaps a foot across, eight inches deep and four inches tall. It had a lot of ornamentation on it, but as far as he could see, no opening.

Yet as soon as the wizard touched it, a new light bloomed in the room from the box itself. Runes, that Col hadn't seen before, blazed to life in a blood-red hue.

Col didn't know what the man was doing. The wizard simply stood there, holding the box as the ciphers on it glowed, bathing him in red light. He closed his eyes and seemed to drink in that light.

All the hairs on Col's body stood on end. Something was happening, but he didn't know what. He didn't doubt it was magical, but his knowledge of such things was exceedingly limited. Over the span of a few heartbeats, the light from the box dimmed, and for a moment as it faded, the man himself seemed to be emanating with the same light. But then it was gone, and the torch was all that lit the room again. Col wasn't sure he'd seen what he thought he had. Had the man just sucked the light out of that box?

Was that box what the bogey had sent him for?

The other question that plagued him as the wizard left the room was... was it too late now to do anything?

He hoped it wasn't.

DALIA FELT IT, A BLOOM OF ENERGY, MAGICAL AND POTENT. IT caused her to pause as she drew near the gates.

She was close enough that some guard with keen eyes saw her. "Halt! Who approaches?"

"Dalia Athernon, I have a meeting with the wizard here, Zatharyn."

"Approach no farther or you will be fired upon!"

She shrugged and stayed where she was. Zatharyn could find her here as well as anywhere.

She didn't much care if she was fired upon, she'd put up a shield around herself which would deflect any arrow or crossbow bolt shot at her. She was in no fear of the men on the wall.

In fact, she'd already developed a plan for winning this little conflict with little bloodshed. She'd connected with the two thousand men behind the wall and seen how they were dispersed. A column of five hundred cavalry waited, lined up behind the sturdy gates. It was clear they were there to flood out and surround the attackers once they'd reached the wall. Other than that, the rest was what she'd expected to find, archers and footmen ready to defend the estate. She connected to all of them and wove her magic into them. Now she just had to wait for the right moment to enact her plan.

No, the men did not worry her at all. What worried her was that great surge of power she'd felt. At the same moment, she'd thought she'd heard... voices? When that power had been welling, she'd thought she'd heard faint screams, so many, but sounding ever so distant. She didn't know what to make of that.

Then she had no more time to ponder such things.

Zatharyn was coming.

She sensed his power. It was unlike anything she'd felt before. Almost as if he were more than just himself. Her life sense was befuddled and uncertain. She sensed him well enough, but it was as if there were somehow others with him, not around him, but... in him? It was strange.

Zatharyn had flown from the estate out to her, landing not far away. There was a faint red nimbus of light around him.

"You have come to surrender yourself." It wasn't a question.

"Where is Col?"

"Safe, in my dungeons."

"Release him and we'll talk about me surrendering."

Zatharyn shook his head. "No. I care little if you trust me or not. I will only release him once you have submitted and are mine. Otherwise, how am I to know you will not break your end of the bargain and attack me once you have what you want."

She was planning on doing just that.

"Then we are at an impasse. I will not submit without Col here, free. If you will not bring him, what are we to do?"

She knew what *she* was prepared to do.

Zatharyn stood there for a long moment. "I thought you might be difficult." But he did nothing. There was something in how he looked at her. He gave a faint shake of his head.

She smiled. He was assessing her and didn't like what he saw.

Good.

His eyes went hard. "If you do not submit, I will kill your man now, from here. Do not doubt my power to do so."

It was a bluff. She was surprised at how easily she could read him. The nearly imperceptible clenching of his jaw and puffing of his chest. She knew he was all bravado and no substance.

"If you could do as you say, then there would be no harm in bringing him here and handing him over. Also, if you can kill from such a distance, then why should I hand myself over knowing you could kill Col once I've surrendered?"

"So, you will not submit?"

She smiled. "Will you?"

Again, a faint gritting of teeth... annoyance. He knew he'd lost the war of words.

That meant...

She expected the attack when it came. She already had a shield up and knew the fire he blasted at her would not harm her, but she threw her arms up channeling the attack through her shields to deflect it upward into a geyser of flame.

"That's your signal, Kellan," she whispered. To ensure the commander understood, she reached out through her life sense to him and whispered within his mind. "*Now.*"

She sensed the commander's movement, his command to charge. Now she just had to do her part and make sure the wall was down before they got here.

Zatharyn lifted off from the ground, never letting up on the gout of fire he poured out at her.

"Cavalry attack!" he shouted, and the gates opened. "Attack the girl!"

She been expecting the mounted men to come out and attack, but she'd assumed the assault would be on her army, not on her specifically. It didn't much matter. She could handle it.

Zatharyn let up his flames as the mounted men drew close, but then Dalia sprouted her own wings and floated up and away from them. The horsemen were not armed with bows and could not get to her. She was safe enough here.

"Archers!" Zatharyn called out.

She needed to end this. She waited just a moment longer until the entire column of horsemen had moved away from the gates yet before the archers fired. That's when she sent a wave down into the enemy army. She'd connected to them earlier and it was easy enough now to tell them to sleep.

They all fell as one.

And just in time for her own men to ride through the now open gate.

She turned her attention back to Zatharyn with a grin.

ZATHARYN KNEW HE'D WAITED TOO LONG.

He should have destroyed the girl when he'd had the chance, before she'd come into her power. It seemed his curiosity and drive to understand and control all things had betrayed him. Now, he knew she was too powerful for him to defeat. Her shield alone was like nothing he'd ever seen or faced before. Now she'd laid low his entire army with a single strike of her magic.

He could have woken his men, but he had no time now. Dalia drew nearer, and he needed to find a way to fight her.

He blasted her with fire once again, hoping that would distract her from his real goal. He was also reaching out with his senses to test her shield and see if there might be another way to penetrate it. Yet everything he sent at it slipped off like he was trying to grab a fish.

She was too powerful.

What was she?

If she was fey, he should be able to control her, trap her, but instead, his attempts to do so slipped off as if she were not there at all. If she were human, he should be able to ensnare her as well, but again his attempts were foiled. She was neither fey nor human, but something else. He needed to change his tactics.

He centered himself. He still had a great amount of energy from his last drawing from his phylactery. He just needed to use it effectively. So, he took a moment to consider everything he did know of his opponent.

A smile grew on his face as an idea dawned on him.

33

COL HAD WAITED SEVERAL LONG MOMENTS AFTER THE WIZARD HAD left before daring to come out of hiding. He crept over to the box on the man's desk and reached out a tentative hand to it. Nothing happened when his fingers brushed the cold, silver-inlay exterior... well, nothing happened to the box, no runes lit up. But his finger jerked back as if he'd touched something incredibly cold.

That hadn't happened the last time he'd touched it. Perhaps this was some residual effect of the wizard's use of the item?

He reached out again. This time he forced himself to press his finger to the box for longer. His arm trembled as he felt a searing pain, but there was more... screams, panicked, so many at once as to be indistinguishable. It wasn't heard so much as felt, the pain, terror, and anger.

He pulled his finger away, checking it. There was no mark, no burn, nothing. But the memory of those screams, that feeling of so many trapped and pleading souls, shook him. He stepped back for a moment.

"What...?"

What was this thing?

Col inspected it closely. If it was a box, if it held anything within, there seemed to be no visible door or lid. It was one solid piece of wood set with iron and silver in an intricate pattern.

So, was it solid? Was there an inside at all? Did it matter whether there was an inside if it was magical? He didn't have any of these answers.

He needed more information but knew none would be forthcoming.

He reached out with both hands and grabbed the box.

His mind thundered with the cries of... something, but this time over the din of the multitudinous voices he heard one cohesive message. "Free Us!"

He released the box and stepped back, letting his mind settle. He needed a moment to understand what he'd heard.

Someone was trapped, but where and how?

He gritted his teeth and reached for the box again. Perhaps another round would provide more information.

Tom urged his mount past those in the lead.

The others were stopping to dismount and either survey the unconscious enemies or start gathering them up. He cared little for that. He had one goal only.

As he drew near the estates, he saw a lone figure up on Gariast's balcony.

Good.

Gariast was alive.

He wouldn't be for much longer.

Zatharyn's mind had always been his strongest asset. His

body may be frail, old, weak, but his mind was still able to decipher problems with alarming speed. If Dalia was both fey and human, and yet neither fey nor human, then he couldn't deal with her in ways he'd already established.

He needed to adapt, and that was something he did very well indeed. He'd built his entire success on overcoming great obstacles like this one. So, he had let his mind work through the problem. It didn't take long to find a solution.

He stopped focusing on what she was. That didn't matter. Instead he concentrated on how to deal with, and eliminate, her magic. This time he didn't attack her directly but instead created a great bubble around her. It was an unseen thing of pure magic, meant to contain magic alone.

His grin widened as he shrunk the bubble around her until it encountered her shield.

Now the real fight began.

If she was smart, she'd know what was happening by now and be pumping more power into her shield, which would resist his anti-magic sphere.

He tried pushing in on her shield for a moment, feeling its strength, before adapting again. He added a new element to this bubble. It wouldn't just block or stop magic, it would siphon off magical essence.

This was his expertise. This was how he'd grown in such power. For years, he'd been trapping fey and siphoning off their power to use as his own. He was quite experienced drawing the power from others. If he did this right, she wouldn't even know he was stealing her power until it was too late.

Then, he'd crush her.

~

DALIA WAS STARTING TO GET WORRIED.

Somehow, Zatharyn was blocking her magic. She'd sensed it the moment it happened, or more precisely, she'd felt the lack of her extended senses. She'd been cut off, her life sense not feeling anything beyond a certain radius. She'd felt the magical field contract until it was trying to bring down her shield. That was when she'd started to panic. She pushed everything she had into keeping her shield up. She had the fleeting image of her shield collapsing then... well she didn't know what would happen. She just knew she didn't want her shields to fall.

She pushed harder still against this magic-canceling force, trying to expand her shield.

Nothing happened.

Zatharyn's laughter reached her ears. Not a good sign.

She could feel herself growing weak, expending far too much energy, sapping the last reserves of her magic. It wasn't working.

And only then, as she gave one last push with her magic, did she sense what had happened. She connected with Zatharyn's anti-magic field and saw how it was subtly siphoning her own power away, for him to use.

If she'd caught it sooner, perhaps she could have done something, but it was too late. Her field fell, and the magic-consuming force tightened around her and swallowed her power entirely.

The loss of her magic hit her like a punch to the gut.

Limp and only semi-conscious, she fell from the sky.

The impact with the ground stunned her to life again even as pain shattered through her body. Her head burned, hazy; her body was broken. Her magic was gone.

She felt little—nothing below the waist—only a cold settling over her body. Yet her awareness lingered. Perhaps as some cruel joke, to witness her last moment as Zatharyn touched down nearby.

COL STAGGERED BACK A FEW STEPS.

Every time he took hold of the mysterious box, he got more and more of an impression of what it was, but also, as time passed, whatever it was he was connecting to seemed more and more distant. The discordant screams he heard or felt—he was never quite sure—were now nearly inaudible for how quiet they were. The intensity of his reaction was the same, but the ability to hear or connect with those who were trapped was nearly gone.

Again, he figured that whatever the wizard had done to the box, what magic he'd used, was dwindling now. Soon, the box would be just a box again.

What he'd gathered was a horrific, if still uncertain, scenario. Somehow, hundreds, if not thousands, of fey had been trapped... somewhere... by the wizard. He was using their power, the very magic that was their life essence, to fuel his own spells. This box contained some deep reserve of power and if fully drained, which Col was sure had recently happened, that wizard would be an incredibly puissant force. He hoped Dalia knew what she was going up against.

These fey, mostly sprites, were kept in some strange place between worlds, where the wizard could tap into their power when he wished by using this box to siphon off what he needed. It was a constant torture to these creatures, who had never known such confines, and should be free to keep the chaotic balance of the natural world.

No wonder that bogey had chosen Dalia to become... something else. They had needed someone who wasn't fey to fight the wizard because every fey who went up against him was trapped and added to this power source.

The bogey...

Col's eyes widened. Could it be that simple? How had he not thought of that?

He took out the key he'd been given. There was no keyhole in the box, so he simply touched the key to the wood and hoped.

There was a blinding flash. Col staggered back as a flood of raw energy blasted forth from the box. The key in his hand vanished even as he'd dropped it. It was no longer needed.

The energy swirled around the room and, after a moment, coalesced into shapes. There were hundreds of sprites and other fey, their inner light dim. They were all so very weak, but their joy at being free was a palpable thing which filled Col with giddiness. At the same time, without words, the fey conveyed their thanks in raw emotion, and Col was nearly overwhelmed with the wave of gratitude. He fell to his knees, tears in his eyes, weeping with delight. It was all he could do.

The great vortex of fey then swirled up through the stone of the dungeon and out of the room.

He was alone, but he knew he'd done what he needed to do.

The wizard would have no more power.

Through his tears, he choked words he knew Dalia probably would not hear. "The rest is up to you."

Zatharyn savored his moment of triumph over the tempestuous girl.

"Now, you shall die," he said, though the last word came out as more of a squeak as he staggered to one side as if hit.

His magic was draining away. He could feel it. Something had happened! Someone had broken or opened his phylactery, he was certain of it. Even as he glanced off toward the palace, he saw the great gout of fey stream out from the building and away in a mighty hurricane of power. Power that was no longer his.

"No!" he gasped, falling to one knee.

His power was slipping away... but it was not gone, not fully. He had what he'd taken from the Athernon girl, and that would be enough to finish her, a cold irony that made him smile.

He reached out a hand to blast her one last time.

DALIA DID HEAR COL'S WORDS.

...The rest is up to you.

For a moment, she was so delirious and weak she didn't know what this was, who had said it. When she realized it had been Col, several things sank in at once, despite the addled daze of her thoughts.

The first was simple: Col had done something, but what? Yet even as his words came, she'd seen Zatharyn stagger then fall. Had Col done that? She had to assume that the two events were connected.

The second realization was simply that she could hear Col. This meant her life sense was working, which meant she still had some vestige of magic and that Zatharyn's blocking field was down—possibly because he'd been harmed somehow, it didn't matter.

The third realization was the most important. If she still had magic and her life sense... she could still win this fight.

Instantly, she reached out to everyone around her. Since she'd already connected with the enemy army before it was easy to find them again. Once connected, she pulled as much energy as she could out of them. She made certain not to go so far as to kill any of them. That was far too much energy anyway. Even a small fraction of those two thousand men was enough to fill her with power.

She surged her healing and erected a new shield just as Zatharyn blasted her with fire once again.

The flames arched around her, weakening her shield, but not harming her.

Slowly, she rose to her feet. She was still weak, only just freshly healed from the shattered bones and torn muscles of her fall. But her power was swelling within her and she felt certain enough to take a step.

She walked over to where Zatharyn knelt, his flames blasting at her shield the entire way. The attack only abated as she came to stand over him.

"How?" he gasped. "How can you be...?" His hoarse voice raked the silence of the night.

"You didn't get all my magic. I had enough to take what I needed from others here."

"From people, humans? But how?" He seemed confused, disoriented.

She knelt next to him. "It doesn't matter now." She reached out and touched his forehead. He tried to flinch away but only succeeded in falling back. She touched his weathered and wrinkled skin and tore every ounce of power out of him. She made sure not to kill him, though he'd be unconscious for some time.

He lay still.

Everything was tranquil around her.

A little ways off, the men of Kellan's army were wandering among the unmoving forms of the enemy.

Trentin approached her.

"You fell from the sky. It didn't look like you meant to. How are you doing?" He looked down at the wizard as he stopped next to the two of them. "How is he doing? Going to cause us any more trouble?"

She shook her head. "No, he won't." She drew in a long

breath. "And I am... well enough, thank you." She rose and turned, heading for the estate.

"Where are you going?" he called from behind her.

"To find Col."

TOM CHARGED OUT ONTO THE BALCONY. HE'D SEEN A FORM UP here as he'd ridden close and guessed it might be his prey. As he drew closer, he could see the form crumple to the ground in a heap from where it had been leaning against the railing.

He approached carefully, wary. There hadn't been many guards in the estate, certainly none around the room. If this was Gariast, he had been confident enough to send his men away, which did not seem like the man he knew.

Tom inched forward next to the form and kicked it, rolling it over.

It was Gariast indeed.

"Who...?" The man's voice was weak. He didn't seem like he could stand at all.

"Don't you recognize me?" Tom said softly. "You should." He spat out the vile taste in his mouth at the words he was about to speak. "I'm your son."

Gariast laughed, though it was a hoarse and wheezing sound. "A bastard," he gasped. The man was actually grinning.

Tom drew out the coin Gariast had given his mother.

"Not just any bastard." He dropped it on Gariast's chest. The man didn't even move to retrieve it. Whatever had been done to him, he was in no state to fight at all. That was fine with Tom. "The bastard who is going to kill you."

"What...?"

Tom drew his sword back, his hands shaking, sweating on

the grip. There he paused, hesitated. The man before him was so weak and frail.

He shook his head, lowering his sword. "I can't kill you like this."

Gariast laughed. "Then you're no son of mine!"

Tom heard those words and let them sink in.

"No." He found a grin spreading on his face. "No, I'm not."

Then he went to get something to bind the man with. Gariast was so feeble he was still struggling to rise when Tom returned. It was easy enough to bind him. He made sure to pull the ropes tight. As much as he couldn't kill Gariast, he wasn't against causing him a little pain.

Gariast grunted, saying nothing.

"You'll face justice soon enough," Tom said. "But it won't be from me."

COL STARTED AWAKE WHEN SOMEONE TOUCHED HIM.

He hadn't realized he'd fallen asleep. All he remembered was feeling overwhelmed with emotions: joy and gratitude. Perhaps it had been too much, and he'd blacked out.

But he opened his eyes to find Dalia smiling down at him.

"Hello," she said softly.

"Hi."

"Would you like to leave now? I've... sort of... blasted the door to cinders."

"I'd love to. Just let me go get my brothers."

"They're here?"

"Yes. You don't happen to have keys for the cells down here do you?"

Dalia put out a hand, palm up, and a gout of flame appeared. "I think I can manage something."

He smiled, getting to his feet. "I take it we won?"

"Yes, thanks to whatever you did that weakened Zatharyn."

He embraced her. "Good." He'd tell her about the box and its horrid contents, but now wasn't the time.

She held him tightly, her body pressed to his. He couldn't think of anything better in the world than this feeling.

"Dalia, will you marry me?"

She laughed lightly. "Yes, Col. Though my father will probably have a fit that I'm not marrying a nobleman."

"The king owes me a thing or two. Perhaps I'll ask for a title."

"It doesn't matter. I'd marry you no matter what my father, or the king, or anyone else said."

Then she kissed him and demonstrated just how much she meant it.

34

Tom couldn't stop himself from trembling.

Valeesa, her arm already around him, squeezed a little tighter. "You did the right thing," she said softly so as not to disrupt the proceedings.

Tom knew it. He'd kept himself from killing Gariast. He didn't even think of the man as 'his father' anymore. In truth, he didn't know if he was trembling from anticipation, or rage, or anxiety.

"I know," he whispered back, and leaned in to kiss her softly. "I know."

Then he turned back to watch the gruesome ceremony.

"Lord Vandar Gariast, you are accused of high treason for conspiring to murder the Crown Prince of Santhine, as well as negligence in your duties to your vassals and serfs, as well as the murder of the Rossferol family and their servants, as well as innumerable accounts of misconduct of a lord of your station." Col's words were stiff, formal. Tom could see the cold fury that burned beneath the surface of his friend and leader's face. "How do you plead?"

"You have no authority to judge me!" Gariast spat out. He had regained his strength from whatever had happened to him that night on the balcony. Two men restrained him now as he struggled to free himself.

"How do you plead," Col asked again, undaunted.

"I've done all those things you've said, but there is no power in this kingdom that can stop me! I own the king! He's the one who should be judging me, and that spineless coward would never think to punish me. He needs me!"

"The plea is guilty." Col didn't even seem to notice Gariast's ravings. He nodded to the men holding Gariast, who forced the man to his knees, bending him forward.

Col drew out his sword.

"By the authority of King Halviar of Rovalia, I pronounce your sentence: death."

"You have no authority! You—"

Col's sword fell swiftly ending Gariast's tirade.

Next to Tom, Valeesa gasped looking away. Tom forced himself to look. This was death. This was justice. He felt a little cold inside. It was done. He too turned and led Valeesa away from the scene.

Once they had put some distance between them and the site of the execution, Tom stopped. He held Valeesa close. "Thank you," he said softly.

She returned the embrace just as urgently. "For what?"

"You told me... You said I was nothing like him. It was your voice that stayed my hand when I could have killed him. He was helpless, and I could have... I wanted to... but... I heard your voice, and I knew if I did, I would be just like him."

She hugged him tighter. "It wasn't me." Her voice was a little muffled with her face in his shoulder, but he heard her well enough. "You're a good man. It was you who did this. Trust yourself, Tom. You saved me when no one else would, not even my father."

He had.

He squeezed her. "Then... thank you for just being you."

She laughed, her body moving against his. "That, I can do, anytime." She pulled away enough to give him a kiss on the cheek then look him in the eye. "I'm glad you are who you are as well."

Their next kiss was a little longer and was quite quickly dispelling the horrible images of the day.

DALIA KNELT NEXT TO THE STILL FORM OF COL'S BROTHER, BERRIS. Jaidan and Rissa were similarly asleep and laid out peacefully on beds. They were in the largest room of the Dusty Road tavern in Kilian's Hollow. Rissa, Col's sister, had been here since they'd freed her, and Col had thought it best to bring his brothers here instead of trying to bring Rissa back to the estates. That might be too much for the girl.

Dalia had said she could heal them of their torment, but it would be easiest if they were all in the same place.

Col waited outside.

Ayneii, despite her discomfort at being outside of her forest, had come to help and guide Dalia.

Dalia touched Berris' forehead and delved into his memories and emotions.

"It will be best to simply remove everything from their time in that place," Ayneii said, hovering nearby. Dalia's eyes were closed, but she heard the instructions clearly enough. "They will have a gap in their lives, but from what Col says, that is far better than the alternative."

Dalia went about sifting through Berris' mind. Searching back further and further to the last pleasant memory he had before being taken by Gariast's men.

"Sometimes, there are people who fall asleep and don't wake up for years," Ayneii said softly. "That will be the equivalent of what they shall experience."

Dalia let her connection to Berris guide her. In his own way, he knew what she was doing and knew what to let go of. It took time, for nothing on this scale was easy or quick, but eventually, she drew herself out of Berris' mind and opened her eyes.

"It's done," she said with a sigh. There was sweat on her forehead and she felt drained, but she went on, moving next to Jaidan.

With her connection to guide her and Ayneii there for further support, she cleansed the minds of the other two as well, ensuring their bodies were returned to a healthy state with not so much as a scar.

By the time she finished, she was exhausted. It had taken most of the night.

Col met her as she left the room. He hadn't slept during this time either; she could see it in his eyes and feel it through her life sense.

"Well?" he said simply.

"When they wake, they shall remember nothing. Their souls and minds and bodies are free of the horrors inflicted upon them. It will be as if the last couple of years never happened for them. They will probably be curious. Tell them what you will."

He nodded.

"I'm tired," Dalia said softly, "But I could use a bit of a walk if you're up for it. I need to stretch my legs and get some fresh air. Then I'll sleep for a day or two."

He gave a short laugh and nodded, taking her hand.

They left the tavern and walked a short distance to the woods that clustered close behind it, at the edge of the town. The day was slowly growing brighter. It was a beautiful morning, still and quiet. No one else was up yet.

They didn't say a word to each other, simply walked, hand in hand through the trees.

Then as they turned to head back to the town and the tavern, there leaning against a tree not far off, was the bogey.

Dalia and Col stopped, uncertain.

The fey approached them.

"It is time, Dalia," he said gravely.

"Time?" But she knew what he meant.

"Time to give back what I gave you. You defeated the wizard as you were meant to, and I let you keep it a little longer to help those you could, but it's over now."

"Over?" Col said. He looked from her to the fey. Then Dalia saw awareness dawn behind his eyes." You have to give up your abilities?"

She nodded.

She'd wondered if this would happen. If she would be allowed to keep the power she'd acquired. A part of her had hoped, now that she had come to accept it, that she might be able to keep it. Yet she knew it wasn't right. She was an unbalancing force in nature.

Still, it seemed unfair. She'd only just come to her full potential a few days ago, and now it would all be taken away.

She sighed. As unfair as it might be, she knew she couldn't delay.

"I know. How do we do this?"

The bogey held out a hand. "Give me your hand."

She knelt, for he was much shorter than she was, and took his small hand in hers.

"It is done."

With those words, her world closed in. Her life sense was gone, and everything else had gone with it.

She rose and felt a little unsteady, much more... human.

"Perhaps," the bogey said wistfully. "If there is need again within your lifetime, the mirandine might make a return, but I do not think it likely."

She agreed.

She had a question for the bogey. "I couldn't find Zatharyn when I returned to where I'd left him. Was that you?"

The bogey nodded. "He will face the judgment of the fey for what he did."

She nodded again. "Good."

She rose with a sigh. She was human again. For the past couple weeks—had it only been that long?—this was what she'd wished for. Now she had it.

"Thank you," she said. "For that small time as something... special."

The bogey laughed even as he faded into nothingness. "Oh, you're still pretty special."

She shrugged. "I wonder what that means."

A hand on her shoulder startled her, without her life sense, she hadn't known Col was right there next to her. She reacted without thinking. Grabbing his hand, she pulled him closer, then knelt and bent forward, flipping him over onto his back. He landed with a thud and a puff of breath as she twisted his wrist, locking it.

She stayed crouched for a moment trying to figure out what had just happened.

A disembodied voice which sounded a lot like the bogey said, "I may have left you with a little muscle memory." Then a laugh.

She couldn't help but laugh as well, though she did check with Col. "Are you alright?"

He nodded. "I know not to sneak up on you now." He laughed as well.

"Probably a good idea," she said through her laughter. It felt good to laugh with him. It even felt good to not know how he felt, to instead see it in his smile and eyes. She'd miss the special connection she'd had with him, with everyone really, but mostly with him. Yet she was happy to be just human again. Well, maybe more than 'just' human.

He pulled her down next to him and they laughed in each other's arms. Then they stopped laughing and began kissing.

∽

"Don't worry. I'll be back," Col said to an over-agitated Ayneii. "I have a life here. If that changes and I move away, I'll have to come back here to get what few things I have."

"And me," Ayneii said with a squeak of a voice.

"And you, of course." Col sighed. He knew things were going to be changing. Perhaps now was the best time to explain that to the sprite. "Ayneii... I... it's up to you, of course, but I might not be living in the Sandren anymore after this. I know you're uncomfortable outside of your forest." He didn't quite know how to say the words. What came out instead was. "I could come visit... often."

Ayneii dipped and peaked in a chaotic zigzagging pattern around him. "I... I could go outside the forest. I could... really."

"I didn't think you sprites cared that much for humanity."

"We don't." This was a new voice.

Col looked over to see Tom and Riiku approaching. He was surprised Riiku was allowing herself to be seen. Col had so rarely seen Tom's sprite.

Riiku continued her thought, "But you specific humans are... interesting." Riiku's sidelong glance at Tom made it clear that

that wasn't meant as a compliment. "We'd... miss... you." That sounded like it took a lot for the fiery-hued sprite to admit.

"And Dalia, I'd miss Dalia," Ayneii added. "And playing tricks on some of the others, I'd miss that. Oh, and entertaining the little ones, I'd miss that too." There weren't many kids in the forest camp, well there hadn't been at first, but the camp had grown a lot in the last few weeks. All of those people would be leaving now.

Col wondered, "Why don't you like leaving your forest?"

"We make bonds here," Ayneii said quickly.

"The plants we tend and the animals that roam our lands, they call to us," Riiku added.

"And if you were to tend new plants and animals?"

"They would call to us too. We'd make new bonds," Ayneii said. "So, if we went with you, we could do that! It would take time for us to feel more comfortable there, and we'd want to still return to the Sandren to visit our bonds, but it could work."

Col turned to Riiku. "What do you think?"

Tom was grinning as the sprite squirmed. "That... sounds horrible... but I could be convinced to do it... maybe."

Col nodded, trying to hide his grin. "Then it's settled. Once we know what we're doing and where we're going, we'll come back and get you and you can start making new bonds wherever we end up."

"Yes! That is a great idea. Thank you, Col!" Ayneii swooped in and hugged his arm, her tiny arms not even able to get all the way around.

He reached up and patted her carefully.

"I don't know what life would be like without you, Ayneii." A lot less interesting for sure.

She released him and zipped back up, now flying in a much less agitated way. "Well, now you won't have to find out."

"No, I won't."

"I have some things I need to do to get ready!" Then she was gone, and Riiku with her.

Tom sighed. "You could have asked if that's what I wanted."

Col grinned. "Something tells me we never really had a say in it."

Tom nodded. "You're probably right."

35

THE CARRIAGE ROLLED THROUGH THE PALACE GATES, AND DALIA felt a slight thrill. She'd been to the royal palace in Roval a few times as a child. This would be her fourth time going through these gates, but never before had she felt like this. She'd been some nobleman's daughter before, but this time she was going to see the king herself and be recognized for what she and Col had done. She squeezed his hand, and their eyes met.

He smiled.

"Never really thought I'd see the inside of the royal palace," Tom said quietly. "They say Queen Genehra is the most beautiful woman in Rovalia. I can think of one who might be more beautiful..." He looked at Valeesa sitting next to him. The two of them sat across from Dalia and Col.

Even with her shorter hair, Valeesa was radiant. She'd trimmed and styled the shorter cut well to frame her face and looked every bit the noblewoman once again.

Valeesa blushed. "You can say that here, but don't you dare say that inside. I don't want you beheaded by a spurned queen before I can marry you." She was looking rather splendid in a gown of green, much more daring than Dalia would ever wear, off the shoulders with a plunging neckline. Then again, Valeesa had a bit more of a figure to show off.

Tom laughed. "Understood." They leaned in and kissed.

Dalia herself was in a blue dress, which supposedly set off her eyes. Yet next to Valeesa, she just felt frumpy and 'flat' and plain. That said, she didn't miss the men's clothes she'd worn for so long. She didn't need to be ready to fight at any minute anymore. Those clothes had made her feel even more unsightly and outcast at first, but then... When she'd been mirandine, she'd come to feel beautiful and special. It hadn't mattered what she wore. Now that she was human again, a lot of that confidence had fled. She was having to work to get it back.

Dalia looked at Col, and he smiled. It made her smile too. Any thoughts about how she might look in her dress dissipated. It didn't matter. Col loved her, she saw it in his eyes, and that was all that mattered. He'd loved her as an outcast, when she hadn't known what she was. He'd loved her as a mirandine, and he loved her now.

That went a long way toward helping her regain her confidence.

There was another carriage following behind them with Trentin, Kellan, and Grunston—the fur trader through whom Col had been communicating with the king.

The carriage came to a stop under a great covered area at what was known as the "Rain Port" entrance to the palace. This was a common entrance for more mundane visits as opposed to the formal entrance at the front of the palace with the great wide steps up to a massive door.

Dalia followed Col out one side as Tom helped Valeesa out the other.

Dalia had found she'd retained a certain amount of fluid movement and grace from her abilities, perhaps more of what the bogey had called muscle memory. She didn't need Col to help her out of the carriage, but it was nice. She may have been awkward in many ways before all this, but now her movements were smooth and elegant.

Some things had changed for the better.

Once inside the palace, they headed to the lower level of the Great Hall.

The king was waiting for them with his queen and their three daughters. They were all dressed in subdued finery, and the queen was indeed beautiful. Lord Armalan, Lord General of the King's Army and First Captain of the King's Guard, stood to one side of the throne, holding a large sword, but it was the other man in the room who captured all of Dalia's attention.

"Papa!" she cried out and ran across the great hall to him. He swept her up in a tight embrace, lifting her from the floor, tears in his eyes.

"Dalia! Gods, but I thought you were dead! I don't care what you did. I'm just glad to have you back."

He set her back on the floor and through her tears, with a voice thick with emotion she said, "Oh, Papa, it wasn't me, not that horrid thing with the Rossferol's. That was Gariast!"

"Yes, we know." This from the king. Dalia recalled that there had been several messages back and forth from Col to the king in the days since they'd taken Gariast's estates.

Dalia suddenly remembered where she was and who was here. "I am sorry, your majesty," Dalia said with a formal court curtsey. She stayed down until she heard the customary, "Rise, my child."

She got up as Col was approaching her.

He put an arm around her. She heard a faint grunt from her father as Col embraced her, but that could wait for a moment.

"Halviar," Col said, addressing the king in the most informal way possible, by his given name. "It's good to see you again."

"And without your sword at my throat," the king said evenly. That brought about a few gasps from others in the room.

"A lot has changed since then." Col grew more serious with these words. He turned to Dalia and said, "I've explained everything to the king already. He knew I was bringing you, so he must have invited your father." Col looked up at the king. "That I hadn't been expecting, but it is a pleasant surprise."

Dalia whispered a quick, "thank you," to Col, then to the king said, "If I might have a moment, your majesty?"

The king nodded again, a bemused smile on his face.

Dalia, still in Col's arms, turned back to her father. "Papa, this is Colric of Haverstal. We're to be married."

Her father's brows shot up. "What? You're just a girl and he's a—"

"Commoner? I don't care." Dalia grinned at her own brazenness. Apparently, she'd kept more self-assurance than she'd thought. She'd never have interrupted her father before.

Her father gaped at her.

"And I'm not a girl anymore, Father, not after what I've been through. I can tell you the full story later, but for now, please trust that I am a woman who can decide for herself who she loves and wishes to be with, and that is Col."

Her father drew in a long breath, lips pressed tight, but when he let it out, a hint of a smile caught his mouth. Then he laughed, a clipped expression of relief and release. "I'm just glad to have you back. We can talk about the rest later, as you say." He gave Col an assessing look. "If this young man is everything his reputation says he is, then perhaps I can live with your choice. That, too, we can talk about later."

Col extended a hand. "It is a pleasure to meet you, Lord Athernon."

Her father took the offered hand and they shook.

"Now," Col said, turning back to the king. "To the matter at hand?"

"Yes," the king said, having had a moment to regain his composure. He rose from his throne and stood tall and confident, regal and unruffled. "I summoned you to congratulate all those who helped to defeat Lord Gariast." He swept his gaze over the lot of them. "Because of you, a stain on our kingdom has been removed." A rather relaxed smile spread on his face. "Also, because of you, I have finally managed, with Lord Athernon's help, to regain control of my Council of Lords. We will retain the council as advisors to the king, but their power shall be... reduced." The king drew in a long breath. "My kingdom has been restored, the lords are in line, and I have you all to thank for it. Ask your reward."

A silence hung over the hall. Who would speak first?

Oddly it was not who Dalia expected. It was the furrier, Grunston.

"My liege, I seek nothing but the continued favor of the court. I didn't do that much anyway."

The king laughed. "The court's favor you have, and shall continue to have, for as long as you, or your offspring, are in business."

"Oh, well... thank you, your majesty."

Next, it was Trentin. "My king. I was a nobleman once, with a modest keep and some small lands. I ask only for that in return."

The king nodded. "I am afraid you will not get your request, Sir Edwir." Dalia looked over at Trentin, who was nodding stoically, lips pressed tight.

"I understand, my liege."

"Do you? I think not. I am not giving you what you requested, instead, you shall be burdened with far more than what you had. You can keep your... keep, but the lands that you oversee shall be expanded. Finding lords I can trust is a rare thing, and such lords are rewarded well. I raise you to the title of Duke and give you one third of the lands which Gariast once ruled. Also, this shall grant you a place on the Council of Lords."

Dalia watched Trentin's jaw drop as these words hit him. He finally stammered, "Thank you, your majesty."

There was another heavy silence before Kellan spoke. Oddly, he seemed hesitant to come forward. "Sire, I too only wish to serve as I always have."

The king nodded. "And so you shall. However, I am promoting you to Lord General of the King's Army and First Captain of the King's Guard."

"Sire, is not that rank held by Lord Armalan?" Kellan nodded to the man standing erect on one side of the dais on which the king and his family were placed. There was gray in the man's hair and clean-cut beard, though not much.

"Indeed, it is. He will stay on for a period to transition the role to you but has let me know he wishes to retire soon. I couldn't think of a better replacement."

Kellan bowed. "Yes, your majesty, thank you."

That left Col and Tom.

Col opened his mouth, but Tom spoke first. "Your majesty. I can't say I've lived a life that was always lawful. I was a horse thief, and I've raided my fair share of lords' caravans. But if you could see your way to forgetting about those things, I'd be much obliged. Oh, and I wouldn't mind being allowed to marry this young lady." Tom put his arm around Valeesa, who leaned into him affectionately.

"You are the one called Tom Willow, yes?" the king asked.

"Yes, your majesty."

"I pardon you of all crimes. As for the marriage... do you require a royal decree for that?" The king peered closer at Valeesa. "Do I know you, child?"

Valeesa spoke up. "I am Valeesa Tandor, your majesty. I

believe Tom's request comes from concern in marrying a noble-woman when he has no title. Though, perhaps that is a concern for my father."

The king laughed. "There you are! Half the kingdom is looking for you." He turned to a young page. "Go fetch Lord Tandor, he'll want to be here." He turned back to the couple. "Your father came to me earlier today to enlist my aid in searching for you. He feared you had been stolen away by some rogue with ill intent."

Tom shrugged. "I am a rogue, your majesty, but my intent was entirely pure. I promise."

The king laughed again.

Tom was a bit soberer when he spoke next. "I'd overheard that Valeesa was to be sent to Lord Gariast. I feared for her safety and sought to help her free herself from such a fate. As it happens we..." He looked Valeesa in the eye at that moment and smiled. "We found a strong affection for each other in the interim."

The king nodded. "Colric has told me of your exploits and everything you did to help bring order to the kingdom. If it would help, I have a title I could provide you."

Tom looked conflicted at this. He looked from the king to Valeesa, and some whispered words passed between him and her. It was a moment before he finally answered. Oddly, he seemed quite reluctant. "I would accept that, your majesty."

"You are from the village of Kilian's Hollow, yes? How would you like Gariast's estate and some of the surrounding land? You'd be close enough to your home."

Tom seemed to turn green. His answer was even stranger. "Would I have to live in the estate, sire?"

The king looked a bit perplexed. "You'd be a lord. You could live wherever you wished. You could have the estates torn down and rebuilt if you wished."

Tom nodded. "Good, thank you, then I accept."

The king nodded. "Approach the throne, Tom Willow." The stoic Lord Armalan also strode to the king and presented his sword. The king took it and asked Tom to kneel.

The king rested the sword on Tom's right shoulder. "Do you swear to uphold and adjudicate the laws of the realm and protect all those under your care?"

"I do, your majesty."

"And do you swear your full loyalty and fealty to me, the king, and my successors, as long as we too are keeping our pledge to protect the kingdom and uphold its laws?"

"I do."

The king moved the sword to Tom's left shoulder. "Then I dub you Sir... Tom Willow, Lord of Killian's Hollow and surrounding lands. Rise, Sir Willow."

Tom stood.

At that moment, a large bull of a man came charging into the great hall, Lord Tandor. He scanned it and locked eyes with Valeesa. "My daughter, you're safe!"

But even as he made his way to her, she became stony, her words stern. "No thanks to you, Father!" That stopped him. "You were going to send me to Lord Gariast! You would sell your own family rather than betray a corrupt lord?"

Lord Tandor was frozen. He glanced at the king. The King said nothing but gave the man a stern look. It was Valeesa who spoke next.

"I am willing to forgive you, Father, with one condition."

He cleared his throat. "What is that?"

"I decide who I will marry."

Tandor's shoulders slumped; it seemed partly in defeat but partly in relief as well. Perhaps he felt like he'd gotten off easy. "Agreed." He took another step toward her before her next words stopped him again.

"Good, then I'm going to marry Lord Willow."

"Lord Willow? Never heard of the man."

Tom chimed in. "Nice to meet you again, Lord Tandor!" He stepped down from the dais, strode across the hall, hand extended toward his father-in-law-to-be.

"You! You're the one who stole her away!"

It was the king who interceded. "From you, because you were making a poor choice at the time. Besides, he's a lord now with lands to rival your own... and not far from your own. Your daughter will be safe with him."

Tandor's bluster vanished, but he couldn't seem to take his eyes off Tom. "But you... your name wasn't Willow before..." Tandor seemed confused.

"I was lying, about a lot of things. Time enough to explain all that later, but I am a lord now." Tom was grinning and had his hand extended to Lord Tandor.

The lord nodded, still seeming uncertain, but took Tom's hand. "Take care of her." It sounded more like a threat than congratulations.

Tom's reply was earnest. "I will."

Tandor nodded, and only then did he proceed to his daughter who he caught up in a great hug. "It's good to see you again. I'm sorry, my darling."

Valeesa's reply was lost, muffled by her face in her father's shoulder.

The king turned to Col. "Which leaves only you I believe."

"Myself and Dalia yes."

The king raised a brow and looked at her. "Dalia? Is there something you wish from the crown?"

Dalia gave Col a frustrated look. He only smiled at her.

"To seek permission to marry a non-noble." She glanced at her father who frowned for a moment, but then sighed heavily and nodded as he met her gaze.

"Don't worry, that will soon be rectified as well, Dalia. If it's Colric you wish to marry, he'll be a noble soon enough. Is there anything else you desire?"

Something occurred to her then, another surge of her growing confidence. She'd gotten used to men seeing her as an equal, as capable. "Yes. I do not wish to simply be some lord's lady." She glanced at Col who had a single brow raised, still smiling. "I wish to hold as much weight as my husband with as much say on any matters of state or on any lord's council."

The king stared at her for a long moment. His gaze moved to Col.

Col looked from the king to her then back. He shrugged. "I'd do as she asks if I were you. If it comes to a fight, she'll win. She always wins."

The king looked a bit dumbfounded. "I had heard tales," he said slowly. "Were they all true? Could you really fight like a man?"

Before she could respond, others did.

"Better than any man I know," Kellan said evenly.

"She beat me repeatedly," Trentin added.

"It's a long story, that we'll tell you some time," Col said. "And when you hear it, you won't believe it, but it's all true."

The king sighed, considering. "I'm not entirely sure how to give you what you wish, Dalia. Ladies have ruled in their husband's stead in the past, if their husband was away at war or dead. But usually this is for a limited time. I wouldn't know how to give you both the same power without instigating confusion among your peers and vassals."

Dalia stood her ground. "There need not be any confusion," she said stern, stoic, and decided. "Think of Col and me as one unit. We will speak with the same authority, pass judgment, and enforce laws equally. It actually works quite well if you think about it. If one of us is away, the other is there to keep the peace.

I may not be able to ride to war as he can. Well..." She shrugged. "At least not yet, but it will mean I'll be experienced at maintaining our lands while he is away if it comes to that. We will be one voice from two mouths—our word taken as law, our actions always for the betterment and protection of this kingdom."

The king was nodding slowly. "Perhaps..."

"As for any confusion among the other lords, I'll leave that to you to work out."

The king laughed. "Will you? How kind." The king considered for a moment longer. "And what if, heaven forbid, you might disagree with each other on a ruling or decision?"

Dalia glanced at Col. He shrugged. His look was thoughtful. She knew well enough that they were different people and might have different ways of thinking, make different choices. "That will be up to us to work out together, away from the public so as to always appear as a united ruling couple."

The king nodded, as did Col.

"Well said," the king said. After a moment of thought, he went on. "I do not think the title of Lady will suit you then. If you and..." the king smiled, "...your man wouldn't mind approaching the throne."

She glanced at Col and they walked over, hand in hand, kneeling before the king.

"First, Colric of Haverstal, I pardon you of all crimes against the kingdom. I also name you first Advisor to the king. You have ever been an honest man and forthright with me; I could use more of that. To this end, I grant you full right-of-speech."

'Right-of-speech' was full freedom from the formality of addressing royalty and nobility. It was usually reserved for the most powerful of nobles or the most trusted and true of advisors. It was a great honor.

Dalia saw Col smile. He knew he already had that, but now it was formal. "Thank you, your majesty."

"Next, the Baron of Haverstal is an old man with no heirs. Colric, I give you all his lands... for now."

Col looked up, confused.

The king waved the unasked question away. "I'll explain shortly. I'm realizing some things that make this whole idea of Dalia's a little more complicated."

Col shrugged.

Dalia wondered what the king was talking about.

The king set his sword on Col's shoulder. "Do you swear to uphold and adjudicate the laws of the realm and protect all those under your care?"

"I do."

He moved the sword to Dalia's right shoulder and repeated the question.

"I do," she said evenly. Trembling with excitement. This was actually happening.

"And do you swear your full loyalty and fealty to me, the king, and my successors, as long as we too are keeping our pledge to protect the kingdom and uphold its laws?" The question was posed to both of them in turn, and their reply was the same.

"I do."

"Then I declare you both, Lord of Haverstal and heir to all the lands possessed of Lord Athernon."

Dalia blinked. Had she heard that right?

The king went on. "Rise Lords of Haverstal." They did, and the king looked Dalia in the eye. "As you now possess all the rights and obligations of any man of the nobility, and as your father's only child, you are now the heir to his estates and lands. You shall have Haverstal and all Athernon lands, both of you, once he passes."

That sank in.

Her father's lands were vast and rich. "Oh," she said slowly.

The king gave her a wry smile. "You asked for it."

"I did." She nodded. "Thank you."

"That was more than I had expected," Col said slowly. "But, thank you."

The king turned that same smile on him. "Blame her."

Col turned to her and grinned. "This is going to be interesting."

She embraced him. "We can do anything together."

"I suppose we can," he said, returning her embrace.

Once the ceremony and official business was done, Dalia had a moment with her father. As he looked at her, there was something in that gaze she couldn't place.

"What is it, Father?" she asked.

He seemed to consider her words for a while before he spoke. "I had thought you a girl, but I was wrong. You are a woman. I can see that now." He smiled faintly, as if he was losing something, but gaining something else just as valuable. "When I first learned that your mother and I could have no more children, I was quite upset that my lands would fall to some other lord when I passed. Now... that is no longer a concern. You are truly an amazing woman, I wish you... and Col well. And do visit soon, your mother misses you."

"I will. And... thank you, Father."

THE KING PULLED COL ASIDE WHEN DALIA WENT TO SPEAK WITH her father. Tom and Valeesa were speaking with Lord Tandor. The rest were mingling with the royal family.

He put an arm around Col's shoulders and spoke softly. "Thank you, my friend. I had wondered if anything or anyone could bring down Gariast. I am glad I put my faith in you."

"In some ways, it was more Dalia than me."

"Truly?"

"I won't ever lie to you." The king nodded to that. "I was trapped in Gariast's dungeons for the final battle. Dalia, Trentin, Kellan, and Tom were the ones who ended this."

"And they would not have been a team if not for you, Col." Col nodded to that. "And... I just wanted to apologize again. I should not have betrayed you. I cost you years of your life and brought so much pain to your family. I am so sorry, Col."

Col drew in a long breath. That was all behind him now. "You have given me so much to look forward to. Thank you."

The king nodded. "I look forward to your candid advice."

"You'll have it. We'll see if you come to regret it."

The king smiled. "We'll see."

The king left as Dalia found him again. "I promised my father we'd come visit. You need to meet my mother if we're to be married."

"When do you think we should do that?" Col asked.

"Get married?" She considered. "The king could do it now if you like?" She grinned. "But my mother would never forgive me for not being here. My father could perform the ceremony. We could do it first thing once I return home. How does that sound... Lord Haverstal?"

He kissed her lightly on the cheek. "Sounds good to me, let's do it... Lord Haverstal."

She laughed, and with that sound, everything in his life fell into place. He was the king's outlaw no more, and he had everything he could desire.

"Now, the real question is..." Dalia said, putting an arm around him. "Does your right-of-speech extend to me since we are equal, one voice and all? Because I have a few things I'd like to suggest to the king."

It was Col's turn to laugh. "I do believe it does and I'm sure he'd be happy to hear them."

OTHER BOOKS BY R. MICHAEL CARD

TALES OF THE SEVEN KINGDOMS

The Goblin King

The Swordmaster's Apprentice

GUARDIANS OF LIGHT

Book 1: The Last Scion

Book 2: Scion Rising

Book 3: Scion's Sacrifice

The King's Outlaw

ABOUT R. MICHAEL CARD

R. Michael Card has loved fantasy since he read his first Dragon Lance book so many years ago. He has been writing for twenty years but has only recently decided to start sharing his work with the world. He has always enjoyed the lighter side of epic fantasy, the grand adventure, and has infused that love into his works.

He lives near Toronto, Ontario with his beloved wife and their cat. He has had a plethora of careers, working in software, insurance, trades, and education, with jobs ranging from washing cars to career counseling.

www.ingramcontent.com/pod-product-compliance
Lightning Source LLC
Chambersburg PA
CBHW031156020726
47499CB00002B/390

* 9 7 8 1 9 8 8 1 1 5 4 9 8 *